I0772899

An Unlikely Phoenix

An Unlikely Phoenix

Frank Saverio

AN UNLIKELY PHOENIX
By Frank Saverio

©Copyright 2018 Frank Scalise

Published by Code 4 Press, an imprint of Frank Zafiro, LLC

Cover Design by Eric Beetner. Revised by Frank Scalise
Book Design and Layout by Frank Scalise

ISBN: 978-1-962889-05-6

Previous editions attributed to Frank Zafiro and Frank Scalise, both pen names for Frank Scalise.

As this novel is set in the future, all events are clearly fictional. All characters depicted in this novel are likewise fictional, including future fictional depictions of existing celebrities, whose words and actions contained in this novel are fictional and should not necessarily be construed as representing their current or past real life personas.

For Malcom,
that your world is far different than this.

The only thing necessary for the triumph of evil is for good men to do nothing.

Edmund Burke,
Irish Statesman

Author's Note

Regardless of what shelf (virtual or otherwise) you may have found it on, *An Unlikely Phoenix* is a difficult book to categorize. It is at once a near futuristic, dystopian sci-fi crime fiction thriller, a social and political commentary, and a satire. Above all, it is *fiction*, and so by definition, all of the characters are also fictional.

This includes fictional, futuristic versions of real people. In this novel, these people may or may not resemble much of their current selves. Probably more *may not* than *may*. Likewise, you may or may not agree with their fictional depiction. You may be tempted to say, "So-and-so would never do that" or "So-and-so doesn't talk that way." And you know what? You might be right. But with regard to futuristic depictions and scenarios, I consider such statements to be in much the same league "that would never happen." This is a fictional future in a work of fiction, so within that context, it could *all* happen, at least in this alternative, fictional world.

So please remember that fact, in the event that your reaction is to be offended or angry. These characters are all fictional, even the future, fictional versions of actual people. If you don't like what they say or do in this tale, you have several options. You may read on, and simply endure (which is most definitely my preference). You may stop reading (not my preference, but it's cool if you do). Or you can write your own book (also cool) and in that book, people can act and events can go exactly as you determine.

You see, in each of these instances, it's your *freedom of choice*. We still live in a world and in a nation that has such freedom, and that is a glorious thing, is it not?

Prologue

They say the eyes of history judge harshly, and it is true. But it is also true that the eyes of history are always changing, and therefore what is seen – and how it is perceived – changes yet again. Immensely popular people in their own era are examined more objectively through the lens of time and distance and perhaps brought down to earth, while underappreciated figures are eventually given their due. And while the perspectives of each historian are colored by the era in which s/he writes, time and distance usually paint a balanced picture of persons and events in a way that is virtually impossible for most to see as they happen.

The 2030s were, by all accounts and by any objective measure, a catastrophic period. Few historians, even the most stolid, would call that description hyperbole. The world teetered on the brink of utter annihilation, our collective toes over the edge of the abyss. One could easily argue that we toppled off that cliff, only to catch a hand on an outcropping of rock, before scrambling back to the top, not unlike an action movie (the non-interactional, visual medium that was a primary source of entertainment at the time).

Much has been written of that period, including Daniel

McCollough's magnificent 2076 work Desolation Averted. The wars, the political maneuvering, and the sheer scope of human struggle of that decade have not been better captured so succinctly, so eloquently, or so completely. What McCollough writes about are events that are firmly engraved in the minds of any and all aware citizens of the world. The 2030s were a watershed moment in human history, rivaling the rise and fall of the empires of Rome or China, with the suddenness and the impact of the Second World War from 1939-45, and McCollough covers it brilliantly. I will not attempt to rival his work here.

Instead, my focus will be on the events leading up to that monumental conflict, one which has dwarfed all previous conflicts in size and import. It is instead my intent to examine the late 2020s. Despite the fact that all of the seeds of what was later reaped were clearly sown in this decade, it is underrepresented in the field of academics. Some of this is due to the sheer volume of propaganda that an historian must sift through in order to find the objective (or at least less subjective) truths of what occurred. A totalitarian state is difficult to pierce from the outside, whether as a contemporary or when looking backwards across the expanse of time. The decades since have both served to open possibilities and to cloud facts, and so, while a fascinating period and a case study for human behavior, this era is less attractive to many historians and, frankly, to most readers.

The average reader, even an intelligent one, seems to be more drawn to the compelling narrative that is the 2030s (and McCollough's stellar prose only accentuates this tendency) than the more complex one of the previous decade. The wars of the 2030s, once engaged, shed much of the ambiguity of what led to the fighting on all sides, seemingly providing a clear picture of good versus evil, and that is a story that humanity has always embraced. However, a careful examination of the 2020s reveals as stark a division between what we contemporarily see as right and wrong as existed in the wars that followed. The division lurked beneath the immediate surface of a nation that had enjoyed a dominance not unlike that of Rome two millennia prior, only to ultimately suffer a fate not dissimilar.

"The past is prologue" is a well-travelled adage, but here it is doubly true. When one delves into the question of how a world superpower – very briefly the sole world superpower – became a nationalistic dictatorship, the answer lies in the past becoming the present. In truth, the first and easiest parallel is the historical path of Rome herself in which a successful, longstanding republic was supplanted by a megalomaniacal leader who inspired his followers to unfaltering loyalty and replaced that republic with an emperorship that lasted another 400 years. Thankfully, the American dictatorship more closely resembled the brief tenure of England's Oliver Cromwell than the Roman example. But if you were to say to anyone in the world as late as 1800 that the metaphorical phoenix of the Roman Empire would rise out of a small nation in the "New World," a former colony which had only achieved its independence due to French intervention…well, you would have to forgive the look of utter disbelief that would meet your prediction.

And yet, the United States rose to the status of world superpower and, once you correct for changes in civilization in the roughly thirteen hundred years since its western demise, mirrored the Roman Empire in a plethora of ways. Along with

China, the United States between 1830 and 2030 is among the pantheon of truly powerful nations. And while the argument exists that Rome lasted almost eleven hundred years, it was at its zenith for only a portion of that time, and one must account for the speed at which the world changed (or did not change) in ancient versus modern times. Clearly, there is a case to be made that the United States was a modern Rome, or as close as it is possible to be.

But there is a second, more recent parallel to the rise of American prominence (and nationalism) that is unavoidable. While the ethnocentric belief that the United States was the country that defeated Nazi Germany in the Second World War conveniently ignores or undervalues the much longer and more impactful efforts (not to mention sacrifices) of the First Soviet Union, there is no doubt that, much like the First World War, the entry of America into the war effort swung the tide and forced the eventual Allied victory. With this in mind, and coupled with the fact that the national psyche of the United States remained steadfastly convinced for three quarters of a century that it had defeated Nazism almost singlehandedly, it is particularly ironic that this nation would ultimately serve as the ashes from which that hateful movement would rise once more.

How much should the public have seen coming? Were the early indicators of ego and a disconnect from reality in the President's first term warning signs that the populace should have keyed upon? Would the surge of white supremacy, coming immediately on the heels of the nation's first black president, have occurred without the initial, tacit encouragement from the new president? Is there any argument that the rebranding of Nazism in all but name became a political tool for the president to solidify his power base, ultimately leading to the repeal of the Twenty-Second Amendment to American Constitution and allowing a president to serve more than two terms?

It is at once difficult to blame those who were in the moment for what could be perceived as their blindness and equally difficult to forgive their apparently reluctant, sluggish response to the rapid changes made to the nation's fabric. Admittedly, it is difficult to see one's own time clearly while simultaneously being part of it, but most historians who study the era tend to agree that American apathy played a significant role. Never considered the worst of sins, the truest lesson of what followed might be to revisit apathy and its true venality.

Much like Julius Caesar and Adolf Hitler before him, the last President of the United States rose to his position within the legitimate confines of the existing structure by capitalizing on a disaffected, disillusioned political base, and used that powerful minority to usurp that structure and create a dictatorship. And while at least the Roman example is replete with those who actively opposed Julius Caesar (indeed, those who eventually assassinated him), the German example is sparse in this behavior. A large majority of the population at the time simply went along with the minority that had seized power, trading some measure of normalcy and peace for their feigned or self-imposed ignorance of actual events that were happening around them, and regarding how terrible some of those events were. In 1940 Germany, you would be hard pressed to find someone who publicly criticized the Fuhrer.

By 2028, in the United States of America, things were very much the same.

— From the Introduction of *An Unlikely Phoenix* by Reed Ambrose, published by Oxford Press. First Edition, 2081.

Part I: RYAN

St. Louis, Missouri

USA

May 2028

…[C]ops don't expect to hear the words "thank you" very often, especially from those who need them the most. No, the reward comes in knowing that our entire way of life in America depends on the rule of law; that the maintenance of that law is a hard and daily labor; that in this country, we don't have soldiers in the streets or militias setting the rules. Instead, we have public servants-police officers-like the[se] men who were taken away from us.

Barack Obama,

44th President of the United States,

From a eulogy for fallen officers in Dallas, Texas in 2016

Chapter 1

When the President nationalized all of law enforcement in 2026, it was viewed by many within that career field as an affirmation of his support for their efforts and their role in society. No one looking back now would argue that the six decades from 1960 to 2020 weren't difficult, tumultuous years for law enforcement. Public unrest during the Civil Rights era and the Vietnam War (two events that current historical wisdom see as intertwined), and the police actions in response to that unrest marked the beginning of the deterioration of public respect for law enforcement. The so-called War on Drugs initiated during the Nixon Presidency contributed to this division as well, and had the added impact of the greater militarization of police, a trend that continued for the remainder of the nation's history. Racially charged (and many have argued, racially-motivated) events such as the widely televised beating of Rodney King in the early 1990s in Los Angeles, the shooting of Michael Brown in Ferguson, Missouri more than twenty years later, and the race riots of 2026 in several large

U.S. cities further eroded that police-public relationship. That vital partnership has always been pivotal to the successful mission of any law enforcement entity, and yet, by the 2020s in America, the regard for police was at the very least polarized, and most certainly degraded in many corners of the nation. Even independent, outside investigations such as the Department of Justice review of the Michael Brown incident, which ruled it as a justified shooting, did little to assuage the damage.

The sad realization that one makes when afforded the luxury of years and hindsight is that while most of the events that drove the damage between many U.S. police agencies and their respective communities were at the very least initially concerning and merited the attention they received, these moments represented a tiny percentage of the membership and good work of those agencies. With the notable exception of a very few departments mired in corrupt city-wide cultures, a careful examination of historical evidence bears this out. Simply put, in the late teens and early twenties of this century, most cops worked hard, were honest, and dedicated to the people they served. But such things were understandably lost in the maelstrom of media and public attention to those anomalous events.

As a result, it is not surprising that the last President of the United States enjoyed wide support amongst the rank and file of law enforcement. When someone of that stature publicly recognizes underappreciated efforts by a frequently maligned group, the psychological response is always likely to be one of tremendous support. 'Finally,' many in law enforcement must have thought, 'someone in power gets it.'

This support was not unanimous but was certainly the

majority. A survey of law enforcement labor unions and fraternal orders in 2025 showed that over 76% supported or strongly supported the President, while most of the remaining 24% were indifferent or apathetic.

While the nationalization of all police in 2026 ostensibly left day to day operations in the hands of the individual agencies and the city, county, or state it represented, in reality this move gave the President direct authority over every police officer in the country. Eventually, this provided him with the ability to force or maintain order among all but the most outspoken or active dissidents. For the latter, the tool of professional law enforcement also served well, as long as the activities of those targeted were a violation of law. And since the President enjoyed strong control over Congress and many state governments, such laws were not difficult to enact.

Did these men and women become unthinking soldiers in the President's political army? Did they cease to be the honorable individuals that our research indicates most of them were? Or were they such supporters of the man that they adopted his policies as their own? Or, like the thousands of police officers who preceded them, did they continue to uphold the laws of their community, subjugating their own personal views on those laws to their sacred duty to enforce them?

No one of these answers is likely true of all members of law enforcement. Some refused to capitulate, especially when party membership became almost mandatory for career advancement. Others seem to have simply focused on their day to day jobs, responding to the calls for service, investigating the crimes that occurred within their jurisdiction, and abstaining from politics. There were, of course, a few who saw these developments as an opportunity for personal advancement, and who

---

R yan Derrick stood at ease, waiting for roll call to begin. He recalled a time when they sat around rectangular tables, conversing easily and raucously until the sergeant came in. During those early days of his career, the veteran cops groused about how roll call used to be more disciplined. How they stood in squads, lined up, and showed proper respect to the sergeant and lieutenant. Uniforms got inspected and no one left the station looking like a rag bag.

Now here he was, grousing about the laissez faire days of yore. At least he kept his gripes to himself, sparing today's rookies the burden of listening to them.

It was more than that, though, he thought bitterly. You had to be more careful what you complained about these days, and to whom. Law enforcement had changed a lot in the past ten years.

Everything had.

"They announce the detective's list yet?" Marcus asked him quietly.

Ryan glanced over at his sometimes partner. The big man's biceps strained at the short sleeves like a bull in the chute, barely contained. He sometime teased Marcus about always wearing his little brother's shirt to show off, but he knew that showing off the merchandise did more than get the man a few phone numbers. It served as a warning to those suspects who were on the fence about whether or not fighting their way out of a situation was a good idea or not. If Marcus got hold of them, it never was.

"S'posed to be today," he answered.

"Today's almost gone."

Ryan's gaze flicked to the green numbers of the digital clock high up on the wall at the front of the room. 2059, it read. Marcus was right. In three hours, it would be tomorrow. "I guess the bosses like to create some suspense."

Marcus let out a subdued snort of contempt. "If they spent any time out on the street instead of sitting in their offices, conspiring and kissing each other's asses…"

"…they wouldn't be brass, then, would they?" Ryan finished.

"Truer words were never spoke."

Ryan let the conversation die. In the patrol car, he might have tacked on a couple more exchanges, because no one could overhear and he knew he could trust Marcus. But in the drill hall, ears were everywhere, and some people liked to make a big deal about every little thing. He didn't need that. Things were tough enough already.

The door swung open. The officer nearest to the door called the assembled group to attention, and everyone snapped to the position, standing ramrod straight, staring directly ahead.

Sergeant Potulny took his time getting to his place at the front of the room. Only after he'd set his iPad on the lectern and cast a discerning gaze across the assembled shift did he give an almost reluctant, "Stand at ease, men."

Ryan, along with the rest of the officers, relaxed, training his eyes on Potulny. He stood in the second row, his view of the sergeant partially obscured by the braided head of Jennifer Koslaw, one of his academy mates. He wondered if the universal use of the term 'men' still bothered her, or if that forced social convention had just become one more adjustment to make.

Sergeant Potulny read off the district assignments. He and Marcus had the sixth, which had become the norm over the past year. Potulny liked to say the sixth district was high crime committed by low people, a phrase he'd taken from the shift commander, Lieutenant Schwab. Nothing said kissing your boss's ass like repeating his pet phrases.

Pet phrase or not, it was an accurate assessment of the sixth. When the city redistricted, creating eleven smaller districts instead of the original six, the borders were gerrymandered to ensure that the sixth district held most of the high crime areas. This allowed much of the city to boast good numbers while mostly ignoring the bad numbers coming out of the sixth.

Ryan knew they drew that assignment as a passive form of punishment, but he didn't care. He liked to work, and there were plenty of opportunities in the sixth to do just that. Besides, while the inhabitants in the sixth might be 'low,' as Lieutenant Schwab and his lackey sergeant described them, Ryan found them more honest than most people these days. Not about their criminal activities, of course, but about most everything else. It was actually refreshing to only be lied to about crime.

"Now, some of you might be wondering about the promotional list for detective," Potulny said, his reedy voice barely filling the drill hall. "Command has informed me that the list will be posted on the department intranet before midnight. Final list position were determined based upon the last two assessment categories. For those of you who aren't aware, those categories are political affiliations and commander's review."

Potulny gave Ryan a dark glance. Ryan couldn't tell if it was because he was happy or unhappy with the results, and where Ryan had eventually landed. He thought he might have read a sense of satisfaction in the sergeant's eyes, which could only mean one thing – he'd dropped down in the rankings.

The sergeant moved on, detailing some subversive activities in a park in the eleventh district, which was the posh area of downtown that had been heavily gentrified over the past five years. Ryan was secretly relieved he didn't have to deal with the so-called subversives or the complainants. It wasn't what he thought of as real police work.

When Potulny finished the briefing, he gave the room another meaningful assessment. "Be safe out there, men." He called the assembled officers to attention again.

"Honor your city and your president," Potulny said, snapping a salute to his brow.

Much of the room followed suit, returning Potulny's salute. When the shift salute was introduced a year ago, after the President officially nationalized all police departments, it had been characterized as voluntary. Ostensibly, it still was, but Ryan noticed fewer and fewer officers demurred. Those who did, looked down at the ground, avoiding the harsh gaze of the sergeant. That action, meant by many as a gesture of disgust, was re-cast as an expression of shame, and now those who didn't salute were dubbed "shamers" by those who did.

"MAGA, brothers," Potulny said with conviction. "Making America Great, Always."

"MAGA," intoned the assembled saluters.

Potulny dropped the salute and the officers did the same. "Dismissed," the sergeant said curtly.

Ryan turned immediately to the back of the room and gathered up his duty bag. Marcus did the same. Sergeant Potulny remained at the lectern, watching. As Ryan walked past, headed toward the door, Potulny held up his hand stopping him. "How long are you going to stay a shamer, Officer Derrick?"

Ryan considered for a moment, then said, "I just choose not to salute, sergeant. That's my right, isn't it?"

"It is," Potulny admitted. "But why you'd choose not to be a patriot is beyond me."

Ryan didn't respond.

"You're a smart man, Officer Derrick. Anyone can see that. But you might want to get with the program, before the program gets with you."

"Thank you, sergeant."

"Don't patronize me," Potulny snapped.

"No, sergeant."

Potulny scowled and shifted gears. "Maybe when you see the promotional list, you'll start to figure things out. Stop wasting your talent and get on board."

Ryan didn't reply. Most of the time, he'd found that to be the best response.

"Go on," Potulny snapped. "Get to work."

Ryan obeyed, leaving the room while Potulny glared after him.

Marcus was waiting for him in the basement sally port with the car. "What did Pot Belly want?"

Ryan glanced around to make sure no one heard, then shook his head. "Same as always. To mess with me."

Marcus shook his head in disgust. "All the time with that guy."

Ryan put his bag in the trunk and closed it. "A man needs a hobby."

"I suppose. And if he wasn't screwing with you, he'd be torturing pet mice or something."

Ryan opened the driver's rear door to the car's armory. A pair of bright orange, less lethal shotguns and jet black assault rifles were secured against the cage. When he reached for the first one, Marcus said, "Already cleared, locked and loaded."

"My man."

"Don't say that."

"Why?"

"Makes you sound ridiculous."

Ryan closed the door and went around to the passenger side of the patrol car. The prisoner compartment took up the passenger half of the back seat. He popped open the door, searched under the plastic covered seat to make sure the previous prisoner hadn't dumped something there, then gave Marcus a thumbs up. Ryan settled into the front seat, ensuring that the sliding partition in the shield between the front and rear was closed. Two nights ago, he'd been driving and Marcus forgot to close it. Once they had a prisoner in the back seat, the man had proceeded to spit at them through the opening.

Marcus fired up the engine. Twelve cylinders of raw power rumbled to life. They pulled out of the basement sally port and headed to the sixth.

On the way, Ryan logged them into the Mobile Data Computer. He quickly perused the calls that were holding, then switched the tab to the intranet announcements page.

Nothing.

"What do we got?" Marcus asked. "Anything good?"

Ryan toggled back to the calls holding screen. "A few burglary reports, two stolen cars, an assault report and a trouble unknown."

"Let's go with the mystery before the dispatcher tags us with paper."

Paper. He could hardly remember writing police reports on actual paper, even early in his career, and no one did now. But some terms died hard deaths, and this was one of them.

Ryan selected the trouble unknown and self-dispatched them. The address was on the far side of the district and would take at least ten minutes to get there. He switched back to the announcement page and hit refresh.

"You know, checking every three seconds ain't going to make it pop up any sooner," Marcus told him.

"Keep your eyes on the road."

"Just saying."

Ryan hit refresh again, then settled back in his seat.

"Why you want to be a detective anyway? Working patrol is where it's at. Something different every day and when you go home at the end of it all, you're done. Clean slate, every day." He shook his head. "Detective goes home, he comes back to the same case files, plus maybe some new ones stacked on top of that. It never ends."

"Maybe. But detectives work day shift."

"Not robbery/homicide. They work the whole clock, just like us."

"Well, I won't be going into robbery/homicide, will I? New dicks get property crimes, and property crimes works a straight day shift with weekends off. You know what that means?"

"Yeah. It means you get boring and fat, all at the same time." Marcus snorted derisively. "Day shift," he muttered.

"What it means is family time. Normal family time. And that's something Nathalie and I have never had."

"You've got family time now. Just because it isn't based around whatever everyone else's schedule is like, so what? You tuck your little girl into bed before you come to work, don't you?"

"Yeah, now. What happens when her bedtime isn't eight o'clock anymore?"

"You kiss her on the forehead and tell her good night before you leave, and let Nathalie do the tucking. Melina won't mind."

"I mind."

"So you're just being selfish, then."

"I'm not being selfish. I don't sleep with my wife, Marcus."

"Neither do I, and you don't see me carping about it."

"You're funny. Can you be funny and drive at the same time? Because I didn't think you were talented enough to do both."

"I'm just saying."

"Look, I just want a normal life, okay?"

"There is no normal."

"Fine," Ryan conceded. "Then I want a different life than this."

Marcus was quiet for a few moments. When he spoke again, his tone was more serious. "You know you didn't get no political points. You're not even on the supporter rolls, much less a party member."

"I know."

"And if you think Lieutenant Schwab gave you any more points than the absolute minimum he had to for seniority and your performance record, you're dreaming."

"I know I'm not dreaming, because I'm stuck with you."

Marcus refused to take the bait, and remained solemn.

"Did you score high enough on the written exam and the skill segments to offset that?"

"I don't know," Ryan admitted. He thought about what Potulny said about the list coming out, and added, "Probably not."

"Then stop checking the announcement page, and just do police work."

"All right."

"Let's make the MOST of it, brother."

Ryan grinned. Their private joke stood for Making Our Sixth Tolerable, and was a jab at the MAGA lemmings they worked with.

"My man," he said, and when Marcus started bitching about *that* phrase again, he almost forgot about the detective promotion, the politics of the job, all of it. Instead, he was just a patrol cop headed on a trouble unknown call with his partner, nothing else to worry about except whatever was waiting there for them.

Chapter 2

In 1829, Sir Robert Peel famously drafted his Nine Principles of Policing as a guide to the newly founded London Metropolitan Police Department, the first concerted attempt at modern policing. In one of these principles, Peel contended that 'the police are the public and the public are the police.' This seemingly simple concept is one from which, arguably, the law enforcement profession strayed considerably during the late Twentieth and early Twenty-First century. The development wasn't a sudden shift, but rather a slow drift. The advent of motorized patrol vehicles in the 1940s signaled a beginning of a slow detachment between many law enforcement agencies and their respective communities. Rather than frequently interacting with a police officer on a foot beat, community members saw these same police officers drive by in squad cars. This created a social distance that gradually but eventually grew into a divide. Citizen interaction with police became largely limited to either being victimized by crime or perpetrating it. This social divide increased by another factor when the so-called War on Drugs was launched in the 1970s. This drug war was driven by federal emphasis and supported with federal dollars, though admittedly it was met with enthusiasm by most state, county, and municipal agencies. This concerted federal effort included the sale or granting of excess military equipment to these various agencies, regardless of actual need. It should have come as no surprise that this trend ultimately led to the greater militarization of the police and further exacerbated the estrangement of the police and the community members. An uptick in social unrest intensified the issue, and the race riots of 2026 unfortunately presented a stage upon which this hostility played out. When police agencies responded to these instances of unrest, one should not be surprised to learn that they did so utilizing the tools at their disposal, including the military-style equipment and weaponry that the federal government had provided. Images of police that were virtually indistinguishable from military members engaged in conflict with rioters may not have been widely broadcasted due to increasing media controls, but still photos and snippets of video inevitably leaked out. Violence is always unpleasant to view, and even legal and proper uses of force appear brutal in nature. The riots of 2026 in multiple cities were brought under control, but accomplishing this restoration of order came at the cost of using tactics that police would cite as necessary and that many in the community called abusive. As a result, relations between these two factions continued to deteriorate, and at an accelerated pace.

Certainly, this phenomenon was more pronounced in some areas than others. Urban centers, particularly those with a larger minority population that already had a history of poor police relations, were especially susceptible to this development. By the time the aforementioned race riots of 2026 precipitated the President's move to nationalize all police, the gulf between

---

T he trouble unknown call turned out to be nothing showing, and when Ryan contacted the original complainant, even the man's description of what he found suspicious was vague and confusing. When Ryan got back into the car, Marcus gave him a questioning look.

"Six to five the complainant's on drugs and none of what he saw happened," Ryan said.

"What did he see?"

"A couple of guys talking."

"And that's suspicious because…?"

"Because the complainant's on drugs."

"Ah."

They caught a domestic dispute next, and it was textbook. The couple wasn't married but had two kids together. Both were drunk and there were no other witnesses. She had a red mark and swelling on her cheek. He claimed she did to herself. There was no way to know, and the law was clear that with the evidence they had, the situation required a mandatory arrest. When Ryan explained this to the man, he started to get worked up. If he'd been drunker, he might have gone, but when he cast an eye at Marcus' hulking frame, thought better of it.

As soon as they finished booking the DV suspect into

jail, a fight call came over the Mobile Data Computer and the air at the same time. Marcus buried the accelerator.

"Why are you hurrying?" Ryan asked him.

"Not this again," Marcus grumbled.

"Seriously," Ryan said. "The dispatcher said this looked like a mutual. Why risk everything that can go wrong by driving fast just to interrupt a couple of knuckleheads who are smacking each other?"

"Because that's our job," Marcus told him, cutting hard around a corner. "That's what we do."

"It's *definitely* what we do." Ryan braced himself against the door as Marcus completed the turn and punched it again. "I don't know for sure if it's our job."

"Keeping the peace is our job."

"So is keeping the public safe. You think it's safe to drive like this when you don't have to?"

"Man, you're looking at it all wrong. This here, is what I sometimes *get* to do. Drive fast, fight bad guys, and take them to jail. It's *fun.*"

"We should take our time getting there, let these two tire each other out."

"Where's the fun in that?"

"Safety can be fun, my man."

"Oh, come on. Stop saying that."

When they rolled up on the two men, they were standing at the curb, clutching at each other like a pair of heavyweights in the eleventh round. A small crowd stood around, half-heartedly watching the event. Marcus man-handled the two men apart and each officer cuffed up one side. It took fifteen minutes of translating drunk-speak before they could confirm that it was a mutual fight, that no one was seriously hurt, and neither one wanted to press charges against the other. By that time, the crowd had vanished. Ryan figured that was good. All they needed was some witnesses to complicate things.

He gave each of them stern warnings to go in separate directions and to go straight home. Then he and Marcus leaned on the hood of the police car and watched the two stagger off, arm in arm.

"Thank God they weren't brothers or cousins or something," Marcus grumbled. "We'd be going back to jail on DV charges."

"What were they even fighting about?" Ryan asked. "Did you get that from your guy?"

"Something political. Or some woman. I couldn't quite tell what the dude was saying half the time."

"We should have called them a cab."

"They should know when to stop drinking." Marcus shook his head. "This is St. Louis, baby, not St. Day Care."

After the two fighters were out of sight, both officers climbed inside the car. Ryan immediately accessed the announcement page. A link reading DETECTIVE PROMOTIONAL LIST sat at the very top of the queue.

Ryan glanced over at Marcus.

"Yeah?" the big man said. "Well, then go ahead and click on it. You got to know or you'll be crazy the whole rest of the night."

Ryan selected the link and the screen instantly filled with a list of names. He knew that at least three hundred had taken the exam, but only the top fifty were ever posted on the promotional list.

He started at the top and scanned downward.

And stopped.

"No way," he breathed.

"What?"

"I'm still at nine."

"Nine?!"

"Nine." He didn't believe it, either. The sheer mathematics of it stunned him. Without party points and the extra bump from the commander, he didn't figure to make the top twenty-five. He knew his other scores were high, but he must have been in the number one or two spot with a healthy margin before these figures were factored in.

"Are you sure it's not nineteen?" Marcus asked. "Because even that would be…"

"Amazing," Ryan finished. "But no, I'm sure. I'm number nine."

Marcus stared at him. He stared back. After a few moments, they both broke out in laughter.

"You might just make it," Marcus said. "Nine might just be high enough."

"There's a chance, at least," Ryan agreed. He reached for his phone. "I gotta call Nathalie and tell her."

"Hell with that. Call Pot Belly."

Ryan laughed, remembering the sergeant's words from earlier in the night. "He made it sound like I was going to be lucky to even make the list."

"Maybe he didn't know."

Ryan shrugged. "Maybe." It was also possible that Potulny knew where Ryan had started on the list and figured the drop was extreme enough to warrant what he said. He shook his head. "Who cares? Within a year, I'll be working case files instead of working for him."

"Unless he transfers to Investigation," Marcus said.

"Always a ray of sunshine, that's you."

"Sorry, brother. Forget I said that. Congratulations. Seriously. You deserve it."

"Thanks, my man."

Marcus feigned a scowl, but before he could say anything, an alert tone sounded.

"Burglary in progress," she said, her tone clear and emotionless as she listed the address.

"That's eight blocks away," Ryan said, but Marcus was already dropping the accelerator.

"Complainant has hidden in the bathroom. At least two suspects were seen. She believes they are in the bedroom now."

Marcus covered the distance in no time flat. As they drew close, he cut off all of the lights, and piloted the car to the curb a half block from the victim's address. Ryan was out of the car and loping down the sidewalk before the engine even died. He knew Marcus would catch up. For a big man, he moved fast.

The house was a small brick box, a vestige of the post-war boom in the time of his great-grandfather. The entire block was full of similar houses, and only the white numbers above the door told him for sure that he had the right place.

Ryan slowed his pace, drawing his pistol and pressing close to the side of the house. A moment later, Marcus lumbered up beside him. Peeking around the corner, he saw the front door standing a few inches open.

Marcus tapped him on the shoulder and motioned to the far side of the door. Ryan nodded. As one, they approached the front door, splitting up at the last moment to take up position on opposite sides. Ryan squatting low on his haunches while Marcus remained standing. They exchanged another look, and Marcus shrugged, motioning his head toward Ryan.

His call.

Ryan considered briefly, then decided to maintain their advantage of stealth. He shifted his stance, reached out with his right hand and slowly swung the door open. The hinges remained silent, and the only response to his action was the dim light from the street spilling across the small living room.

He listened, straining his ears for the sound of a voice, or the scuffle of movement, but there was nothing. He glanced at Marcus, who shook his head. He wasn't hearing anything, either.

No choice but to go in, he decided. He met Marcus' eyes and slowly bobbed his head in a three count. On three, he slipped through the threshold, buttonhooking to the right with his gun leveled at the room

A moment later, Marcus came behind him, his large frame filling the doorway.

Gunfire erupted from the kitchen, filling the small house with flashes of light and explosive sound. Ryan saw two figures in the quick, strobe-like clips of light as they fired their rifles at them. Instinctively, he returned fire, squeezing the trigger at the dancing figures. He heard his own voice crying out in surprise and anger, melding with the crash of shots fired, and the screams of the men shooting at him.

"…fascists!"

"…occupiers…"

"…mother-*fuckers!*"

Ryan kept squeezing until his slide locked to the rear. Without thinking, he dropped the used magazine and slapped in a full one. His whole world was focused on that one simple action, and it seemed to take an hour. The sound of the slide going forward and chambering a round clanged in his ears like a jail cell door.

"Marcus," he gasped, surprised that he could hear his own voice.

That was when he realized that the room had become still. He realized the attackers had used up their ammunition, too. Impulsively, he took the opportunity to take the fight to them. They wouldn't expect it, and this was the only chance he'd get.

Ryan lunged forward to charge, but his legs had no strength. Instead, he collapsed to the ground. He struggled to breathe, lifting his eyes towards the darkened kitchen, raising his gun to shoot.

Moonlight shone through the open back door.

Ryan blinked at the sight, trying to process it.

His eyelids were heavy. A warmth enveloped him, and with it came blackness.

Chapter 3

While Party membership never became an official requirement in most government agencies, by the late 2020s, it was in reality an unspoken, de facto policy. Operating in much the same fashion as the reputed 'good old boy' networks of the previous century, membership in the New American Party opened the door to significant benefits and opportunities. Not being a member closed those doors, and in some cases, invited ill treatment with little or no redress.

— From *An Unlikely Phoenix* by Reed Ambrose

All of the sounds he heard were muffled, and all seemed to come from far away. He tried to move toward the sounds, but he was tired, more tired than he could ever remember being. Still, he'd make some progress, but then was just too weary to continue, so he'd drift away for a while longer.

Later, the sounds became more distinct. Beeps. The hiss of air. An occasional voice. He tried to hold onto those sounds, to grasp them firmly and let them buoy him back to the surface, but he couldn't. For what seemed like the longest of times, he was only able to hear small snatches of sound and try to attach some kind of confused meaning to it. But there was no meaning where he was.

Only darkness.

When he woke up, he wasn't sure at first whether or not it was still a dream. The room seemed unnaturally bright, and every object had an indistinct fuzziness around the edges. But then the nurse was talking to him, explaining something to him that he couldn't quite grasp. He nodded slightly in response, unsure of why he did so, other than out of habit. The nurse asked him something, and when he nodded again, the nurse smiled slightly. He patted Ryan on the forearm and promised to bring the doctor soon.

"Marcus?" Ryan tried to say, but his throat was dry and he could only manage a raspy wheeze.

The nurse didn't answer, only adjusted the flow on a tube leading to Ryan's arm. Soon after he left, Ryan fell back into soft darkness again.

He slipped in and out of awareness for some time after that. Sometimes the room would be empty except for the machines monitoring him. Other times, the same nurse or a different one would be present. Once he thought he caught sight of the doctor, conversing with the nurse at the foot of his bed. When they realized he was looking at them, the doctor tried to talk to him but after a few short exchanges, he seemed to realize Ryan wasn't up for it.

Nathalie was there once, holding his hand and watching him. Their eyes met, hers that deep dark brown hue that had bowled him over the first moment they met. Those eyes filled with tears and her lips moved. He couldn't tell if she was speaking or only mouthing the words, but there was no mistaking what she conveyed.

I love you.

He tried to say it back, but could only nod before falling back into the dark sleep that held him. He fought it, unlike the other times, struggled to stay with her just a little longer, but he was too weak.

He knew he was finally going to stay awake when opening his eyes was accompanied by noticeable pain. It didn't overwhelm him, only nibbled at the edges of his awareness. Even so, he could feel how ravenous those bites were, how large the actual pain must be, and despite the darkness that whatever drugs he was on had imposed, he was grateful for them.

"Back amongst the waking, I see?" The doctor was older than Ryan by at least twenty years, but fit and tan. His blond hair had the slightest touch of gray, which along with his square jaw, only reinforced his force of personality. The small American flag pin on his lapel was a foregone conclusion. Ryan stared at it, letting his mind clear before answering.

Of course you're a Party member, he thought. You're perfect.

"Water?" the doctor said.

Ryan nodded.

He thought the doctor might bring it, but he motioned to the nurse, who hustled out of the room.

"Don't try to talk just yet," the doctor said. "You were intubated for a while, so your throat is going to be sore, and I know you're dry. The water the nurse is bringing will help with that. We've been keeping you on a fair amount of medication for the pain, but the time has come to start tapering off on that. It's always a delicate balance with narcotics, weighing the pain management issues versus potential addiction and other side effects." He smiled. "But I imagine you know about the issues with drugs, Officer."

Ryan nodded again.

"Do you feel up to talking about your medical status right now? Or at least listening to me talk about it?"

Ryan dipped his chin repeatedly. Information. He needed information.

"All right. I'll fill you in, and after you've had some water and a little time to process what I've said, you can ask me any questions you might have."

Ryan only had two questions burning in his mind, and neither one had to do with himself. But he forced himself to wait for the water, and to hear the doctor out. He'd dealt with enough medical professionals to know that they went about things in a certain way, and there wasn't much you could do about it even if you had the illusion of power.

The doctor glanced down at Ryan's chart, then said, "You may not feel very fortunate at the moment, Officer Derrick, but in some ways, you are. Your attackers fired on you with AK-47 assault rifles, and you were struck with several bullets. Five, actually, which is pretty amazing. Just the kinetic energy alone that your body absorbed was potentially fatal. Your fitness level and your ballistic vest mitigated this somewhat, but you truly are lucky to still be drawing breath."

The nurse arrived with ice water and slipped the straw between Ryan's lips. "Slowly," she said in a quiet, firm tone.

He sucked in the cold water and felt it slide down his throat. The sensation was wonderful, and for a moment, that became his entire world. He soaked it in, and felt marginally more alive.

"Good?" the doctor asked.

Ryan nodded, sipping again.

"Go slow, and don't try to talk just yet," the doctor said. Then he continued, "One of the shots barely struck you, creasing your left triceps." He touched his own left triceps with the tip of his pen to demonstrate. "Two others were through and throughs on your right quadriceps." He pointed to two separate places on his right, outer thigh.

Ryan listened without emotion. The fuzzy edges of his reality were more distinct and clear than before, but he still felt strangely detached, as if he and the doctor were discussing someone else, not him.

"The other two, unfortunately, did more damage. One bullet struck your femur, breaking it." He moved his pen to the center of his leg. "Now, I say *break* because *shatter* is probably too strong a description, Officer. But the break wasn't clean and there were multiple fractures.

Somehow, your femoral artery wasn't damaged, or you likely would have bled to death before emergency medical responders arrived on scene."

It's just that close of a thing, Ryan thought absently. *The veil between life and death is a sheer, wispy curtain.* A moment later, he wondered where that thought had come from.

"The leg is secured. So is your hip. That's where the final bullet hit you." The doctor traced the pen to the opposite hip. "For that injury, I can safely use the word *shatter*. Now, my team and I have performed three separate operations on you since you were brought in the night of the shooting. One was to set and brace the femur. The other two have been on your hip. The first was to clean out bone shards that would eventually do more damage and cause significant pain if they remained. The second was to rebuild and repair as much of that area as we could." He gave Ryan a matter of fact gaze. "The reality is that our actions were mostly a stop-gap effort. You will eventually need a full hip replacement. But we've repaired things to the point that you can live with functional, if modified, mobility until you're eligible for that procedure."

Ryan nodded slowly. He understood it all perfectly, but felt nothing about any of it. He thought that this should disturb him somehow, but all he heard were facts. Facts to be lived with, facts to be addressed and handled.

He sipped his water.

"Usually, these procedures are several years out, but you being law enforcement actually helps you out in that regard." The doctor tapped the flag pin in his lapel. "We can usually make some accommodations for deserving public servants. I'm sure the Party will endorse moving your name up the list."

Ryan didn't bother to correct him. He let the straw slip from his lips, swallowed once more, and then let out a single, rasping word.

"Marcus?"

The doctor managed to keep a poker face, but even in his diminished state, Ryan could read the micro-expressions there. He felt a stab of pain in his chest.

"I think it'd be best if your commander briefed you on the law enforcement aspects of what happened, don't you? Let's just stick to your medical issues."

"Please," Ryan whispered, his throat feeling like he'd swallowed crushed glass.

The doctor considered for what seemed like a long time. He glanced over at the nurse and motioned with his head. She stepped forward and adjusted something next to Ryan's bed. He knew what she was doing, knew the darkness was coming back, but he battled against it, his eyes boring into the doctor's.

"Your partner died at the scene," the doctor said quietly. "I'm terribly sorry for your loss."

Somehow, the pain doubled upon hearing the words. Ryan was glad for whatever the nurse did, and he welcomed the darkness.

Chapter 4

The slow whittling away of civil rights that began near the end of the 2010s and accelerated during the 2020s was largely accomplished under the guise of a pressing need for increased security. The specter of terrorism remained a convenient straw man, and the picture of what a terrorist looked like eventually went from a crazed Middle Eastern Muslim male armed with a suicide bomb to anyone who was not an American. As the crisis approached, even being an American did not immediately absolve one of potential suspicion. Near the end, party membership remained the only litmus test that truly mattered.

— From *An Unlikely Phoenix* by Reed Ambrose

The next time he woke, Nathalie was there. She sat in a chair next to his bed, asleep, her slack hand holding his. He watched her for a long while. She was seemingly never at peace, his wife. Even in her sleep, she scrunched her brow repeatedly as if tackling an obstacle or perceived injustice. Even frowning, though, she was beautiful. Her cocoa skin was a perfect mixture of her Senegalese mother and her Greek father, and the lines of her face were elegant, resilient, haunting.

Much of Nathalie's beauty came from her eyes, though. Her natural curiosity and compassion were buttressed with resolve, and all of these qualities were captured in a single glance. Very different from the perfect model of an American beauty, he mused, which these days seemed to require either a blonde bombshell or Latin lovely. Nathalie's complexion was too dark, too indistinct in a time and a place where being ethnically ambiguous drew suspicion.

Ryan frowned. Why did he let such thoughts creep into his head? Nathalie was beautiful. That was all. It didn't matter what the rest of the country thought or didn't think, so why was he letting these goddamn mind worms eat at him?

The entire train of thought made him drowsy. He could feel sleep coming back on, but whereas it used to be a tidal wave, now it felt more like a change in tides. He couldn't stop it, but he could hold out for a while.

He watched Nathalie.

I'm lucky, the thought. *Lucky to still be on this crazy planet, watching this beautiful woman sleep.*

He'd been watching her for several minutes when she stirred and opened her eyes. She saw he was awake and smiled. Her eyes shone with tears.

"Hey, *vous*," she whispered.

"Who, *moi*?" he replied automatically. His voice sounded strange and he felt his dry lips crack when he smiled back, but it all felt wonderful.

"Yes, *toujours toi*."

"Always you," he said back.

It was an exchange that hearkened back to his aborted attempted to learn French, the language of her parents. He figured he'd start there, because her father was Greek, and even his limited foreign language knowledge base told him that Greek was even harder. She tried to teach him herself, but the furthest they ever got were pidgin exchanges. Eventually, he gave up, grateful for her ability to speak English. But he still loved the trace of her French accent that held on, despite her years in country, and the small exchanges that became part of their marital language.

"We thought we lost you," she said, squeezing his hand.

"You're not getting rid of me that easy."

"Tough cop, *non?*"

"Just love you too much to go anywhere else." His throat was rough and torn. He reached for the water on the bedside table, but Nathalie was quicker. She held it for him while he drank through the straw.

"The doctor says you need sleep," she told him. "Lots of it. But he says we're past the dangerous stage now."

Ryan imagined what might lay ahead of him. Marcus' funeral, the investigation, the questions from his own department. The physical danger might be past, but he knew plenty of other dangers still lurked in his future.

Then he realized he hadn't even considered his own recovery. There'd be physical therapy, and…

He pushed away the thoughts. Tomorrow would take care of tomorrow. He needed to focus on today.

"How are you holding up?" he asked, his voice temporarily stronger after the water.

"Me? I'm fine?"

He looked at her, waiting.

She returned his look, unwavering. "I am fine, truly. Everyone has been very good to me. To us."

"Who is everyone?"

"Our neighbors. Some of them at least. Art and Maggie have sat with Melina whenever I've been here."

"And how is she?"

"Scared," Nathalie admitted. "And a little confused. I'll bring her next time, so she can see you're going to be all right."

"That'd be good."

Nathalie smiled again. Then she said, "Your brother flew out from California. He stayed for several days, and barely left the hospital. He wanted to be here when you awoke, but he finally had to go. There was pressing business in the state capitol."

"The busy life of a state senator," Ryan wheezed.

"You shouldn't make fun. He was very concerned."

"If you say so."

"I do."

"Well, then it must be so," Ryan said. Then he struck on something. "Wait, did you say *days*? How long have I been here?"

She cocked her head and calculated. "You were hurt nine days ago."

Ryan's head sunk back into the pillow. "Nine," he repeated in disbelief.

That meant they'd already buried Marcus. He'd

missed it. He'd missed the chance to say goodbye, to see the department honor him with all of the pomp and circumstance he deserved.

He felt the tears streaming down his cheeks before he realized he was crying. His chest shuddered, and his throat locked up. He was vaguely aware of Nathalie's hand tightening around his, and he focused on that sensation, letting it anchor him to this world. Even with it, he slipped back into sleep, although he couldn't be sure if it overtook him or if he rushed toward it.

He woke and slept, slept and woke. At some point, he realized he was starting to do at least as much waking as sleeping, and it was around that time people started coming to visit him.

Nathalie was often there, and her presence made everything better. Sometimes she brought Melina, and even though the beauty of his little girl's face was marred with concern, her smiles still warmed his heart.

The doctor visited daily, updating him on his progress, which seemed slow but steady. At some point, the man's demeanor shifted subtly from collegial to strictly businesslike. Nathalie noticed it, too, and when she asked Ryan about it, he just shrugged. "I think he must have found out I'm not a party member."

"Why would he think you were in the first place?"

"I'm a cop," Ryan said. "Most of us are these days." He smiled. "Just like most of your journalists aren't."

A shadow crossed her face and she frowned. "You'd be surprised. More and more are."

"More editors, maybe."

"Like I said, you'd be surprised."

Ryan felt a twinge of regret at bringing it up. "I'm sorry, babe. I know it's a sore point."

Nathalie's job at *The Archway*, the weekly free newspaper magazine, was a far cry from the mainstream *St. Louis Dispatch*, both in terms of income and prestige. Her refusal to abandon her principles when it came to reporting all of the news, and not just the part that the party wanted reported, eventually led to her dismissal. Of course, no one would admit that, just like no one would admit the passive capitulation of much of the mainstream media. But Nathalie was convinced of it, and Ryan thought she was right. Even her work at *The Archway* was severely muted, but she seemed to hold out hope that some small piece of her voice got through all the editing. At least they ran stories the larger, mainstream news sources wouldn't.

Nathalie gave him a soft smile and squeezed his hand gently. "Let's just focus on getting you better, okay?"

"You got it."

Sergeant Potulny showed up a couple of days later. Ryan was initially surprised to see him, but Potulny kept things as impersonal as possible. He gave Ryan some paperwork to sign, placing him on medical reserve status.

"What's that mean, sergeant?" Nathalie asked him.

Potulny appeared mildly annoyed by her question. "It means that he remains on paid status but has no arrest powers. It'll be up to the doctors to determine if he's able to return to full duty."

"If?" Ryan asked. "You mean *when*."

Potulny shrugged. "That's up to the doctors. Your injuries are pretty severe. Your doctor has indicated that they might be career-ending."

"Why is his doctor sharing medical information with the department?" Nathalie snapped. "That's confidential."

"Some of it is," Potulny fired back. "But his overall status and the projected results are not. The department has a right to know what those are. For planning purposes."

Nathalie bristled but said nothing.

"I'm coming back," Ryan told him.

"We'll see."

"Count on it."

Potulny shrugged again. "Time will tell." He cleared his throat. "You should focus on your recovery, Officer Derrick. On behalf of the Metro Department, the Party, and your President, I wish you well." He lifted his hand to his brow in a stiff salute. "MAGA," he said, barely suppressing a sneer.

Neither Ryan nor Nathalie responded, and after a few moments, Potulny dropped the salute. "Internal Affairs will schedule an interview with you as soon as you're physically up to it," he said, all business again.

Ryan had known that was coming, but the idea still sent a chill through him. "I should be all right in a couple of weeks."

"Your doctor says in about three days." Potulny smiled humorlessly. "So we'll just pencil that in."

"Fine," Ryan conceded. He wanted to get the experience over with, anyway.

"But if he gets tired, the interview stops," Nathalie interjected.

"Of course," Potulny's flat smile didn't waver. "We just want what's best for him. And the truth, of course." He turned his gaze toward Nathalie. "The truth is everything. I think that's something our professions have in common."

Nathalie stared back at him. Ryan could almost hear the rage-filled reply that had to be roaring inside her head, which made it even more impressive that she held her tongue. Telling off a party hack like Potulny might feel good in the moment, but they'd both pay for it in the end.

"Thanks for coming, sergeant," Ryan said. "But I think I need to get some sleep now."

Potulny nodded. "Certainly. I'll see you in a few days, then." He turned to the door and left without looking back.

"That man is trouble," Nathalie said once the door had snapped shut behind him.

"He's a drone, bucking for the next promotion."

She shook her head. "No, he's more than that. He's a believer. He worries me."

Ryan took her hand. "Forget him," he said, but he knew neither of them could. Not Potulny, and not all he stood for.

The next day, he met Andrew, his physical therapist. The first moment Ryan saw him, he had an image of Marcus coming toward him. Both men were large, and both were black. Andrew even wore a similar, open expression on his face. Once he was closer, though, Ryan saw that his features were very different, and the timbre of his voice deeper, too. He held out his hand and Ryan took it. Andrew gave him a gentle, unthreatening squeeze.

"So," Andrew said, "I hear you're a mess."

Ryan laughed weakly at that, and immediately trusted the man.

For the first several days, they worked from a seated position. Andrew called it warming up the machine, getting the lubrication moving. He pushed Ryan, but watched carefully at the same time to make sure he didn't go too far, too fast.

The first day, Nathalie watched on while he worked, but he quickly decided that her presence distracted him too much. As ridiculous as it seemed, he had a desire to impress her, and Andrew sensed that early on. He asked Nathalie to stop coming to the sessions, and she reluctantly agreed.

Andrew was a realist wrapped up in an optimist. He didn't promise Ryan anything except lots of sweat and some pain, but he offered some hope.

"What's your goal?" he asked Ryan early on.

"To return to the job."

"Police officer, right?"

"Yes."

Andrew nodded slowly. "That's going to be tough. You know that, right?"

"I know. But it's possible."

"It is. You might need another surgery. And being a

cop, you're probably high up on the list."

Ryan shook his head. "No special treatment. I'm on the list, but it'll be a while."

Andrew cocked his head at him. "With you being a cop, I figured you were in the party."

"Lots of people do."

"But you're not."

"No."

"Why not?"

Ryan was surprised at the question. Most people didn't ask it. "That's a long story, my friend."

"We appear to have some time on our hands."

Ryan smiled a little ruefully. "Well, then, we'll see."

That seemed good enough for Andrew.

Internal Affairs appropriated an empty room on the same floor as Ryan's. When his doctor gave his approval, they waited until a time when Nathalie wasn't around to come and get him unannounced. A silent orderly wheeled Ryan in and left him there to wait. A single, plain table and hardback chair were the only pieces of furniture in the room. Up high at the ceiling, a pair of cameras perched in the two corners facing him. He ignored them.

Fifteen minutes later, Potulny arrived, entering without knocking and taking up a position near the door. Ryan experienced a flicker of concern when he saw the gaunt man who followed Potulny into the room. His sunken eyes appeared black and dead, and he was preternaturally thin.

Gleeson.

Investigator Gleeson of Internal Affairs had a reputation at Metro that bordered on something between a comic book villain and an urban legend. Rumors swirled around him like smoke. He could supposedly smell a lie, and had the passive ability to hypnotize.

Ryan didn't believe most of it. For being such a fact-driven profession, cops were notorious gossips and entertained more than a fair share of superstitions. He was reasonably certain that most of what people whispered about Gleeson was utter bullshit.

Most of it.

Gleeson took a seat across from Ryan, taking his time and moving with very precise motions. He folded his hands in front of him on the table and gave Ryan a contemplative look. When he spoke, his voice was like cream poured over broken glass.

"What shall we talk about?"

Ryan took a moment to answer, trying to force any tension to drain from his own voice. "Whatever you need to talk about, Detective."

Gleeson let a tiny smile touch the corners of his mouth. "I'm a captain, actually."

Ryan shrugged. He'd heard that rumor, too.

"Normally," Gleeson said, "once they start promoting someone past the rank of sergeant, that person ends up in the command pool. He gets kicked around from unit to unit like some sort of offering basket in church, getting experience at this and that, looking for that next promotion. But they didn't do that with me. I made sergeant, and I stayed here. Lieutenant, then captain, still here." He leaned forward slightly. "Any idea why that might be, Officer Derrick?"

"You're the Chief's brother-in-law?" Ryan deadpanned.

Gleeson's tiny smile spread into a tight-lipped one without humor. "Funny. Sadly, no. I've had to earn my brass on merit alone."

"Good for you, then."

"Good is the operative word, officer. I am still here because I am too good at my job to be wasted running the motor the pool or a bunch of property crimes detectives. I am here because I get results. I get the truth."

Ryan watched Gleeson as he spoke. He saw the man's vanity, and his confidence. "You won't have to work at it," he told Gleeson. "I intend to tell the truth."

"The problem with that statement is that quite literally everyone I sit down with says exactly that."

"I bet."

"Of course, if the person is being honest, then it isn't an issue. But if that person is being deceitful, I have to bring my considerable skills to bear. The problem is that the only way to know is to put things to the test. So unfortunately, that leaves me in the difficult position of having to assume that everyone is lying, and proceed accordingly."

"You make it sound like you're going to torture me."

Gleeson just blinked at him, letting the moment draw out. Then he said, "Of course not, officer. That is ludicrous. I am merely going to ask you some questions about the death of Officer Marcus Washington, and whatever culpability you might have in that event."

A shot of electricity exploded at the base of Ryan's

skull at those words. He had an insane thought that Gleeson was somehow responsible for the sensation, that he was hooked up to an interrogation apparatus in the wheelchair. But he recognized it as adrenaline even as it flooded his body.

"Culpability?"

Gleeson shrugged. "Perhaps."

Ryan swallowed thickly. "You know what? I think I'd like to have my attorney present."

Gleeson gave him a look of pure disappointment. "Why is that, Officer Derrick? Did you do something wrong?"

Ryan set his jaw. "Lawyer," he said. "Or I'm not talking to you."

Gleeson shook his head sadly, then glanced up at Potulny. "Sergeant?"

Potulny stepped up to the table and placed a sheet of paper in front of Ryan. "Officer, these are your administrative rights. Follow along as I read them to you."

"I-" Ryan began.

"That is an order, officer."

Ryan stared at Potulny's hard face. The man's contempt was clear, perhaps only overwhelmed by the fact that he clearly enjoyed being in control. Ryan was going to get no quarter from him. He picked up the paper and read as Potulny spoke.

"Officer Derrick, you are hereby compelled to completely participate in an interview with the Metro Police's Internal Affairs Division. Said interview will continue as long as the interviewer or his commander's discretion determines is necessary in order to properly identify all salient facts regarding the matter at hand.

"You do have the constitutional right to remain silent during this process. Electing to exercise this right, however, will immediately result in your termination from employment.

"You do not have the right to an attorney during this process, unless the interviewer or his commander determines that you are officially a suspect in a crime. At such time, you will be granted a reasonable period of time to secure representation. Reasonableness will be defined, without appeal, by the interviewer or his commander.

"You do not have the right to union representation during this process, unless the interviewer or his commander determines that your responses or the fact pattern make it likely that you are susceptible to internal discipline. At such time, you will be granted a reasonable period of time to secure union representation. Reasonableness will be defined, without appeal, by the interviewer or his commander.

"You are required to answer all questions honestly and completely. Any deceitful answer or a lie of omission will result in your termination from employment and may further result in criminal charges, if appropriate." Potulny looked up from the form. "Do you understand these rights as I've read them to you?"

Ryan shook his head. "I can't have a lawyer here? Since when?"

Potulny pursed his lips. "You are a federal employee, officer. We all are now. That comes with certain advantages and responsibilities." He lifted the paper.

"This is one of the responsibilities."

Ryan glanced down at the paper again. Then he shrugged and set it on the table. It didn't matter. He hadn't committed a crime, and he hadn't violated policies. He could afford to let Potulny be the bureaucrat he was and for Gleeson to flex his ego.

"I understand," he said.

Potulny put a pen on the table and slid it to Ryan's form. "Sign it, then."

Ryan grabbed the pen and scrawled his name on the signature line. Then he dropped the pen with a clatter. "Ask your questions."

Gleeson waited until Potulny had collected the form. Then he gave Ryan a withering look. "You should come to one realization right away, officer. Things will go much easier for you if you can manage that."

"What realization is that?"

"You are not in charge."

Ryan didn't answer. That much was obvious.

"Actually," Gleeson continued, "you could say that your kind isn't in charge anymore."

"My *kind*?"

"Yes."

"And what kind is that?"

Gleeson glanced up at Potulny. "How would you describe people like Officer Derrick, Sergeant? A shamer who refuses to salute his city, his nation, his president? Marries a foreigner? Won't join the New American Party?"

"I can think of a lot of things to call people like him," Potulny replied, his voice dripping with contempt.

"I'm certain you could." Gleeson met Ryan's eyes. "Sergeant Potulny is a true believer. A true American. You, on the other hand, are something less than American, wouldn't you agree?"

"No, I wouldn't." Ryan felt the anger brewing in the pit of his stomach, threatening to explode. "I'm as American as either of you."

"Oh, I'm sure you're correct," Gleeson said. "Legally, anyway. At least for now. But if we're judging a man based on his actions, you…" He wagged his bony finger at him. "You are very suspect, Officer Derrick."

"Is that what we're here to talk about?" Ryan asked. "Politics? I thought we were going to talk about what happened on the job."

"We'll get to that. But you're making a common error in your thinking, officer." Gleeson waited a few moments, and when Ryan didn't respond, he completed his thought. "*Everything* we do is politics. If you understood that, you wouldn't be in the situation you're in."

"What are you saying? That if I understood politics better, I wouldn't have been ambushed? My partner would be alive?" Ryan shook his head, anger welling up. He was so tired of the arrogance of these party members, thinking that in just one short decade, they had completely remade America, changed all its people, and that somehow all of it was valid. "Pardon me for saying so, but go fuck yourself."

Gleeson gave him a disappointed scowl. He pointed a bony finger at the cameras behind him. "That sounds like insubordination, officer. Or conducting unbecoming. Perhaps both."

"If you're going to discipline me, I'll take that union rep now."

Gleeson dropped his finger. "We'll let it pass. This time. You're still upset about the passing of your partner. And perhaps you are lashing out because you feel some measure of guilt."

Ryan's anger dissipated almost as quickly as it flared up. Gleeson was right on that count. He harbored a great deal of guilt. But it wouldn't pay to let the investigator see too much of that.

"Let's talk about the incident," Gleeson continued.

"Fine by me."

"Whose decision was it to respond to the call for service?"

"I don't remember."

"Who was driving?"

"Why would you ask me that? You know Marcus was driving." Not only were there cameras inside the car that were activated by the lights or siren, but each officer's badge contained a GPS chip. Figuring out who was behind the wheel would take about three minutes of investigation.

"How about if I ask the questions, officer? Would that be all right?" Gleeson's silky tone had a light sarcasm to it. "You just concentrate on answering them."

"Fine. Play your little game."

Gleeson exchanged a glance with Potulny that seemed to be a confirmation of all of Ryan's shortcomings. Then he asked, "Who was driving?"

"Officer Washington was driving," Ryan said, his own tone formal.

"And so you were handling the mobile data computer system?"

"I was handling the mobile data computer system," he parroted.

"So you decided to answer the call." Gleeson's tone had no hint of a question in it.

"It was a mutual decision," Ryan said. "An unspoken one."

"What do you mean?"

"We heard the call come out for a burglary-in-progress. We were close. So we responded." He gave Gleeson a hard stare. "That's what cops do. We answer emergency calls."

Gleeson ignored the jibe. "Yes, of course," he persisted. "But let me be clear: you were the one who hit the keys on the computer system dispatching your patrol unit to the call in question?"

"Yes, I was."

"And upon arrival, who formed the tactical plan to approach the residence?"

Ryan shook his head. "It doesn't work like that."

"Oh? You don't make plans? You just stumble into dangerous situations?"

"We didn't need to," Ryan growled. "Marcus and I have been partners for a few years now. We – "

"Were," Gleeson corrected.

Ryan stopped. "What?"

"Were," Gleeson repeated. "You and Officer Washington *were* partners. You are not any more. Officer Washington is now deceased." He squinted at Ryan. "You do understand that, do you not, Officer Derrick?"

Ryan gritted his teeth. "I do. Is this also a psychological evaluation?"

"Hardly. We won't require one of those until the question of your return to duty becomes more immediate, and let's face it: that is a ways off, isn't it?"

"A long, long ways off," Potulny added.

Ryan didn't reply. He suddenly felt weary, worn out, weak. He sat motionless, waiting for Gleeson's next move.

The investigator finally gestured with his thin fingers. "You were saying there was no need to formulate a tactical plan."

Ryan blinked, collecting himself. Then he continued, "We knew what to expect from each other. We worked as a team."

"Who was in charge?"

"It was a partnership," Ryan said.

"But you are the senior officer."

Ryan shrugged. "By years of service, yeah. I guess so."

"When you reached the door, what did you see?"

"It was ajar."

"How much?"

"Just a few inches."

"What did you make of that?"

Ryan took a deep breath and considered. What *had* he made of it? All of his actions had been automatic that night. He hadn't stopped and broken down each piece of data as he received it, merely reacted based on his training and experience. "I took it as a validation of the original call of a burglary in progress," he said, trying to recreate his automatic thoughts at the time. "I thought it possible that the burglars had left the door open to escape more easily, or that they had simply forced it open and it swung back but didn't close entirely."

"Which?"

"Which what?"

"Which possibility did you think had occurred?"

"I didn't know. It was possible that either had occurred. It was also possible that neither had, and the door was standing open for another reason entirely. On patrol, we encounter mysteries like this all the time."

Gleeson didn't react. "Who made the tactical plan for entry?"

Ryan tried to remember, wishing he could consult their badge camera footage. He knew any inconsistencies in his statement could be construed as intentional deception. "I believe Marcus made the decision as to what side of the door each of us stood, though that was a pretty standard tactic for us."

"Why?"

"I'm left-handed. He's a righty."

Gleeson blinked at him, a fleeting confusion seeming to cloud his eyes.

"That puts us each on our gun side," he explained. "That way we each expose less of a target when we lean in for a shot."

"I know that," Gleeson said shortly. "I've been a cop for twenty-seven years."

You've been employed by the Metro for twenty-seven years, Ryan thought, *but you haven't been a cop for a long time. You've been riding a desk, investigating real cops.*

"What happened next?"

Ryan closed his eyes, trying to envision the scene. "I pushed the door open wide. We looked inside, but couldn't see anything. I looked at Marcus, gave a three count, and then we button-hooked through the door."

"So it was your decision to go in?"

"There wasn't a decision. We had to go in."

"Please answer the question, officer."

"Yes, goddamnit," Ryan snapped. "*I* gave him the head motion, *I* made the three count, and *I* went in first."

"And then what?"

Ryan took a deep breath, trying to control his frustration and a cavalcade of other emotions coming right behind it. He let it out, then said, "Nothing, at least for a second. Then Marcus came through the door and the shooting started."

"Did you see the shooters?"

"I saw flashes. Shapes. No one I could identify."

"Did you return fire?"

"You have my gun. You know I did."

"How many shots did you fire?"

"I don't know."

"Officer –"

"I...do...not...*know!*" Ryan looked at him, exasperated. "As many times as I could. They were trying to kill us."

"They did," Gleeson said, matter-of-factly. "Or one of you, at least."

Ryan swallowed, his emotions a mess. His guilt for failing Marcus battled his anger at Gleeson for his transparent tactics and accusations, and the resulting swirling maelstrom seemed to have nowhere to land. An immense weariness settled over him.

"I think I'm done for today," he said, quietly.

"That's not for you to decide."

"I am not medically fit to continue," Ryan said, forcing his tone formal.

Gleeson hesitated. It was a fine line that he was treading, Ryan knew. Despite the prominence of the American Party, and the requirements laid upon Ryan as a police officer, Gleeson still had to play by the rules. Appearances still mattered, and bullying a wounded man had potentially bad optics.

"We will resume tomorrow morning after breakfast," Gleeson said.

"What else do we need to cover?"

Gleeson gave him a tight smile, but didn't answer. He reached for the call button on the table, then hesitated. He looked at Potulny. "Sergeant, I believe there is one more piece of business to address? Now is as good a time as any."

"I'm tired," Ryan said. "Whatever it is, it can wait."

"This will only take a moment," Gleeson insisted. He motioned to Potulny.

The sergeant stepped forward into Ryan's field of view. "Your wife isn't an American citizen, is she, Officer Derrick?"

"You know she's not," Ryan snapped. "What's with all the ridiculous questions?"

Poltulny ignored the outburst. "What's her status?"

"She's a resident alien."

"Planning to return to Senegal? Or is it Greece? I forget which parent is from where, but I suppose it doesn't matter. Where is she planning to go?"

"Nowhere. She's planning on staying here with our daughter and me. She's applied for citizenship." He glanced at Gleeson, then back at Potulny. "What's with this? What do you care about my wife?"

"It's my job to care."

"Last time I checked, you were St. Louis Metro, just like me. Not Immigration."

Potulny shook his head. "I'm federal, remember? The President made us all federal. And I got an agent assist request from Homeland Security and Immigration."

"HSI doesn't have local agents?"

"They're busy. So I'm helping out here."

"Helping with what?"

"With your wife."

Ryan flexed his fist open and closed. "What about my wife? You want to get to the point, *sergeant*?"

"The point is simple. I've been asked to update her file for HSI. Make sure she's still working, isn't involved in criminal activity, or anything subversive." He gave Ryan a hard stare. "You don't have a problem with that, do you?"

"No," Ryan said, his mind spinning. He hadn't considered that Potulny would try to use Nathalie somehow to get to him. He tried to imagine what the sergeant's play would be. "But she's complied with everything for almost six years now. She gets her citizenship in just over a year."

A slow smile full of malevolent joy spread across Potulny's face. "Oh, you don't know yet, do you?"

"Know what?"

"She didn't tell you?" Potulny shook his head. "That surprises me."

"What the hell are you talking about?"

"While you were recovering, the President has started rolling out his immigration reform policy. Lots of changes, and most of them long overdue."

"Get to the point!"

"Watch your tone, officer." Potulny said but his tone remained amiable. "The point is that there was a change that affects you pretty directly. Well, your wife anyway. You see, effective three days ago, any foreigner who marries an American citizen doesn't have to wait seven years for American citizenship." His smile broadened. "Now they have to wait twelve."

Potulny may have said more, or perhaps it was Gleeson who spoke. But Ryan did not hear their words. He sat, frozen in his wheelchair, staring at the wall, until both the investigator and the sergeant finally left. The silent orderly entered a few moments later and returned Ryan to his room.

Chapter 5

It has been said that the core beliefs of any organization – whether a business, a social club, a political movement, or a nation – around which the organization is founded and which drive it to greatness…those same beliefs also ultimately become the reason for its own downfall. This concept of 'active inertia' essentially argues that success creates its own set of pitfalls, including strategic blindness and an unwillingness to adapt or change with the evolving external events. This was not necessarily the case, however, with the United States of America. Instead, it is particularly ironic that it was the corruption of one of the founding elements of America – a core belief if you will – rather than adherence to it that became the catalyst for its greatest crisis.

That fundamental element was immigration.

— From *An Unlikely Phoenix* by Reed Ambrose

"You should have told me," Ryan said to her that night.

They sat in his room, an untouched tray of dinner off

to the side. Nathalie's hands were folded in her lap, and she seemed to be waiting to see how Ryan would react. Anger had never been his first approach, but he could sense that emotion lurking around the edges of his mood, the remnant of a grim shadow hanging on from his meeting with Potulny and Gleeson.

"It wasn't important," Nathalie said quietly.

"Not important? How can you say that? Nat, this is our family we're talking about here."

"*Oui*, I know this." Her tone remained low and non-confrontational. "But you must forgive me. I was more concerned with whether my husband was going to die or not."

That stopped him cold. Like any good cop, he understood prioritizing things during an emergency. Her citizenship must have seemed like a minor issue compared to his life and death struggle. Except…

"It is important, Nat. If I *had* died, what would you have done?"

"*Mon Dieu*, shut up with this talk."

"Answer the question."

"It is a stupid question."

"No, it's important."

"How can it be important? You didn't…you lived."

"But if I hadn't?"

"Are you trying to torture me?" A hint of frustration crept into her tone. "Fine, then. If you had died, I would mourn. Melina would be crushed. There, are you happy now?"

Ryan held out his hand toward her. She hesitated only a moment, then took it. He squeezed softly. "If I die, what happens to your citizenship application? You'd be a resident alien with no means to become a citizen. With a child who *is* a citizen. Which means that you would eventually have to leave the country, and that she may not be allowed to leave."

"They could not keep my child from me."

"The Minority Safety Act has a clause in it that precludes a parent from taking a child who is an American citizen out of the country to an unsafe destination."

Nathalie snorted. "Greece is not unsafe."

"Senegal is. And let's be honest about Greece…it isn't the most stable of nations, either."

"I don't see your point."

"No, you don't want to see it. Put your journalist eyes on it. How hard would it be for them to say that the danger of you returning to the land of your mother instead of your father?"

"There would be no proof."

Ryan gave her a look. "They don't require proof. They can say whatever they want. That is what this government has become."

"Why would they do this?"

"Power," Ryan said. "Control." After a moment, he added, "Revenge."

"For what?"

"For me."

They shared a long look, and he could see that she understood everything that those two words entailed. His lack of party compliance, his quiet resistance while maintaining a position with the police, was all a major affront to people like Potulny. And people like Potulny, Ryan had reluctantly come to understand, were running things now.

"Then you had better not die," Nathalie finally said.

"No plans."

"Good." She squeezed his hand, then pulled her own away and clapped her hands together. "Then we must plan for what is happening today."

"You have any ideas? Other than waiting for almost six more years?"

She nodded. "The ACLU is going to appeal the law to the Supreme Court as soon as the legislation is passed by Congress."

"It should take them about five minutes," Ryan said. "Unless they've got their rubber stamp already out and on the desktop."

"It doesn't matter. Sooner is better, anyway. The law can't be appealed until it is passed and then applied to someone."

"The Supreme Court," Ryan mused, shaking his head. "How many of those justices did this president appoint?"

"Five."

"So there's his majority."

"Two of the others usually concur as well. The other two usually dissent."

Ryan snorted. "For all the good it does."

Nathalie looked him in the eye. "Sometimes dissent is its own reason, regardless of what it accomplishes. Otherwise, wouldn't you be saluting at roll call every night?"

"*Touché.*"

"Ah, your French is improving. Have you been using Rosetta Stone behind my back?" She smiled gently, and took his hand. "I've already spoken to Annalise. If the ACLU fails in their appeal, she will draft an individual appeal on the basis that my application was already in progress. She called it a – "

"Grandfather clause."

"Exactly so, yes. She believes that may be the compromise the White House concedes in order to overcome resistance to this bill. If they do agree, I will still gain citizenship in March."

Ryan considered. He wasn't a political scientist, he was a cop forced to pay attention to politics. Nathalie was the political expert, but she was partially blinded by hope and desire. Still, he admitted the concession might occur. People throughout history have seemed perfectly willing to allow governments to pull up the ladder once they were safely in the treehouse.

"Then we'll hope for Plan A and prepare for Plan B," he said.

"Yes," she agreed. "But mostly, like I've been saying all along, we will focus on getting you healthy again."

Andrew helped with that. Each day, he worked Ryan to the point where Ryan felt like he'd reached his limit, then pushed him a little farther. His personality seemed to be a cross between Ryan's Marine drill instructors and a personal trainer, but behind all of it was a genuine kindness that Ryan was grateful for.

Kindness was not what he received from Gleeson.

Every day or two, the investigator returned to the hospital and repeated his questions. Sometimes he asked new ones, and Ryan was often unable to see the relevance of the questions. But while he feared the power that rested within Gleeson's conclusions, he knew he hadn't done anything wrong, and so he simply did as he always had – he answered truthfully.

The truth was undergoing a lot of changes, however.

Once he was walking again, albeit very short distances and with the help of the parallel walking bars, Andrew asked him about his pain tolerance and medication.

"Normally, that's a doctor question," he explained, "so feel free not to answer. But my recommendation is to use only as much pain relief medication as you need to be able to function. I know pain is unpleasant, but it is also a good indicator of where things are with your body. Sometimes it takes knowing where it hurts to know best how to fix it."

"A philosopher," Ryan joked.

"It takes philosophy to survive these days," Andrew said quietly, and with a smile, but his eyes shot left and right when he said it to make sure no one else was within earshot.

"Let's hope that's enough," Ryan said, grimacing as he took another step and settled his weight on his bad hip.

"It's always enough," Andrew said. "It just doesn't always save a man."

Ryan opened his mouth to ask what that meant, then closed it suddenly because he thought maybe he understood.

The next day, Gleeson asked him if he knew his assailants.

"How many times do you want me to answer the same question, Captain?"

"As many times as I ask it, *Officer*. If you're telling the truth, this shouldn't be a problem, should it?"

"The only problem is that it is tedious," Ryan grumbled, rubbing his eyes. Andrew had been especially hard on him that morning, and he'd been looking forward to a light lunch and a nap before their afternoon session. Gleeson's visit interrupted those plans.

"I'm sorry you find the search for your partner's killers to be tedious," Gleeson replied.

"I didn't mean it like that."

"Just answer the question, please."

Ryan sighed. "No, Captain, I did not know my assailants. I could barely make out their figures in the darkness. If it weren't for the muzzle flashes, I couldn't have even said it was men with any certainty."

"So you're certain none of your attackers were women?"

"I meant men in the general sense. Human, not automated gunfire or something."

"I see. Now you said you heard these figures shouting phrases at you and Officer Washington, correct?"

"Yes, I've told you that already."

"And do you remember those phrases?"

"Not exactly. It was hard to focus on anything but the

gunshots."

"*Allahu Akbar?*"

"No, I don't think so."

"Was it in English? Arabic? Greek?"

Greek? Ryan struggled to disguise his reaction. Was Gleeson trying to somehow find a way to connect Nathalie, based on her parentage? Or use this attack on him to hurt her citizenship application.

He tried to shake off the thought, but it clung to him. Ten years ago, he would have thought it ludicrous, but as Potulny had reminded him in their first post-shooting interview, all police were now federal. Gleeson could be working at more than one purpose.

You're being paranoid.

"Officer? What language was it?"

"English."

"Are you certain?"

"Pretty sure. I thought I heard them say 'fascists.'"

"Not *fascistes*?" His voice took on a slight French accent, then shifted to one Ryan didn't recognize. "Or *fasistes*?"

"I don't think so."

"But you aren't certain."

"No. It could have been another language. But they called us *motherfuckers*, too, and that's a pretty uniquely American word."

Gleeson didn't appear at all ruffled. "Do you know what the dark web is, Officer Ryan?"

"No."

Gleeson arched an eyebrow. "No?"

"You seem surprised."

"You have been a police officer for ten years. I would have think you'd have come across the reference."

"It sounds like a cyber-crimes concern to me. I was in patrol. I answered emergency calls, like a real cop."

"And in heroic fashion, I'm certain." Gleeson smiled tightly. "All right, then, a brief education. The deep web is a site that does not appear in a search engine, but requires a direct link. This mechanic is not necessarily subversive in itself and has some practical, legitimate uses. Your bank account is deep web, for instance. The dark web, however, is another matter. It exists on the Internet but requires special software and passwords to access it, or even be aware of its presence. This level of deep secrecy on the 'net has been the bane of law enforcement for the last twenty years, providing a safe harbor for drug dealers and child pornographers alike."

"What does this have to do with me?"

"Of late, seditious parties have utilized this medium to further their agendas and spread propaganda."

"Seditious?"

Gleeson's tight smile remain fixed. "Traitorous."

"I know what it means. But last time I checked, the First Amendment is still in effect. So who gets to decide what qualifies as sedition?"

"A thorny question, to be sure. Some things do hover right on the edge of the borderline, in the gray area, so to speak. This can cause a great deal of disagreement. But many of these groups are considerably more radical, and far from ambiguous. One of them released a video yesterday. Would you care to see it?"

"You're not asking, so let's not pretend I have a

choice."

"Point well taken. But I will warn you, it is a bit disturbing." Gleeson turned to the television hanging on the wall and used a remote to turn it on. The image that appeared was already cued and paused. A hue of green light bathed the entire scene, showing a modest living room and a front door.

The door was slightly ajar.

"Do you recognize this setting?" Gleeson asked.

Ryan cursed softly and averted his eyes. "I...don't want to watch this."

Gleeson was quiet for a moment. Then he said, "You know what I find interesting? That many people in America today have the luxury of seeing and living in the world the way that they want it to be. They exist within a bubble of their preferred beliefs, inside of an actuality created by carefully constructed scenarios, untouched by any inconvenient reality." He paused for effect, then continued. "Now, they are able to do this because other men and women are willing to sacrifice that luxury for themselves, and live within a much more true reality. Police officers, firefighters, emergency room doctors and nurses, and even politicians...all of them must live in the world the way that it truly *is*. Those truths are forced upon us at every turn, and if we do not acknowledge them and face them and ultimately resolve them, then that pleasant fiction that the rest of the world gets to live in is exposed and destroyed."

Ryan barely heard his words. "I was there. I don't need to see it a second time."

"I think you do, Officer Derrick. Because you chose to

live in the world as it is, not as you would like it to be."

Ryan rose clumsily, reaching for his walker. Sweat immediately popped out on his brow and ran down his spine. His legs felt shaky.

"Sit down," Gleeson commanded. "Before you fall down."

Ryan lowered himself back into the seat. He reached for the call button. The silent orderly could help him walk out of the room.

"Leave that alone." Gleeson's voice was cold. "Here's what's going to happen. I'm going to play this clip, and you are going to watch it. And then we're going to talk some more. If there's any doubt in your mind about all that, know that you are being compelled to participate in the remainder of this interview as a condition of your continued employment."

Ryan fired a hateful stare at him. "You enjoy this, don't you? It's a power trip for you."

"I enjoy doing my job well. If that conflicts with your desires, forgive me if I think the needs of the Metro and the citizens of our nation are more important."

A petty man wrapped in patriotism, Ryan thought, but held his tongue. There was no profit in continuing to poke at Gleeson, and Ryan knew that, right or wrong, his job did hang in the balance.

When he didn't answer, Gleeson took it as acquiescence, and started the video clip.

Ryan watched, his stomach clenched, as the door swung open. Then he saw himself button-hook through the door, sweeping his pistol across the field of vision but seeing nothing in the dark. A moment later, the large figure of Marcus Washington filled the doorway, and then loud shots erupted.

His partner actually made it through the doorway and fired several shots of his own as he fell, something Ryan wasn't aware of. Little of what happened inside that room had been shared with him. Seeing Marcus crumple to the floor, Ryan battled several waves of competing emotions. Devastating grief rose first, having barely receded below the surface. But anger flared as well, and a small flash of pride. Marcus Washington was a warrior, and he fought to the very end.

There was a moment of stillness when the shooting stopped, then the field of vision swept to the left and toward the back door, before Gleeson paused it.

Ryan forced himself to unclench his jaw. Rigid tension filled his entire body, and he took in a deep breath and tried to release it from the muscles in his back and shoulders. Only then did he realize that his face was streaked with hot tears. He wiped at them, unashamed.

"Did you catch it?" Gleeson asked.

"What was I supposed to see?"

Gleeson shook his head. "Not see. Hear."

"All I heard was gunfire."

"Then close your eyes," Gleeson instructed. "I'll run it again."

"I don't – "

"Close your eyes."

Ryan obeyed, focusing on this breathing, and listening intently. He heard the slight squeal of the door hinge, then the eruption of gunfire. And then…voices.

"Die, you fascist occupiers!"

"Nazi cop motherfuckers!"

The shooting and the yelling was followed again by that eerie silence. Ryan opened his eyes and saw that Gleeson had paused the video as before.

"You heard it?"

Ryan nodded. 'Nazi' had become the newest 'N-word', equally offensive to both liberal and conservative alike.

"Does that sound like free speech to you?"

Ryan considered. "It could mean a lot of things."

"Pray tell."

"They could be anti-Federalists, or just anti-police. It's hard to say for sure."

"You seem very calm when talking about the men who maimed you and murdered your partner."

"Believe me, I'm not calm."

Gleeson pursed his lips, watching him. Then, wordlessly, he started the video clip again.

The scene changed. The green night vision was replaced by a bright corona of light that surrounded a shadowy figure whose features were indiscernible. When he spoke, his accent was distinctly American, but Ryan couldn't place the regional dialect.

"What you have just seen is the beginning of a revolution," the shadowy man said. "For years, more and more power has become concentrated with the federal government. Because of this, we have seen the rights of many citizens further eroded. In the United States of America today, unless you are white *and* a member of the New American Party, you have become a second class citizen in your own nation. Those poor souls who were somehow less than that before have become even more oppressed. Young black men continue to be shot and killed by the police in even greater numbers than a decade ago, and there is even less scrutiny of these murders. The police have become the indiscriminate instrument of the state, doling out a warped sense of social, criminal, and racial injustice. This will not be allowed to continue. Unless the federal government takes immediate steps to rectify this situation, we will be forced to continue such actions as those you saw here. It is with a heavy heart that we carry out these missions, for despite the hatred on the surface in this nation, we recognized that we are all, in the end, brother and sisters. Let us hope that our leaders listen sooner, rather than later."

The scene faded to black and a logo reading BASTARDS OF LIBERTY appeared.

Gleeson turned it off. "This was broadcast widely on the dark web. No legitimate news sites are running it, of course, but that doesn't mean no one is seeing it."

"They're...terrorists," Ryan whispered, realization sinking in.

"They are. And attacks like the one on you and Officer Washington happened in sixteen other cities, all within twenty-four hours of each other."

"Sixteen..." Ryan shook his head, disbelieving. It didn't seem possible.

"These terrorists are protesting the necessary consolidation of proper authority in its proper place. They are attacking the institution that protects that authority and provides order in this nation. Now, do you see that behavior as residing in the gray area of free speech or can we agree that it is clearly seditious?"

Ryan didn't answer. He couldn't. The grief and anger welled up again, blocking out everything, and leaving him temporarily immobilized. These men had ambushed him and Marcus over a political idea. They didn't know him, or anything about him, or Marcus. If they had, they never would have chosen either of them as targets.

Gleeson continued. "Perhaps now you can see why Sergeant Potulny and I have…pressed certain issues with you, Officer Derrick. More is in the balance than just an officer involved shooting. In many ways, you could argue that the future of our country is in jeopardy. And with those stakes, where you stand is of critical importance, don't you think?"

Ryan swallowed. "I…I don't know what you want from me."

Gleeson opened his mouth to reply, but the door buzzed, cutting him off. Potulny strode in with an air of self-importance. He gave Gleeson a wave of dismissal, and stood waiting impatiently for him to comply. Gleeson showed a hint of irritation, but rose dutifully and left the room.

Potulny settled into Gleeson's seat. "Let me ask you a simple question, Officer," he said, without preamble. "Did you know your attackers?"

"Of course not."

"You didn't know this attack was going to happen?"

"What the hell are you talking about?"

"Officer, we lost a man in this act of domestic terrorism," Potulny answered sharply. "*That* is what I'm talking about. I'm talking about whether you are in any way complicit with that."

"Well, I didn't."

"Then you wouldn't have any problem making a public statement condemning this assassination?"

"Why?"

"People know about these attacks. They're understandably outrage. You survived. People will listen to what you have to say. It's an opportunity for important messaging."

"What kind of messaging?"

"The truth, of course," Potulny said. "That a valiant man was assassinated by terrorists. That we should remember that, and more importantly, him."

Ryan hesitated, then nodded. "Yeah. I'll do that."

Potulny nodded triumphantly. "Good. Good to finally have you on board."

Chapter 6

It is the particular hubris of the historian to look back upon the events of the past and point to the singular event, that glaring catalyst, which sparked the descent into war and madness, and proclaim it obvious. Such proclamations are clear only in retrospect, however. While the significance of an event may be evident to many contemporarily, its true impact can only be measured with the passage of time. In other words, just as it is patently unfair to judge men and women outside of the context of the period in which they live, it is likewise unfair to judge their contemporary understanding of events against the greater understanding we have achieved with fifty years of perspective. Even more to the point, we know how things turned out, and those in the midst of these happenings lack that luxury. Simply put, a mystery that seems simple once solved was still difficult while being investigated.

And yet, is it hard to imagine the polarized reaction to the American Immigration Act of 2029? Is it entirely unfair to wonder how many people suspected that this would be the match that lit the tinder? Even a generous view of the contemporary man or woman of the 2020s would suggest not.

"Did you know?" he asked Nathalie, and her eyes told him the answer.

It was the second time Nathalie had kept something from him. He didn't like it, and told her so.

"*Je suis désolé,*" she apologized quietly. "But it is like I told you before. All I cared about was you getting better. The doctor said that anything that upset you was counter-productive to that goal. And you were already devastated about Marcus."

"They murdered him!" Ryan blurted out.

"I know this."

"Over politics," he went on, shaking his head in anger and disbelief. "They didn't even know us. Didn't know Marcus' politics. Didn't know mine. Do you know how much shit I took for not saluting at roll call? For not joining the party?"

"I do. I've been here all along, remember?"

Ryan hesitated, realizing how he sounded. Nathalie's career had suffered for her convictions, too. Working at *The Archway* was a far cry from the *St. Louis Dispatch*, and while the journalists had never been asked to physically salute the President, more subtle means of compliance were required. And much like he had refused to salute and instead looked downward, and been labelled a shamer, Nathalie's fact-based reporting and incisive manner of questioning the status quo ultimately led to her being among the first victims of the newspaper's 'restructuring.'

"I'm sorry," he said. "I know you have."

"Our country is slipping away from us," she said. "It has been for a long while, I think, but now momentum is gaining. There is division everywhere, and no one seems to listen to anyone else."

Ryan smiled then, despite it all. He loved her fight, her brutal honesty. "You sure you still want to become a citizen, with everything going to hell?"

"It saddens me," she answered, not returning his smile. "You were born here, Melina was born here, but I *chose* America to be my home. She is becoming something different than the nation I fell in love with many years ago."

"Maybe we should leave," Ryan suggested.

"Where would we go?"

"Greece? You still have your citizenship there. I could apply. We could start over. If Greece is unsafe, perhaps Britain, or –"

"What about Senegal?" Nathalie asked quietly. "You don't even consider the land of my birth?"

Ryan hesitated. Senegal had once been a stable democracy in Africa, but in recent years had been usurped by a military junta. All foreign assets were seized and nationalized. People of his complexion were not particularly welcome.

Nathalie took note of his hesitation, and his silence. "Ah, yes. I have forgotten. Senegal is one of those places the President so wisely labeled as shithole countries. Why would we go there?"

"Nat-"

"It doesn't matter. I will not leave my home, *mon amour*. I will not let them take it from me. From us."

Ryan lay back on his bed and stared at the ceiling. His mind flitted over the events of the past twelve years, and he sighed. "Maybe they already have."

"Do not say such things. That is how they will win, if enough people believe this."

Ryan let it go. She wouldn't surrender, he knew. At least, not when there seemed to be a chance. It simply wasn't in her to give up, and arguing about it here would accomplish nothing.

"All I can control," he said, "is getting better, right?"

"Right," she agreed.

He nodded at that. "Right," he repeated.

Ryan stared down at the piece of paper in front of him. Potulny and Gleeson waited while he read it. When he finally finished, he looked up at the two of them. "I can't say this," he said simply.

Potulny frowned. "Why not?"

"It's party propaganda."

"Be careful, Officer."

Ryan shrugged. "That's how I see it. You asked me to condemn the terrorists that killed Marcus. I'm willing to do that. But I'm not going to spout all of this…party line agenda."

"What is your objection?"

"Almost all of it. It reads like a party recruiting pamphlet."

"It reads like truth," Potulny insisted.

"Christ, you even have me calling Marcus a party member." He shook his head. "I can't lie about his life, or his death. I loved him too much for that."

Without a word, Potulny opened a folder and removed a piece of paper. He slide it across to Ryan. Ryan looked down at it, then did a double take.

"What's this?"

"What does it look like?"

Ryan peered more closely. It was a membership application for the New American Party. The blanks were filled in with Marcus Washington's bold, firm script.

"No," Ryan said. "I don't believe it. He wasn't a party member."

"Associate member, technically," Potulny said, taking the application back and replacing it in the file. "His membership was still pending when he was murdered."

Ryan stared back at Potulny, his surprise not fading. He tried to imagine Marcus embracing the ideals of the NAP, and it didn't make sense to him. If he hadn't seen his partner's handwriting on the form, he would have refused to believe it at all.

"So you were wrong about your partner's party membership," Potulny pointed out. "So can you allow that you may very well be wrong about other parts of the statement that you object to?"

"No," Ryan said, automatically. His mind was whirring. He wished he could have asked Marcus about this, wished he could have understood. But even as this thought occurred to him, so did another. Marcus already had one thing going against him – his skin color. Maybe he had joined in name only, just to take some of the pressure off or remove one more obstacle.

It didn't matter. He knew who Marcus was and what he truly stood for, and it wasn't the New American Party. He knew that from a thousand conversations, and any reason the man might have had for filling out that form didn't change that knowledge. The last thing he was going to do was let his partner get used as propaganda for the party.

"I think we're done here," he said, his voice low and grim.

After that, Potulny and Gleeson stopped hounding him about the statement. Their meetings became less frequent, and seemed to focus more and more on any mistakes he might have made during the ambush. He tried to ignore the potential consequences of a negative outcome of the investigation, and worked with Andrew every day, sweating and pushing through pain. As the days passed, he switched out the walker for a cane, and abandoned the parallel walking bars altogether. Slowly, he reached a point where he could take several steps without any support, and walk from the bed to the bathroom only using the cane.

"You're doing well," Andrew told him.

"I've got a great coach."

"Nah, you're a hard worker. That makes a big difference."

Ryan developed a strong sense of trust in the physical therapist, and while they kept their conversations careful, he got the sense that the two of them had similar beliefs. But they stayed away from volatile subjects, including politics and policing, and how Ryan was injured, even when they were alone. One of the things he'd learned in his police career was to believe the adage that "there's always a camera." Besides, he wouldn't have put it past Gleeson or Potulny to actively spy on his therapy sessions.

Thinking that made him feel overly paranoid, though he'd come to view a healthy paranoia as a self-preservation strategy. Still, the sessions with Gleeson slowed down, and though they were always at least mildly contentious, he felt like the investigator had backed off. Ryan welcomed this development.

He and Andrew were working on a weight machine the day the President made his immigration policy speech. Ryan had known there was something coming ever since Potulny had taken delight in telling him about the naturalization requirements shifting from seven to twelve years. But he'd forgotten the speech was scheduled for that day.

The White House spokesman was on screen when he

looked up, moving his lips, but there was no sound. Closed captioning followed along, advising that the President would be out shortly to deliver a momentous policy change.

"Turn it up," Ryan suggested.

Andrew glanced at the television. "We got one more set to do."

"Turn it up," Ryan repeated. "We'll watch the speech, and I'll give you two sets."

Andrew frowned, but didn't argue. He found the remote and turned up the volume.

"-will be no questions at the conclusion of his speech, though there will be a private consultation at the White House with members of the Majority party in order to plan how to properly proceed with the implementation of the President's policy."

The spokesman adjusted his glasses, then absently touched his earpiece. "And I'm now being advised…yes, of course…ladies and gentlemen, the President of the United States of America."

A recording of *Hail to the Chief* played as the forty-fifth President strode to the lectern. The trademark swoop of his hair was impossibly blonde, not showing any sign of graying, even after three complete terms of office. Ryan remembered seeing the before and after pictures of previous office holders and shaking his head at how much the responsibility of the position had aged each of them. Somehow, this president seemed immune to this phenomenon.

Once at the microphone, the president took a moment to make eye contact with a couple of his favorites, even smiling briefly and pointing at one. Then he removed a sheaf of notecards from his interior jacket pocket and placed them on the lectern, before staring meaningfully into the camera. His expression grew serious and sank into what Ryan always felt looked more like a scowl than the presidential affect he was sure the chief executive was going for.

"My fellow Americans," the President began, and then stopped. "My. Fellow. Americans. What does that even mean?" He turned up his palms and pantomimed a theatrical shrug. "I mean, past presidents have been starting important speeches with that phrase for centuries, but has anyone ever stopped to really ask what it means? What it means to be American?"

Something small clenched in Ryan's stomach, and he had a vague premonition of something dark.

"I'll tell you what, folks. No president in the history of our country, of *any* country, has been faced with such difficult times when it comes to answering that question. Or running a nation, for that matter. You have no idea." His hand swept across the top of podium dismissively. "No one really does. I mean, sure, there are still two former presidents alive who might have an *inkling*." The president held his thumb and forefinger up, showing just a tiny space between them. "Maybe that much. But they didn't face the kind of situations we've faced, and let's not kid ourselves, folks…they were Democrats. Yeah, remember them?"

He smirked, and polite rumble of laughter came from the assembled crowd, even some scattered clapping.

The President smiled at the applause. "Oh, yes, they're

still around, just like my old party. And both claim to represent the voice of the loyal opposition, and all that, but come *on*. We know better, don't we?"

There was more applause. The President was clearly pleased by it.

"But put that aside. I'm not here to divide. No, I'm here to unite. Unite all Americans. Because we all need to be together these days. These are dark, perilous times. Both out in the world and within our own borders. So let's talk about those borders. That's probably the best place to start."

He glanced down at his note cards and seemed to be ruminating what he read there. Then he looked back into the camera, his serious, presidential expression returning.

"When I campaigned for election for the very first time, our border was a very important issue. And I was very clear about my position on protecting that border. I proposed a wall that would serve both as a symbol of how we viewed our nation's sovereignty and as a practical way to enhance our ability to protect our borders. People laughed and made fun back then. Do you remember this? There were all kinds of doubters. But we did it. I did something no other president has ever even come close to doing. I built that wall."

"You built a sieve," Andrew muttered, next to Ryan.

"And as I promised, through our trade agreements, the money to pay for that wall came from Mexico. That's only fair, isn't it? Their country was causing the problem, so they should pay for the solution. And they did."

Applause broke out, then gained momentum. The president spoke loudly over the rising tide, punctuating his words with a jabbing finger. "I said it before, and I'll say it now, either we have a country or we don't."

The applause swelled to the point of the Congress members standing, and went on for almost thirty seconds. The president basked in the adulation before finally raising his hands to signal them to sit down again.

"Now, some people don't get this concept, folks. They like to say that wanting to protect your country is somehow racist or whatever other nonsense. But they're wrong, and true Americans know it. You know it. And time after time, everywhere I go in this country, these Americans are telling me that is what they want. An America for Americans.

"Hey, you deserve it. We all do. Don't let people call you a white supremacist or other derogatory terms because you're a patriot. Nowhere else in the world is being a patriot painted as a bad thing. Every other country can say 'France for the French' or 'Russia for Russians' and it's viewed as their right. But we say that here in America and the liberals and even some of these same countries that are doing the same thing all jump up and down and cry like little babies. Racist, they say. Unfair, they say." The President shook his head. "Well, frankly, I'm sick of it. And the American people – the true American people – they're sick of it, too. And it is high time we did something about it. Because that's what government is for, folks. Carrying out the will of the people.

"You wanted me as your President twelve years ago, and so you voted, and the process worked. The people got what they wanted.

"You wanted trade agreements that were actually fair to our nation and to our business people, and you got it.

"You wanted a tax plan that was fair to honest working people and business alike, and I gave you that plan right off the bat, in my first term.

"You wanted an end to reckless foreign aid, just pouring money into holes in the ground all over the world, and I heard you.

"Under my leadership, government carried out the wishes of the people.

"In fact, I did such a good job of carrying out your wishes that when the end of my second term was drawing near, you people didn't want me to leave office. You thought it was a stupid rule that a President could only serve two terms. It wasn't always that way. What if he's doing a great job? No other president was asked to go for a third term, but the American people wanted me to continue in this office. What was I to do? How could I say no? And so the government responded to your wishes. The New American Party was formed, and we put legislation before the people to repeal the Twenty-Second Amendment, and it sailed through faster than any Amendment in the history of Constitutional law. And I got to stay as your President, doing the will of the American people. For which, I'm deeply humbled."

Ryan heard an up swell of pandering applause that the President soaked in for a few moments, his expression anything but humble. Then he continued. "By the way, and I haven't been campaigning like I usually do because I've been too busy doing the work you hired me to do, but do please remember that we have another election in just a few months. I am seeking a fourth term as your president, and if you elect me again…" He smirked. "And you will. Why wouldn't you? I'm doing a great job. I'm doing the will of the people. But when you elect me again, I will officially surpass FDR as the longest tenured President in the history of our country. And I'm very excited about that. I've already done way more in three terms than FDR did in four, but it will be especially satisfying to pass him up."

More applause, and then more standing. The President let it go on for a little longer this time, so much so that it actually receded on its own. He glanced down at his note cards before continuing.

"All right, so the American people have made it clear who they want to lead them, but they've also been clear on what they want. They want their country back. And I've been working tirelessly for twelve years to give it to them. And I've had great success. Phenomenal success. No president ever before has had so much success. But there's still more work to be done.

"I have been consulting with some very smart people on this issue. Tremendously smart people. And I've put together a plan that is just incredible. You're going to be very happy when you see this plan. You'll be thrilled. We're going to roll it out over the next year, and there are a lot of small details that make it work, but tonight, I am going to give you the big picture. Because things are gonna change, folks. You're going to get your country back. I made America great again, just like we promised, and I'm going to keep making America great, always."

Applause exploded. Some senators and

representatives leapt to their feet. No one remained seated. Ryan heard a few scattered calls of "MAGA" from the crowd.

The President beamed and let it play on for a long while, finally waving them back to their seats. "Let's get to the meat of it. Because that's what matters. Back when I was in business, making my fortune, that's all I cared about. People would come to me, and they'd sing a good game, but all I wanted to hear from them was the bottom line. And the American people deserve the same consideration, because you're smart people."

He stared into the camera meaningfully. "Get ready, because the liberals and the America haters are not going to like this. But all that should do is reinforce for you what a tremendous idea it really is. It is an idea whose time has come, and one all true Americans can embrace.

"Think about that for a second. *True* Americans. Are you one? I know I am. I know I only have men and women in my cabinet who are, and only support men and women in Congress who are. But there are people out there who don't understand what that means, to be a true American. These are the people who want to coddle terrorists." The President began counting off on his fingers. "You've got these musicians and actors who try to tear our country down. And of course, you've got the race riots just two years ago. These people have lost sight of what it means to be a true American."

A cheer built up in the crowd.

The President shook his head vehemently. "Listen, folks...if you call yourself African-American, Muslim-American, Gay-American, or any other hyphenated anything-American, then you're not a true American in my book. Nothing, and I mean *nothing*, should go before the word American. Nothing!"

The audience vaulted to their feet again, giving him thunderous applause. It went on for a full minute.

During that time, Ryan glanced over at Andrew. The black man stared at the television, silent. Anger radiated off of him like heat. When he seemed to feel Ryan's gaze, he turned to meet it, and Ryan looked away. A stab of guilt and shame hit him in the chest, and he felt the weight of the sins of his skin color.

"Tell me you're not buying this shit," Andrew said, through clenched teeth.

"Not for a second," Ryan answered, and that gave him the courage to look Andrew in the eye.

"Yeah, well, you're in the minority these days."

"You're telling me."

That brought a slight, strained smile from the big man.

On the television, the president held out his hands. "Thank you. You're very kind." He waited for the assembled group to sit down, then continued. "So here's what we're going to do, folks. You're going to be very happy with this, believe me. Because we're cleaning house. It's that simple.

"If you are not an American citizen right now, *today*, then I am officially telling you to leave our country."

A swell of applause began in the audience, but the President spoke over it.

The sinking feeling in Ryan's stomach grew.

"Oh, Nathalie," he whispered.

"If you refer to yourself as a hyphenated American,

that time is over. You need to decide which side of the hyphen you want to be on. Either drop whatever is before the word American, or you will be asked to leave *our* country."

The applause grew.

"If you're not an American, a true American, then we simply do not need you here. We don't want you here. We want our country instead. So you're leaving. Within one year, anyone not a citizen or any citizen who claims status as anything other than American will be *gone*. And if you don't go on your own, then we will come for you. We will find you and deport you, and quite frankly, you might not get sent to a country of your choosing. So take advantage of this amnesty period, and get out."

Loud cheers joined the applause.

"We have everything we need within the borders of our own nation," The President continued. "We have all of the natural resources, all of the know-how, the talent, all of the labor, all of everything. We don't need other nations. They might need us, but we don't need them. And so, as part of this initiative, we are closing the borders. We will not be admitting anyone to this country without strict review, and maybe not even then. And the same will apply to Americans leaving the country. Because if we're going to have tight borders, folks, they can't be tight just one direction. That doesn't work.

"Americans will have the next six months to get their affairs abroad in order before the full restriction kicks in, but I am instituting closer scrutiny on every traveler immediately, in or out. This is a necessary move, and quite frankly, folks, it is long overdue. If we'd had this kind of vigilance in 2001, we would have prevented the tragedy of 9/11, I guarantee it. Think of that when people try to argue against this policy. Tell it to them. They won't have an answer, because there isn't one. That's because this is the best move.

"This is all part of a shift in policy." He hesitated, cocking his head, and making a strange expression. Then he gave his head a shake. "You know, actually, that's not exactly true. We've been working toward this policy since my first term. We heard the voice of the people and have been on our way to this point since way back then. Like I said, government is here to serve the people, and that's what we're doing. Serving.

"So the United States is finished being the world's policeman. We have already backed away from being the savior that everyone looks for to solve the problems they created. What did that get us? We poured tons of money into foreign aid and development and disaster relief, and what happened? Everyone expected more, that's what. And they hated us even though we were helping. I don't know about you, but it felt like coming across some kind of bum on the street, back when this was a nation that had bums on the streets. But you remember, if you're old enough. These people, they hold out their hand and ask – no, they *demand* – you give them money. Your money. And why? Because you have it and they don't. It doesn't matter that you worked for it, that you sacrificed for it, or that they didn't do a damn thing. No, all that matters is that they feel like they are somehow entitled to what you earned, and they believe it is your responsibility to give it to them. And what happens when you do? They hate you anyway. Maybe they hate you even more than before. And I'll tell you what else happens, folks. You get more bums coming at you with their hands out."

The President shook his head, affecting an expression somewhere between anger and sorrow.

"So we stopped giving out money. And they hated us for that, too, but what're you gonna do, right? What're you gonna do?" He sighed. "Well, now we're done cleaning up the messes around the world, too. We're going to focus on the United States for a change. Just like we made sure to feed our own people first, now we're going to make sure our own people are safe first. Instead of sending young Americans to die in some other country for some other people, they are going to serve right here within our own borders. Let the rest of the world take care of itself for a change. We're going to take care of each other right here in the U.S. of A.!"

The cheers had been building and now they exploded once more, seeming to be even louder than before. The President soaked it in, his face lifted imperiously as he looked out into the assembled legislators.

"America first!" he yelled, and pumped a fist in the air.

That sent the crowd into a near frenzy, and he smiled at them.

"So make no mistake," he boomed over the cacophony in the Capitol building. "Let every nation know that we shall see to our own needs before we consider theirs. And everyone in this country who is *not* an American…it is time to get your exit plan in order. Because a new dawn is rising in America, a new order, a new way that is the old way, a time of America for Americans! It should have happened a long time ago, but that doesn't matter because it is happening now. It is the will of the people and I am making it happen. I am making America great, always." He raised his fist in salute, then opened it in a brisk wave, turned from the lectern and walked away.

Ryan sat, stunned. He barely registered Andrew turning off the television and joining him in his silence. Nathalie's image hung in his mind's eye, and he struggled to make sense of what he had just heard.

"Damn," Andrew said, his voice low and raspy.

"I've got to call my wife," Ryan said. "We've got to…figure things out."

Andrew nodded slowly. "I imagine so. But from the sounds of it, the man in the White House already did all the figuring."

"This can't be happening." Ryan shook his head in disbelief. "I thought it was bad before, but…"

"But now he's upping his game." He met Ryan's eyes meaningfully. "You best get yourself correct, Officer. Because the only thing that these party dudes hate more than someone who isn't one of them is someone who they think oughta be."

Ryan stood and used his cane to move laboriously toward the door. He had a long way to go and not much time to get there.

Part II:
ALEXANDER

Sacramento, California

USA

February 2029

Freedom is never more than one generation away from extinction. We didn't pass it on to our children in the bloodstream. It must be fought for, protected, and handed on for them to do the same, or one day we will spend our sunset years telling our children and our children's children what it was once like in the United States where men were free.

Ronald Reagan,
40th President of the United States

Chapter 7

As what was viewed by many on the left as the White House's continual march toward extremism progressed, relations between several states and the federal government deteriorated. Long before anyone envisioned an actual war, a political and cultural war came into being. Battle lines were relatively clear, opposing opinions loudly stated (to the point of becoming jingoistic and certainly propagandistic), and this led a slow but inexorable escalation in which all parties found themselves becoming more entrenched as time passed.

California emerged as the leader of the opposition. While Hawaii and Alaska both predated the Golden State in objecting to federal measures and were even the sources of the first rumblings of secession, the overwhelming population and economic strength of California, coupled with its social and cultural prominence, pegged it early on as the de facto leader of a loose, unofficial coalition of liberal states who defied federal mandate. While there were states such as Wisconsin that likewise spoke out, these few states were isolated and ultimately cowed by their very geographic location. Thus, the true division over the proclamations the President made in 2028 and the

— From *An Unlikely Phoenix* by Reed Ambrose

S enator Alexander Derrick wanted very badly to punch Carl Young in the face. In a legal sense, he'd probably get away with it. Technically, Young was employed by the New American Party. He wasn't an elected official and his public profile was negligible outside of the small political circles he moved in. Alex doubted the police would even be involved, much less arrest him for smashing the man's nose.

There would be a political price to pay, however. Young's handlers were still courting Alex, and sending their pet back to them all bloodied would signal an end to that courtship. And while Alex knew that their efforts to win him over would ultimately be in vain, his purpose now was to keep them talking as long as possible.

If they're talking, you're winning.

That little gem came from his brother, who was a cop in St. Louis. Ryan had been wounded in the line of duty nine months ago, and Alex had gone back home to see him then. But it was actually a few years ago at Thanksgiving, after the two of them had knocked back a few drinks, when his little brother dropped this particular bit of wisdom on him. Ryan had grown philosophical, telling Alex that their jobs weren't really that different. Both mostly involved talking, and as long as people were still talking, both of them were winning. It was only when the talking stopped that somebody had to lose.

Alex reminded himself of that every time he wished Young would just shut the hell up.

"Everyone knows it's these fringe elements driving all this talk," Young was saying from the plush, high backed leather chair across from him. "Between the Hollywood types and the Berkeley crowd, they're whipping up all the moderates with their reckless behavior."

Alex glanced over at Miriam Slake. She didn't react, even though her district included exactly the so-called fringe elements Young was deriding. Miriam's face was unreadable, however, as she stared at Young implacably. The only sign of her frustration that Alex could read was in the tight grip of her fingers around her untouched drink.

"I'm not sure why you're talking to me about this, Carl," he responded. "I don't represent Hollywood or Berkeley."

Carl grinned tightly and without humor. The action stretched his skin across his skeletal features. "Let's not be coy," he said. "You carry a lot of weight in the Senate. People look to you for approval. They look to you for direction."

"I think you're overstating my influence," Alex said.

"Is that what you'd like us to believe?" Young's fake smile didn't waver. "That your position as Majority Leader is merely ceremonial?"

Alex shrugged. It was a delicate dance with these people. He had to make them think that he was powerful enough to influence those that they wanted influenced, but not so powerful that he could simply command them to do as he bade. These men from Washington that Young represented had to believe that his influence would work...but only eventually. That bought them all something precious – time. So it was in that narrow space in between too powerful and not powerful enough where he walked now.

"My position gives me a voice, yes," he said. "And so does my seniority. But it doesn't make me an executive, Carl. At the end of the day, I am still just another state senator. I'm not the Governor, or the President."

Young's smile twitched at the mention of the Governor, but he quickly recovered. "No one is asking you to be the President. We're just asking you to be who you are – a senior member of the legislature. And as a senior member, to influence these...radicals within the rest of the legislature."

"Now you want me to reach across the hall to the State Assembly as well?"

"No need," Young said easily. "You show leadership in the Senate and bring these people around, and the Assemblymen from those same districts will follow suit. It's inevitable. It's human nature."

"Do you really think that some of the more dedicated Assembly members are that easily swayed?" Alex shook his head. "You called them radicals, and in one sense, I have to agree with you. Many of them believe in their stated principles very strongly. They were elected based upon those ideals. They're unlikely to readily abandon their positions or surrender their convictions."

Young shrugged. "Some will, some won't. We'll address the recalcitrant ones at a later date."

And how will you do that? Alex wondered, but didn't say it. Instead, he held his hands up in a gesture he knew conveyed reasonableness. "I can only promise to speak with my fellow senators. I can't promise what their eventual course of action will be."

"Who amongst us can?" Young said. "And that is all we are asking of you. To have a *conversation*. To *influence*."

"And I will. I'll talk to the moderates first. Lay the foundation before I approach those with more entrenched views."

"A smart strategy. But don't take too long. The White House is watching the events here with a concerned eye."

Alex had a fleeting vision of the giant, demonic red eye of Sauron atop a black tower in the classic *Lord of the Rings* films he and Ryan watched as kids. That eye had been scarier to him than even the black orcs on the battlefields. Perhaps even at that young age, he had an inkling about the nature of power. The orcs were monstrous and scary, but the power that sent them was even more worthy of fear.

"Something wrong?" Young asked.

"No, why?"

"You had a curious expression on your face just there."

"Oh." He forced a smile. "I was just thinking about how Senator Chavez was going to react to our eventual conversation."

Young returned the smile, but it didn't touch the

suspicion in his eyes. "Of course. I look forward to hearing about it."

"Probably more than I look forward to having it," Alex said, heaving a sigh. "But it must be done. He's the most prominent senator associated with the Mexico Movement. Any road to reconciliation leads through him at some point."

"I hope so. But it should be an interesting discussion, at any rate."

"Because I prefer the Canadian option?" It wasn't necessarily true but Alex enjoyed goading him.

Young's smile faded to a frown. "That's not even funny, Alex. If someone of less…patriotism made a comment like that…"

You'd take them away? No, not yet, my friend. But I'm sure that is in the playbook for the fourth quarter, isn't it?

Alex waved away his concern. "Relax. It's just us three here. And a little humor keeps things from becoming too morose."

"We live in serious times."

"And so we should avoid always being so serious."

"It's the only way to deal with such times."

"*Talking* is the only way to deal with such times," Alex corrected him. "And for that reason, I thank you for coming to me. Let Washington know that I will bring my best efforts to bear." He stood and held out his hand to Young.

Young didn't immediately follow suit. He took a few moments, no doubt to make the point that Alex didn't order him about. He rose before the gesture became rude, however, and took Alex's hand. In typical party fashion, he pulled Alex's hand brusquely toward him, pumping it twice in the process.

Ah, yes. The Presidential handshake.

Alex ignored the move, releasing the handshake as if nothing untoward had happened. Miriam didn't bother standing herself, knowing full well that Young wouldn't offer her a handshake.

True to form, Young gave Alex a curt nod, ignoring Miriam. "I'll look forward to hearing from you."

"I look forward to having something good to share soon." He walked Young to the door and held it open for him. "Have a safe trip back to D.C."

Young smiled coyly. "Oh, I'm not headed back just yet."

Alex raised his eyebrow.

Young ignored the unspoken question and left without another word.

Alex closed the door, then turned to Miriam. The anger she'd been holding inside was on full display now.

"That *bastard!*" she growled, her voice low.

"I know."

"How can you treat with him like that, Alex? He's a slimy, worthless-"

"I don't have a choice," Alex said, his tone brusque. "I'd like nothing more than to smash him right in middle of his smug face, but I don't have that luxury. I have to do what's right for the citizens of California, not what feels good for Alexander Derrick. That's leadership."

"Yes, I know that's leadership," she snapped. "You don't have to lecture *me* on the sacrifices of leadership. Did you see me claw his eyes out when he called some of the finest people I know *radicals*? Or when he completely ignored me and didn't offer a handshake on the way out the door? Not that I'd want to touch that smarmy piece of gutter trash, anyway."

"Then why get angry about it?"

"It's the damn principle of the matter," Miriam said. "I'm a senator for the great state of California, but because I'm a woman, that doesn't matter to him. And yet, hypocrite that he is, he still wants my vote, my influence."

"Neither of which you will give him."

"No, but he can't know that."

"There's a lot he can't know."

"Little piece of bird shit. That's what he is."

"We both know what he is, and who he represents." Alex didn't fear Young. Young was the orc, not the eye. "And now we know what they want."

"We already knew," Miriam said. "Reconciliation. Or whatever you call it when you get back together before actually breaking up."

"I call it survival."

"Do you really think so? This isn't the 1860s, you know. Peaceful separations do occur."

"Name one."

"Czechoslovakia after the Velvet Revolution. They split into the Czech Republic and Slovakia."

"That was almost forty years ago."

"Fine. What about Quebec? And Scotland? Both happened within the last decade."

"And both were only partial secessions. Both retain significant governmental ties with the mother country."

"We've left that option open. The draft of the

Declaration specifically says that."

A secret *draft*, Alex thought, but didn't say. He supposed it was, in reality, something of an open secret in most circles. "No one will hear anything after the word *secession*."

"I don't agree."

"How nice that we live in a nation where we can disagree." Alex shook his head. "We have to slow things down, Miriam. Even if this happens, it can't be something we rush into. There's too much at risk."

"You really believe it would come to war?"

"I think it most likely will. And that isn't even my greatest fear."

"What is?" Miriam asked.

Alex didn't answer. He just stared at her, letting her work it out for herself. When her face turned white, he knew she had.

"He'd...*never*..." She couldn't seem to finish the thought.

Alex wasn't sure, either. But he knew he never wanted to place a bet on what a desperate President would do if defied, and more to the point, if he lost.

"Finish your drink," he told her. "And let's have another."

Because, he thought, *we live in serious times.*

Chapter 8

When a reporter asked about the importance of institutions and tradition during the tense period leading up to the crisis of 2029, Governor Sarandon famously answered, "I believe in tradition. I believe in certain institutions. Tradition and institutions are important, wonderful things in this nation. Until they aren't."
— From *An Unlikely Phoenix* by Reed Ambrose

Alexander checked his watch. He'd been waiting for twenty minutes, and his appointment was scheduled to begin fifteen minutes ago. He suppressed a small sigh. If there was one thing about the governor that he didn't necessarily admire, it was her lack of punctuality. She routinely kept people waiting. Alex didn't believe it was intentional or malicious, and he chalked it up to her long career as a film star. She was used to people operating on her schedule, and he figured she was likely unaware that this wasn't simply the way things were supposed to be. Or maybe they were supposed to work that way, he considered. The time of important people, however you wanted to define that, was more valuable than those who were less important.

Of course, he knew the governor would never say that, or even think of it in those terms. He knew her as a kind woman, usually warm, and an excellent listener. That was often why she kept her next appointments waiting. She gave each person her undivided attention and never hurried a meeting. It was an enviable experience, unless you were the one waiting for the next meeting.

It didn't help that she made Alex mildly nervous, especially in the first few moments of every meeting. At eighty-three, she looked every bit the regal, grand madam of California politics, but sometimes when she smiled at him, he still saw the sultry figure she played in *Bull Durham*. That always made him feel momentarily guilty, as if he were being unduly chauvinistic. It was an uncomfortable experience, and something he went through virtually every time he met with her.

Sitting and waiting outside the door to the governor's office for an extra fifteen minutes didn't help any.

When the door finally opened, the Governor escorted out a young black woman in a wheel-chair. Alex recognized her as one of the Governor's unofficial advisors, Ebby Lawrence. Her area of expertise was computer science. Alex was embarrassed to admit that he had once wondered if the obvious clash against archaic stereotypes gave Ebby an inside track to the Governor's inner circle of advisors. It took all of one meeting with her to scrap that idea. Her knowledge of computers and the Internet was about as advanced compared to his own as any neurosurgeons' knowledge of the brain.

Ebby said something in a low voice, causing the Governor to laugh gently and pat her on the forearm. "I know you will," she told her. "That's why I count on you. We'll talk on Wednesday, okay?"

"Yes, ma'am," Ebby replied, and wheeled away, beaming.

The Governor turned her gaze to Alex, and smiled. The wattage of her smile was only exceeded by its warmth. "Alex! So good of you to come."

"My pleasure, Madam Governor."

She motioned for him to follow her back into her office. "Hold all calls, Harold, if you would, please," she said to her administrative assistant. "Unless, of course, the President has finally been impeached, in which case, do please interrupt us."

"Yes, ma'am."

The Governor waited for Alex to enter the office, then swung the door shut behind them. "Harold is the most efficient desk master I've ever had, but his sense of humor is a bit lacking. I think he might actually be checking the 'net for news of impeachment."

"Mainstream news would never call it impeachment, anyway," Alex said.

"Probably not. Besides, we both know that ship sailed by the end of his first term."

"Yes, ma'am."

She waved away his words. "Get that formality out of the way now, Alex. I get enough of it from Harold and everyone else out there. So sit down, and let's talk." She sat down in one of the chairs in front of her desk and held her hand out toward the other.

"Yes ma'am," Alex said, and felt his face flush warm for a moment.

The Governor laughed. "All right, be stubborn then. But do sit and let's see what we know."

Alex sat down. He could feel his nervousness slip away, as it always did once he'd been around the Governor for a couple of minutes. He wondered how long it would take to get over that first few moments, though. Probably never.

"I understand you had a visit from the bag man," she said, crossing her legs and putting her folded hands in her lap. Her expression was open, but her intelligent eyes were fixed on him.

Alex nodded. "He wanted me to bring the different Senate factions to heel. Or to create some kind of a pro-federal coalition. Hard to tell."

"Perhaps he was sent to sound out your position."

"If so, I gave him nothing."

The Governor shook her head. "Oh, Alex, that's never true. I'm sure he managed to wrangle out something of value. That's what his kind always do. It's how they remain relevant."

"I gave him nothing," Alex repeated, firmly. "As far as he knows, he was successful."

"Why is that?"

"I said I would talk to the moderates first, but I didn't promise anything beyond that."

The Governor cocked her head at him slightly and gave him a wry smile. "Does he have something on you, Alex?"

"No. There's nothing to have."

"Oh, Alex…there's always *something*. I learned that myself the hard way."

Alex shook his head. "There's nothing. I've lived a purposefully clean life, just so I wouldn't have to look over my shoulder for people like Young."

"And yet he came to you." She cocked her head the opposite direction. "Are you playing both sides of the fence, Alex?"

"Of course not!"

She looked at him for a while, as if taking the measure of him. He met her gaze and waited, his conscience clear. After a long pause, she said, "No, of course not. But you'll have to forgive me for asking. We live in treacherous times."

It was his turn to smile.

"What's so funny?" she asked.

"Something Young said to me. He said we live in serious times."

"Also true." She was quiet for another moment, then asked, "Where do things stand in the Senate?"

Alex took a deep breath, collecting his thoughts before speaking. The addition of five new senate seats eight years ago had altered the landscape of the senate, but he'd worked hard to adapt to the changes. More than anything else, the five new senators ensured that the only way a tie vote could occur any longer was if a senator abstained.

"There are at least twenty uncommitted to any form of secession at this point," he said. "Though I think at least half of those could be convinced."

"How?"

"It would take a precipitating event."

"A Sarajevo, you mean?"

He considered the analogy. The death of the Austrian Archduke Ferdinand in the Serbian capital had sparked the First World War over a hundred years ago. The Governor knew her history. "Something like that, yes."

"Well, that's one thing you can say about this President. He does create incidents in his wake. Perhaps one will sway some of those who remain unconvinced. Is there a common theme as to their reasons?"

Alex shook his head. "They're all over the map. Some are Unionists when it comes to secession, and the idea itself is unacceptable to them."

"The kind of person who refuses to get a divorce despite a miserable marriage."

"That's about the size of it."

"What else?"

"There are the pragmatists who believe the danger is too great, that we can never succeed, or that we would simply suffer too much financially. A few are just afraid. And then there are two or three who are Party members."

She wrinkled her nose distastefully. "It's those last ones I can't abide. Who in their right mind can still support this President? And who in their right mind votes for that kind of person?"

Alex considered listing the districts with senators of the New American Party, but she already knew who they were. In fact, she knew everything they'd discussed already, a trend that would likely continue for a few minutes longer. But he understood that this was her process, the foundation of the conversation she liked to lay before delving into darker, unknown territory.

"It takes all kinds," he said blandly.

"All kinds of assholes," she muttered, shaking her head. "Anyway, remind me how are the other twenty-five divided?"

"There are three camps. A contingent of twelve favor secession followed by a petition to join Mexico."

"I believe the term that group uses is *rejoin*."

"It is."

"Not an entirely inaccurate depiction, I suppose," she mused. "And the others?"

"About evenly split between secession followed by a petition to join Canada and those in favor of strict secession and going it alone."

"No one buying into a Pacific States of America?"

"Most of the secessionists are in favor of it, with one or two exceptions. They don't see it as mutually exclusive with their stated preference."

"Meaning we can secede and then join with Hawaii, Alaska, Washington, and Oregon no matter what? Even if we were to become part of Canada or Mexico?"

"Exactly."

"Can I ask you a question, Alex?"

"Of course, ma'am."

The Governor uncrossed her legs and leaned forward in her seat. She motioned for Alex to follow suit. When his face was near hers, she asked in a stage whisper, "Who's to say Canada or Mexico would take us?"

He smiled. "We'd double Canada's population and their GNP."

"And we'd quadruple their problems." She shook her

head and leaned back. "It's a pipe dream. At least at first. If we eventually decide to go this route, we will be in the same position the first thirteen colonies were in. We will need to win our own independence, or at least make a good showing of it before any other nation will risk helping us, even unofficially."

"Well, it worked for those thirteen colonies," Alex suggested.

"Thanks to France."

"But it worked."

"Yes," she admitted. "And it most decidedly did *not* work for the eleven states that tried next."

"Well, the Confederate cause was not just."

The Governor sighed. "If you mean slavery, then I agree entirely. But over my lifetime, I've come to understand that history is not nearly so clean when it comes to motivations, or good and evil. There was another issue that also drove those secessions, one that some have argued was the main reason, and it is one that directly corresponds to our own situation."

"States' rights," Alex said.

She nodded. "I shudder to admit that some of the same arguments those slaveholders made to justify their right to continue that terrible institution mirror some of our own arguments not to be a slave to the federal government."

"Some of the more daring political reporters have labeled it The Great Irony."

"Well, at least reporters are proving to be good for something these days," the Governor said wryly. "My top legal advisor calls it a treasure trove of legal arguments, and not the only one available to us. He seems to think we can litigate our way out of any federal law that clashes with our state law or constitution."

"I agree," Alex said. "What does the Attorney General think?"

"That there's a seat somewhere in Washington, D.C., waiting for him. I can't even have an honest conversation with the man. I might as well just wear an open microphone to the White House." She shook her head. "It doesn't matter. Either we figure out a way to resolve our issues as part of this country, or we will have to fight. There is no way this President will allow us to peacefully secede."

"It's happened elsewhere," he offered helpfully. "Miriam reminded me recently of the Velvet Revolution in Czechoslovakia."

"That was a nation that wanted to separate and had a poet for a president. It hardly applies."

"She mentioned Quebec in 2020, and Scotland, just two years ago."

"And you found those examples compelling?"

He had to shake his head. "No. I argued that they both retained strong bonds with their mother country. Those were technically divorces, but amicable ones."

"All true," the Governor agreed ruefully. "No, the most comparable example remains our own history. And that resulted in four years of war, the bloodiest one in our existence. I'd like to avoid that, obviously."

"Especially since now there's another wrinkle to worry about." He gave her a grave look. "Nuclear weapons."

"And we certainly want to avoid *that.*"

"Yet you're asking me if we have the votes to secede?"

"Of course, I am! If there's one thing I've learned, it's that this White House only responds to strength. If secession is going to be a bargaining chip, the threat has to be real. An empty threat brings empty results."

Alex gave her a curious look. "So, we won't secede?"

"Oh, Alex. You're as literal as Harold sometimes." She reached for a pitcher of water on the small table to the side of them and poured two glasses. Then she handed him one, raising her own. "We will do what we must to remain true to people of the great state of California," she said, toasting.

They drank. The water was cool, and felt good in Alex's throat as he swallowed.

"Now," she said, placing her glass aside. "Here's what I think we ought to do. I think you should very publicly meet as promised with those moderate members and have whatever conversation you need to have so that the White House sees you dancing to its tune. Meanwhile, we need to unify our secessionists, and win over a few more of the non-commitals. If I ever have to slap the President with the open threat of secession, I have to know I have the votes here at home."

"I don't know if we'll ever get the votes for a super majority," Alex said.

"We don't need that. We just need enough to put it to the people. If things ever get bad enough that someone like you or me thinks we need to secede, the average Californian will have to be able to see that, too."

"You'll definitely need a Sarajevo for that."

The Governor smiled grimly. "Somehow, I think this

White House will have no problem giving us that. They've been building toward it for three terms now."

Chapter 9

The further removed we are from an historic event or period, the more emphasis we tend to place on the role of those in higher leadership positions. Much of what is achieved, or what damage caused, is lain at the feet of these leaders. This is surely true of Lincoln, of Roosevelt, of Reagan, and this trend exists throughout world history.

In terms of the crisis of 2030, most eyes tend to come to rest on the sitting President and the Governor of California, who ultimately led the largest opposition to federal power. The impact and influence of both can and should not be diminished, but a closer look at this time period, especially through alternate news sources, reveals additional players whose roles may have been secondary in nature, but which were no less important. They may, in fact, have ultimately been among the most important, as their decisions drove events in a way that even the President and the Governor could not.

— From *An Unlikely Phoenix* by Reed Ambrose

After a day of very public meetings with moderate

members of the senate, Alex felt fatigued. The meetings themselves were not entirely a charade, but progress was limited and glacial, and such things wore him out.

Despite his weariness, he still met with the leaders of the various senate factions that evening. He invited all of them to his home, pouring hard drinks for those who would imbibe, and respecting the wishes of those who did not. By the time the half dozen senators were clustered in his library, it was after nine P.M.

"Can we get this rolling?" James Mallory asked, his tone slightly irritated. "I have an early morning."

"We all do, Jim," replied Héctor Chavez. "Early mornings and late evenings. That's the life of a senator these days."

August Emerson sighed, swirling the bourbon in his glass. "I've been a senator for twenty-six years, Héctor. And an assemblyman for six before that. Trust me when I tell you that early mornings and late evenings have *always* been the life of a senator."

A light, nervous chuckle ran through the group. Alex motioned toward the chairs and small couches in the center of the room, and the senators settled into their seats. Alex purposefully took a seat that could not be construed as the 'head', so as to promote a greater sense of equality. He knew there was a pecking order in this group, like any group, but he wanted to mitigate it as much as possible. Tonight should be about ideas, not personalities. He hoped that would prevail, though he doubted it would be painless.

Alex glanced around the assembled group. Each senator represented a different faction in the discussion over potential succession. Three were in favor, one opposed, and one uncommitted. And then him, of course. An officially uncommitted vote that might sway several others.

Héctor Chavez, Gregory Bell, and Miriam Slake all favored secession, though they differed on what to do once that was accomplished. Héctor wanted to join Mexico (or as the Governor had accurately pointed out, *re*join Mexico). Gregory believed joining Canada was the correct action, while Miriam steadfastly maintained that California should be the premier state in a new nation. August favored conciliation (or, as *he* accurately pointed out whenever possible, *re*conciliation, since even a pro-Union senator had to admit that relations had deteriorated to that point). James Mallory was staunchly uncommitted.

And then there was Alex. The pragmatist. Decidedly undecided.

That's the lay of the land, he thought. *Now let's find out if we can change the topography.*

"I asked all of you here because there are some things that can't be hashed out on the floor of the Senate," he began. "Or better put, there is honest talk that can't happen there. But it can here. So let's talk."

No one replied. The group waited for Alex to take the lead. Except for August, this was something they'd become conditioned to in their careers, and even August had adapted to the changing of the guard. He used to be the Majority Leader, but when the members voted in Alex instead, the veteran senator didn't object. He was nothing if not accepting of the realities of politics. He remained a productive participant in all activities but seemed to oppose Alex whenever his political views allowed.

"We are at a crossroads," Alex began, but August interrupted.

"I daresay we've passed right through the crossroads, Mr. Majority Leader. I daresay it is more accurate to state that we truly stand at the banks of the Rubicon." He lifted his glass slightly to Alex, and sipped.

"Perhaps," Alex allowed. "But when Caesar stood at the Rubicon and pondered what to do next, he had a luxury that we don't. While he may have faced obstacles in *front* of him, all of his people were united *behind* him."

"His armies, you mean," August corrected. Somehow his native Georgian accent, now almost fifty years removed from his state of birth, become more prominent at times like these. And perhaps as the bourbon took effect.

Alex didn't argue the point. "His armies, yes. A major component of the political power of his time. But imagine if he'd been facing that decision with a divided army behind him. There would have been no decision to make in that case, because he would have known anything he attempted without unity would fail. That is the same issue we are facing, gentlemen." Alex glanced at Miriam. "And lady."

"You're right," Héctor said. His suit was impeccable and his dark hair fashionably styled. "But we have been discussing this issue for over a year, and we're at an impasse. What are you suggesting we do?"

"Talk," Alex replied.

"We've been talking," said Héctor, and next to him

James Mallory and Gregory Bell nodded their heads in agreement. "We've talked and talked, and we get nowhere."

"You're right," Alex agreed. "So let's try something else."

"What?"

"Let's listen, instead."

Héctor gave him a baleful look, then leaned back in his seat. "Alex, if you're just going to play word games and insult us, why did you even bother to call this meeting?"

"I'm not doing either of those things. I'm honestly suggesting that tonight, we put aside our own notions as much as we can, and truly listen to each other. Maybe in doing that, we'll find an answer, a path that we can all agree on."

Héctor looked doubtful. "Are you saying none of us has been listening for the past year?"

"Not at all. But I know that I sometimes listen more with an eye towards how I can respond, or I'm looking for a way to counter what's being said, or thinking about what I am going to say when it is my turn to talk. And I like to think I'm a pretty good listener."

"You are," Miriam said, and a couple of the men grudgingly nodded their agreement.

"So if a good listener finds himself falling prey to these things, can we agree that a great listener or a poor listener might as well?" He looked around the group, meeting each senator in the eye. "Look, I know how intelligent every one of you is. If we purposefully focus on really, truly listening to each other tonight, I know we can make some headway. Or at the very least, understand each other better."

There was a long moment of silence, followed by several shrugs.

"Worth a shot," James said.

"Sure," agreed Héctor.

"All right. Who would like to start?"

He half-expected several of them to start at once, but was pleasantly surprised when no one did. *Maybe they really are taking my suggestion to heart.*

"Why don't we start with the most basic question?" Alex suggested. "Should California consider secession from the United States of America?"

Again, no one answered immediately. This heartened Alex even further.

"A straw vote?" he asked, and when everyone seemed in agreement, he pointed to Miriam first.

"Aye," she said.

Alex moved clockwise with his gaze.

"Nay," said August.

"Aye," Gregory said, immediately after.

James hesitated, then shook his head. "Abstain."

Alex looked at Héctor, who nodded. "Aye, of course."

So nothing has changed. Alex wasn't surprised, and he was undaunted. Every game started with knowing where the pieces were on the board.

"August," Alex said, "since you are the lone vote against, I offer you the floor before we go any further."

August gave him a stately nod, and drew himself up slightly in his seat. If this had been on the senate floor, Alex knew they'd all be in for at least thirty minutes of rhetoric. He hoped August would be uncharacteristically brief and more direct than that.

"My fellow senators," the veteran politician intoned, "to consider secession is simply lunacy. I say this not from a philosophical stance, though one could argue such. After all, there are those among us who find it particularly cowardly to abandon one's nation merely upon the basis of political disagreement, especially when the system of government allows for dissent, redress, and change from *within* the system."

"Ostensibly," muttered Miriam.

August shot her a dark look. "I believe I have the floor, madam."

"My pardon." Miriam's tone was unapologetic.

August gave her a tight smile. "As I said, while philosophy and indeed, patriotism, are all enough to stand against the very idea of secession, I reach my conclusion for doing so very much on practical terms before even bringing philosophy and patriotism into the equation."

"Practical terms?" Miriam asked. "Like what?"

August sighed. "My dear Madam Slake, if you are going to interrupt me at every turn, we are going to be here all night."

"I have a feeling we will be, anyway," she said.

Alex held up his hands. "Let's keep this civil," he offered to both of them. "I should have been clearer, however. I see tonight as a conversation, not a series of position speeches. So, please, August, answer the question?"

"If I hadn't been interrupted, I already would have," August huffed. He reached for his drink, taking a deliberately slow sip and swallowed. Once he'd replaced the glass, he cleared his throat and continued. "Practical issues, gentlemen," he said. "That is what we are faced with, not philosophical ones. We serve the people of the great state of California, and to do so, we must live in the real world." August pointed at Miriam. "And so must you, my dear."

"I am not your *dear*," Miriam bristled. "And maybe instead of throwback sexism that reeks of MAGA, you could be a little more specific?"

August clenched his jaw, and Alex thought for a moment that he would jab back at her. Instead, he said gruffly, "The White House will never let us go. Is that specific enough for you?"

"If we vote it, they can't stop us."

"*If.*"

"Yes, August, *if*. And that is what we're discussing here – whether that *if* can or should happen. And you-"

"And I say no on both counts. Curious that you put those terms in that specific order, madam. Can or should? Really, if the answer to the first one is in the negative, then the answer to the second is rather moot, wouldn't you say?"

Everyone was quiet for a moment. Then Miriam said, "I'll play along, just in case you have something new to say. Why *can't* it happen?"

"I've already told you. The Federal government of the United States of America is simply not going to allow a state to secede from the union in 2029. It will not happen. No, the White House will follow historical precedent and prevent the secession by any means necessary. Including military force, if it comes to it."

"I don't believe that," Miriam countered.

"Then you are being naïve."

"Using the military is a violation of law," Miriam said. "It goes against posse comitatus. Federal troops can't be deployed to enforce domestic policy."

"Your reasoning on that point is flawed."

"Oh, really? Do tell."

"There is no need to be snarky, Miriam." August glanced at Alex and back to her. The other three senators looked on wordlessly. "This is, after all, just a discussion."

"Really? Because it is starting to sound like the venerable tradition of man-splaining, but please continue."

August did. "For one thing, the Posse Comitatus Act specifically references only the Army and the Air Force. The Navy and the Marine Corps are not mentioned, and the Coast Guard is given special exemption."

"For law enforcement purposes. Drug traffic interdiction, to be precise."

"Even so, if one were to argue that an act of secession is a violation of federal law, then arguably three of the five branches of the military could be brought to bear without violating the act."

Miriam shook her head. "It's a weak legal argument, and wouldn't survive challenge to the Supreme Court."

"Perhaps, but what is the makeup of the Supreme Court? How many justices has this president appointed?"

"Five," Miriam admitted.

"Five. And two others that are philosophically aligned to these five. A clear majority."

"Yes, and that's a problem when the case is ambiguous," Miriam argued. "But when the issues of law are clear cut, the Supreme Court has no choice but to interpret it that way and rule appropriately."

"My good madam senator," August said, his tone moderately condescending and world weary, "when have you ever known issues of law to be anything other than ambiguous, particularly in the hands of lawyers?"

"Weren't you a lawyer?" she shot back.

"I was, and thus I speak from experience." He shook his head. "But it is a moot point. If California secedes and claims to no longer be part of the union, what standing would she then have to appeal to U.S. Courts? Most would argue little or none. And that leads me to the second point, which is that since the state is no longer part of the union and is a self-proclaimed separate and sovereign political body, posse comitatus would no longer apply. The White House would therefore be free to use any and all military force to quell what would no doubt be labeled a rebellion. And accurately so, I might add."

"That would mean sending American soldiers, some of whom are from California, to fight against other Americans." Miriam's tone was one of disbelief.

"By definition, those others you refer to are no longer Americans, if the state secedes," August said. "And the dilemma you just outlined was the same one many young men faced in 1861."

Miriam shook her head. "I can't believe any President would do that."

"Lincoln did. And he is widely regarded as one of the

greatest presidents this nation has ever had."

"Wait a second," interjected Gregory Bell, the sole black member of the group. "You can't just throw Lincoln around like that. We all know our history, August. That war was over slavery. An unjust cause."

"Unjust, yes, I wholeheartedly agree." August took a sip of his drink, his expression thoughtful. "But history is written by the victors, Gregory. If the Confederacy had been triumphant in that war, I believe you would see history books in the south today speaking very definitively about the moral courage it took to stand up for states' rights, even if the cause of the day was unfortunately misguided."

"Misguided?" Gregory sputtered. "Slavery?"

August waved away his indignation. "I'm not proposing that is the truth of it. I'm simply saying that history is written by the winners and that nations are notorious for employing *ex post facto* rationalizations and deliberate blindness to remain heroic in the telling of their own history. Look at German schoolbooks over the last sixty years, if you don't believe me."

"You'll have to enlighten me on that one," Gregory admitted.

August shrugged. "Suffice it to say that they gloss over the decade from 1935 to 1945, and are prone to their fair share of euphemisms when describing events. It's hardly uncommon. As much as I do love my own country, we are certainly no different in this regard, if we're being perfectly honest with ourselves. Every nation tends to minimize its own evils."

"This is precisely why many of us are unsure about this

course of action," James Mallory said. A thin, orderly man, James reminded Alex of a shorter, more compact Ichabod Crane. "No one wants to end up on the wrong side of history."

"I should think worrying more about right and wrong itself will solve that issue," Miriam said.

James shrugged. "Jefferson Davis thought he was right. That's not the same as *being* right."

"And yet, not making a decision *is* a decision."

"Sometimes," James replied, "it is the right one."

"I've always had a particular loathing for abstention," August said. "It smacks of indecision at best, and at worst, cowardice."

James did not appear ruffled. "I'm glad that things are so black and white in your world, August. The real world is much more gray."

"So sayeth the abstainer."

Alex held his hands up again. "All right, folks. We were doing so well there for a short bit. Can we put the knives away, please?"

August picked up his drink and tipped it toward James and then Miriam. "Forgive me if I was brusque."

There was some momentary hesitation before both James and Miriam raised their own glasses to him, and all three sipped.

"So if I'm hearing your point correctly, August, you're saying that as a practical matter, the federal government will not allow California to secede?"

"Entirely accurate, Alex. And further, that the federal government will utilize military force to prevent such an action from standing. Military force, by the way, that we could not hope to rival, even if we dared consider it."

Miriam shook her head. "I'm sorry. I just refuse to believe that it would come to that. We're talking about going down a path of legal actions to peacefully become a separate political entity. We are not proposing armed insurrection in the streets. With the eyes of the world upon us, I sincerely doubt the White House would turn a legal battle into a military one."

"And that is precisely why I said earlier that you are being naïve," August replied. "I meant no insult by it. But it should be inherently clear to you that this president cares little for what the world thinks, and world opinion will not serve as a restraint when it comes to his response."

"We live in a civilized age," Miriam persisted. "An age of laws. I believe that law will prevail."

"There is plenty of law to be found on this issue," August said. "*Texas v. White*, if you want to start there. The Supreme Court ruled secession to be an illegal act."

"That was over a hundred and fifty years ago!"

"And still a standing precedent. Therefore, law. Therefore, the president could easily justify enforcing said law, up to and including using whatever force is reasonable and necessary to do so." August stared at her plaintively. "Honestly, Miriam, do you not see this? Or do you choose to ignore it?"

"I see it," she replied. "I just see it differently."

"All right," Alex said. "Let us concede that there are significant practical obstacles to a secession."

"That may very well be the understatement of the century," August told him ruefully.

"The century is still young. Even so, if we concede that point for the moment and remove it from consideration, you said you would still argue against secession on philosophical grounds?"

"Yes," August said. "I am an American. I do not run from problems, even if they are of an internal nature. I advocate working from within the system to fix the system. It is a strategy with a long and noble history, and while it has at times been painful, it is always worthwhile. For reference, I point to Martin Luther King, Jr." He glanced almost involuntarily at Gregory, then back at Alex. "I trust no one will argue against the reverend?"

"Not against the man, certainly," Héctor Chavez said before anyone else could answer. "But your analogy is flawed. We are faced with a corrupt system that will not change, August."

"So was Dr. King," August countered. "And instead of moving away from this country or trying to create a black nation, he strove to change the system from within. In fact, he gave his life for this cause, and we are all richer for his efforts."

"Far be it from me to minimize the work of one of my personal heroes," Gregory said. "But I have to agree with Héctor on this one. While Dr. King fought an uphill battle, he had allies in the government who were striving to make the same kinds of changes he was. These were enlightened people who were drawing a somewhat reluctant populace into a higher state of existence. It was much bigger than just Dr. King and his movement, though he was clearly a major driving force. Today is much different. In fact, it is almost the polar opposite.

Rights are being systematically eroded, and quite frankly, this president is dragging a compliant populace back into a simplistic, bigoted state of existence."

"A trend we must reverse," August agreed. "Which we cannot do from outside of the body politic."

"If I had any hope that was possible," said Gregory, "I would be in your camp."

"As would I," said Héctor.

"And I," added Miriam.

"So you are all without hope?" August asked. "That seems a particularly poor place to start when you're contemplating the launch of a new nation."

"Now you're just engaging in rhetoric," Miriam said.

"Forgive me. It is a particular hazard of the profession." He motioned toward Gregory. "You were saying you are without hope, I believe?"

"My hope that this country was on a path to reason or enlightenment has been declining since the 2016 elections," Gregory said. "This president has increased federal power, presidential power, and has shown how dangerous it is to concentrate such great power in few hands. Look at the repeal of the Twenty-Second Amendment, if you want proof."

"In fairness," August said, "the repeal process went according to law, and the requisite number of states did vote to approve it. It was not a violation of law, by any standards."

"Maybe not, but-"

"And California dutifully refused to ratify the repeal of the amendment, I should note."

"Yes, I know. I was there, and I voted no."

"As did I."

"As did seventy percent of the senate and almost sixty percent of the assembly. But enough states *did* vote to ratify, and the Amendment *was* repealed. Now a president can be elected to an unlimited number of terms. *This* president."

"Such is our democratic process," August said. "If you honor the process, you have to accept the outcome."

"An outcome that has led to a tyrant president elected now to his fourth term, and a continued increase in executive powers."

"Once again, I must point out…*elected* by the people in a fair and legal election. Gregory, you cannot at once claim to believe in democracy and then decry the clearly stated will of the people, however misguided that will may be."

Gregory shook his head. "Any hopes I had dwindled to almost nothing when that man was inaugurated again last month. This country is no longer the nation I knew. It has become divided. People's rights are being ignored. Power is more and more centralized. If that's what the people of this country want, August, then I think that alone is a good reason for California to no longer be a part of it."

"We are not the only ones considering this," Miriam said. "Hawaii and Alaska are further along in their discussions than we are. And Oregon and Washington aren't far behind. If we move boldly, we can galvanize all five states. We can secede collectively, and form our own union."

"The Pacific States of America?" August asked,

arching an eyebrow.

"Unless a better name is proposed, yes. The name is not the point. The political clout is the point. With these other four states joining us, we wouldn't appear to be a rogue state. And a united, coordinated move might represent enough strength to keep the federal government from taking any extreme actions."

"Or," August argued, "larger stakes could provoke a larger response."

"We wouldn't have to go it alone," Gregory said. "We could petition to join Canada."

Who says they would want us? Alex suppressed a grin, remembering Governor Sarandon's question.

"If we petitioned Mexico instead," Héctor said, "we might see Arizona and New Mexico join us."

"You might interest New Mexico, but Arizona has long been a red state," August said.

"The population there continues to change, and that political affiliation can change along with it," Héctor said. "Who knows? But even with just New Mexico on board, we might be able sway Texas. There are legal ties between Texas and Mexico."

"Ties broken by revolution," August argued. "In case you've forgotten, Texas seceded from Mexico and fought a bitter war to back up that action. Furthermore, the Lone Star Republic stood as its own nation for almost a decade before petitioning to join the United States."

"I know my history," Héctor snapped.

"Then you know that Texas subsequently seceded again fifteen years later, along with the other states of the Confederacy." He smiled ironically. "Is that your point,

Héctor? That Texas is a politically fickle state?"

"No," Héctor said. "But you're making my point for me. Texas is an historical success story for exactly what we believe to be our most promising path – leaving one country and joining another."

August shook his head. "My fellow senators, you simply cannot mix and match your approach. If you wish to legally achieve separation, then you must strictly remain on that path. If you are relying on the concept of a natural right to revolution and proposing the equivalent of such, you cannot retroactively apply legal arguments to justify your actions. It is hypocritical to do so."

"It is messy," agreed Miriam. "But it is what we are faced with. The White House has become more and more entrenched in political dogma each term. The New American Party has become the numerically dominant party in some states, and where it doesn't have the numbers, it still wields majority-level influence. I don't think I am being alarmist when I point to the obvious parallels to post-war Germany and the rise of another autocrat."

"Miriam!" August snapped. "You go too far!"

"Do I?" She met his gaze, unflinching. "We all remember these comparisons were made early in his first term, back before the eventual stranglehold on the media. Back when the New American Party was referred to by the charming euphemism of the 'Alt Right.' It didn't take learned history professors then to see some of the same dynamics taking place in our country as those that happened in pre-Nazi Germany."

August flinched at the word 'Nazi', as did James.

"Might we retain some decorum, please? There is no need for such language."

"When did Nazi become the new 'n' word?" she asked, glancing almost apologetically at Gregory. He remained stone-faced.

"When it became a political football for the radical left," August answered. "And its meaning therefore corrupted." He shook his head sadly. "I am not a fan of our president, Miriam. I am not a member of his party, and their numbers are thankfully still small in our state government. But I must point out to you once again that he was duly elected to his position. He did not usurp it, or use military force to secure it."

"Neither did Hitler, at first. Check your history."

"Really!" August turned to Alex, exasperated. "I thought the purpose this evening was reasonable discourse with an eye toward a solution to our impending crisis."

"It is."

"Well, you might reiterate that for some of your guests, Alex. It seems more like an opportunity for unbridled political demagoguery." He leaned back, cradling his drink.

Alex didn't reply immediately. He often wondered how much of August's Georgia-born affectation was genuine, but in the end, it did not matter. August was an effective speaker, and he held considerable sway with many senators and assembly members. Alex felt certain that Carl Young had already been to visit the venerable senator. In all likelihood, that was his veiled meaning when he said he wasn't headed directly back to

Washington, D.C.

Alex had hoped for some form of progress this evening, but all that he had achieved was a restatement of positions, along with personality conflicts. He hadn't brought his own influence to bear yet, but he knew better than to waste political capital on a losing situation. He would save his best efforts for when they would count most.

"Senators," he said, "I appreciate your candor, and your time. I don't know that there is much more we can accomplish this evening. However, the Governor has asked each of you to join her and her top advisors tomorrow to discuss this further."

There was a rumbling among his guests.

"Tomorrow?" August said. "Alex, I have engagements, as I'm sure do we all."

"I know. And I apologize for the short notice. The meeting has been scheduled for over a week."

"Why weren't we told?"

"Because up until five seconds ago, you weren't invited." He let his words sink in for a moment. Then he added, "I think it is fair for me to say that I am the Governor's most trusted advisor when it comes to the legislative branch, and my advice to her will be for each of you to be present for a continuation of this discussion. Only you can properly represent your particular views, so if you want them represented, then I hope you will choose to be there."

The senators remained quiet for a few, long drawn out moments, each seemingly lost in their own thoughts. Alex waited patiently, keeping his expression neutral.

Finally, Miriam spoke. "I'll be there. Thank you, Alex."

"I'll come," said Gregory.

"Me, too," said Héctor.

August put his still unfinished drink on the table in front of him. "I will attend," he said, speaking slowly and deliberately. "But I hope, Alex, that you will remember a very important fact."

"What's that?"

"You are a senator, sir. Elected by the people, to serve the people. True, the Governor is the Chief Executive, elected by those same people. But you are not a part of her staff, sir, and I wish to very pointedly remind you that in our system of government, separation of powers is an underlying concept that is meant to check and balance the power of any one branch. It is in the best interests of the people of this state that it remain so." He rose to his feet. "I shall show myself out."

August performed his trademark gesture that was something more than a nod but markedly less than a bow, turned, and left the room. Gregory and Héctor stood, along with James. Each offered Alex a handshake as they filed out. Alex escorted them to the door, thanking them again.

When he returned to the library, only Miriam remained. She stood at the small bar, pouring herself another drink. "That went decidedly worse than we'd hoped."

"And about as well as could be expected." Alex wandered over to his chair, picked up his own drink and swirled the bourbon. "Sometimes I think critics of government have been right all along."

"How's that?"

"All talk and no progress," he said, sitting down. As best that he could see, all of the board pieces were unmoved from when the game began.

But the game isn't over. Far from it.

"I'll say one thing for that pompous bastard," Miriam said, turning around with a drink in her hand.

"What?"

She raised her glass, affecting the same stance and expression August had used in his earlier apology. Her voice assumed an exaggerated, raspy drawl. "He sure knows how to make an exit, suh."

Alex chuckled lightly. "He does. Now, if only we can get our state to do the same."

Miriam settled into the chair opposite him. "Keep the faith, Alex. We'll get there."

Yes, he thought, *but when we do, what will* there *look like?*

He wasn't sure he liked the possible answers that sprang to mind, but he washed them all away with another pull from his drink. Sometimes the best thing to do was to simply forge ahead, and do the right thing.

Especially, he mused, *if one is living in serious times.*

Chapter 10

Freedom of the press was expressly listed in the United States Constitution in 1791 as part of the First Amendment, and along with other personal freedoms, became recognized as a critical element of a free society. And yet it came under assault within the first decade of its existence, beginning with the Alien and Sedition Act in 1798. The institution proved to be hardy, however, and survived, if bloody and battered some, even managing several brief, golden ages in print, radio, television, and ultimately internet journalism. But factionalism in the late 1900s led to readers beginning to seek out the fourth estate for confirmation, not information. This trend continued, and by the time the Internal Security Act was passed in 2023, only a small segment of the public seemed to care, because for most people, it wasn't their news that was impacted.

As a result, most politicians seem to have developed an even greater fear of speaking openly against the President and his New American Party. As the mainstream media became more and more complicit in serving the wishes of the administration, even innocuous, reasoned objections by an elected official could be portrayed very differently when reported by these outlets.

Alex dialed the number using his personal cell phone. The after-market scrambler was installed, and while he suspected it would keep telemarketers and other legitimate businesses from monitoring his activity, he had no illusions about the NSA's ability to intercept the call. Ryan and Nathalie weren't extremists by any stretch, but his brother had refused to tow the party line on the police department, and as a result, was mildly suspect. Nathalie was a journalist on the fringe of the mainstream, and therefore even more suspect. Normally, he doubted anyone would be interested in their conversations, but when his own notoriety as a senator in a potentially secessionist state was thrown into the equation, he guessed enough red flags would pop up to attract someone with headphones on to listen in.

Still, he selected voice only, hoping that the lack of video would make a smaller digital footprint, and perhaps escape notice. He liked to think he didn't care about this internal security, but the prospect bothered him. It smacked of the KGB of the First Soviet Union, and so rankled him. He was old enough to remember a very different America, and he found it frustrating to be exposed to the more recent developments with regard to personal freedoms, or the lack thereof. It seemed more and more pervasive every year, ushered in under the auspices of national security. Even in California, one of the states which had steadfastly resisted the whittling away of these freedoms, he saw things that troubled him. And when a call went out of state, things were even more restrictive.

Ryan picked up on the other end after just three rings. "Hello?" he said neutrally.

"Hey, little brother."

"Alex! How's it going?"

"Same as always. You?"

Ryan didn't answer right away. Then he said, "It's been a little tough, if I'm being honest."

"Your rehab, you mean?"

"That's been going well, actually. I'm not a hundred percent, but I'm starting to get the feeling I'm never going to get back to where I was before the shooting."

"So you're still not at full duty?"

"No. They've got me on modified assignment. I'm on a desk, pushing paper."

"Case work?"

Ryan laughed. "I wish. No, I'm processing found property, community meeting requests, things like that. They're keeping me pretty sequestered these days. Nothing sensitive, that's for sure. I'd need to join the party to get anything better."

"That's the truth of it, huh?"

"That's the truth of it. I'm marked. I don't salute at roll call, so they call me a shamer. Honestly, Alex, if Marcus and I weren't ambushed and shot like we were, I don't know if I'd still be on the job. Party membership is up over eighty-five percent now."

Alex gave a low whistle. "That's high, even for a red state."

"Missouri might be red, but St. Louis has always been blue. But I don't think these distinctions really matter anymore. People seem to be falling in line, especially after the nationalization."

"The president is winning the hearts and minds of the people, then?"

"Maybe. Or maybe cops are just pragmatists. They've seen the writing on the wall, and are going along just to get along."

"I'm sorry."

"So am I."

"How's Nathalie?"

"Good. She's gearing up for the concert tonight."

"Concert?"

"The Concert for Freedom, down at the Homeland

Security Administration Arena."

"Who's playing?"

"Taylor Vera."

"Never heard of her."

"Well, you've heard her pop songs. They're everywhere, including commercials. Anyway, Nate Crider will be there, too."

"Now, there's a show worth going to. Best blues I've ever heard live was him down at BB's."

"Yeah, Nathalie is hoping to get an interview with him for *The Archway*. Oh, and they've got Springsteen on the bill, too."

"Springsteen? Seriously? He's gotta be eighty!"

"The young guard and the elder statesman, I guess," Ryan said.

Alex pursed his lips. Springsteen had never been part of his musical repertoire, but resided more firmly in the music of his parents' generation. But as a venerable rock legend, Alex imagined that had a voice that was difficult to silence. As much as the Party and the President had managed to stifle unfavorable reporting, some people were harder to sideline than others. They'd manage to accomplish it with some celebrities, either by ridiculing them or misrepresenting them to the public. Others cut themselves off at the knees through scandalous behavior, either real or rumored. But some had proven to be impervious to this trend. It took long credibility with a wide swath of the public, and a secure place in rock history. Alex supposed Springsteen fit that criteria easily enough, but he hadn't heard much about him or from him in recent years.

"Seems like they're going a little *too* old school," he mused.

"Says the guy who works for a woman in her eighties."

"I don't *work* for the Governor."

"Well, you work *with* her. Anyway, it doesn't matter. I've heard people say that eighty is the new sixty, or something like that."

"I guess so," Alex said. He figured that at some point, that reasoning was going to fall flat, as math and biology were eventually going to catch up. He changed the subject. "How about Nathalie's grandfather clause appeal of the immigration changes?"

"Still pending," Ryan said.

"What are you going to do if the appeal doesn't come back before the year is up?"

"We don't know for sure."

"Can she go to Greece?"

"Sure, but she doesn't want to. I don't want to. This is our home."

"Of course. I was just thinking you might go for a while, until things can get straightened out."

"They're telling us now that if she leaves the country for longer than sixty days at a time, her application resets."

"The appeal, you mean?"

"No, the whole thing. The twelve year wait."

"What? That's ridiculous."

"That is par for the course these days."

"I'm sorry," Alex said again. "I wish I could help."

"It sounds like you've got plenty of your own to deal with out there."

"True," he admitted. This was typical Ryan. Always focused on everyone else. "How's Melina through all of this?"

"She's a kid. She's not aware of most of it. And kids are resilient. Look at us and what we made it through."

Alex smiled. If the two of them could survive parents like theirs, that was proof that any kid could survive most anything.

"She's the biggest reason we're fighting," Ryan said. "She deserves a future."

"Yes, she does," Alex agreed. "We all do."

Ryan was quiet on his end of the line. Then he asked, "Are you all right, brother?"

Alex nodded, though he knew Ryan couldn't see it. "I'm fine. It's just been a while, and I wanted to check in."

"All right. But I'm here if you need me. You know that, right?"

"I do. And same back at you."

"Fair enough. By the way, the Blues are playing the Sharks next week. I'd say good luck, but I wouldn't mean it."

"I'm always torn when they play," Alex admitted. "Not so much when it's Anaheim or L.A., but San Jose has become my team, you know?"

"You've lived in California for too long, if that's the case. Blues for life, remember?"

"I remember. But it's kinda hard to argue with a Stanley Cup."

"Ouch," Ryan joked. "Traitor."

"I'll watch the game live, if I can. Maybe we can watch at the same time. It'll be like we're watching together."

"As long as you're prepared to cry when your boys get crushed."

"I'll have a box of tissues at the ready."

"Good."

"Though I don't know how I'll be able to hand them to you from this distance."

"Zing," Ryan said. "Nice."

"Good to talk to you, brother."

"You, too. Take care, huh?"

"I will. Give the girls my love."

Ryan assured him he would, and Alex ended the call. A small lump had risen in his throat, and yet he realized he was smiling at the same time. He needed to find a way to go see his family sometime soon.

Alex checked the time, and headed to the Governor's house.

Governor Sarandon smiled at the assembled group. "Thank you all for coming. I'm looking around the room and when I see my most trusted advisors and the leaders of the Senate gathered together to accomplish one end, it warms my heart. I believe this is an important meeting, and I'm grateful that you're all here to be a part of it."

There was a light murmur of agreement in the room.

"We are at a momentous crossroads," she continued. "A time where the future destiny of the people of California will be decided for better or worse. Our job is to make sure it is for the better."

"Better, Madame Governor," said August Emerson, "means without facing war."

"You're right, of course," the Governor replied warmly. "War is ugly. When I was younger…" A small, self-deprecating smile touched her lips. "Much, *much* younger…and along with many others of my generation, we stood against an unlawful war. We gathered on college campuses and we filled the streets, all to try to force our government to stop making war on our behalf."

"Vietnam was a terrible chapter in our nation's great history," August allowed. "But at least it was a *foreign* conflict. What we are considering, and frankly I am astounded that it is even a topic for discussion, is a domestic war. A civil war. For a second time. The first civil war was over a hundred and sixty years ago and wounds from that bloody conflict have yet to completely heal."

"My dear Senator, you speak as if I prefer war, or that it is a foregone conclusion. I assure you, the reason we are all here is to find a path that avoids war."

"The only path that avoids war is reconciliation," August said firmly.

The Governor smiled at him. "Well, surely you will allow that we can disagree on that assessment. And for the purpose of our meeting, will you at least entertain that possibility."

August raised his glass of bourbon. "Of course, Madame Governor."

"Good," she said, then turned to the rest of the assembled group. "Let's start where we can all agree. Does anyone find the ongoing actions of the federal government acceptable? Particularly those of the White House?"

No one spoke up.

"Well, on that we agree, at least."

"If little else," muttered August, loud enough for all to hear.

The Governor ignored him. "I came to politics late in my life, after a long career in acting and a shorter one in activism. Obviously, I wasn't the first actor to be governor of California, and I think it is important to respect the history of this office. I remember another actor-turned-governor who went on to become President. And though I can say that our political beliefs are very dissimilar, I will say this about President Reagan. He believed in what he stood for. He lived it. And we must do the same."

This is surreal, Alex thought. He was sitting there discussing possible secession with Governor Susan Sarandon while she quoted Ronald Reagan. He briefly felt as if he were truly through the looking glass.

"I admired something else about President Reagan," the Governor continued. "Something he and President Obama had in common. They both paid great attention to the lessons of history. So what has history to teach us about our current situation?

"It's not a simple question, my friends. Nor is it one dimensional. We can explore how this President rose to power legitimately and compare it to post-World War I Germany. In many ways, the way the White House has whittled away at our individual and states' rights to consolidate power mirrors that same period. The vilification of people who have some kind of differentness about them is textbook, not just from Adolf Hitler but virtually every despot throughout history."

"Excuse me, Madame Governor, but I must protest." August's face had reddened slightly, though Alex also noticed his glass was empty, so it could have been that. "Are you truly comparing our President to Adolf Hitler? The New American Party to the…" he stopped, refusing to say the word.

"The Nazis?" the Governor tilted her head at him slightly. "Yes, Senator, I suppose I am. At least insofar as the course of history in both instances is very similar. And if that's the case, we can project what our future may look like as a nation, as a people, if we continue on this course."

"I simply cannot agree with that analogy," August said. "I reject it."

"I wish we all could," she replied. "But we must face the world as it is, not as we wish it to be. The way we wish it to be should be our goal."

"I agree," Miriam said before August could reply. "In our draft of a Declaration of Independence, we took your regard for history seriously. Much like the original Declaration made by the thirteen colonies, we outline our grievances so that it is clear why we are seceding from what this country has become."

"Your grievances are valid," August allowed. "But let us give them redress from within the system." He turned to the Governor. "Perhaps, Madame, if you were to consider a run for the White House in 2032…"

She waved his suggestion away with chuckle. "Oh, August, that is no solution. I'm not young enough for that battle, even if it was one we could win. Besides, I've already exceeded my own abilities with the

Governorship."

The group laughed generously, if a little longer than the joke merited. The tension in the room dissipated slightly.

"My friends, I believe that all of the discussion about whether or not California should secede has already occurred amongst yourselves. I know I have had these same discussions with my advisors. We all know what the President has done, and how this impacts our nation. Just considering the topic of immigration alone is enough for us to consider going our own way. And so while I respect those of you who favor reconciliation," she cast a glance toward August, "I would like to have a practical discussion about what would happen if we did choose to secede. How should we go about it? What does secession look like?"

"Like foolishness," August grumbled, then held up his hand. "My apologies, Madame Governor. I shall henceforth curb my inclination to make such editorial observations. You may consider me bringing my full powers of intelligence to bear up on the scenario you propose."

"Thank you." She looked around at the rest of the group. "Now, where do we start?"

"I, for one, will start with a refill," August said, rising from his seat and making his way to the wet bar.

"What about the other states?" Alex asked. "Alaska and Hawaii have been very outspoken, and there's been significant rumblings in Washington and Oregon, too. Have you had talks with the governors of those states?"

"Of course," the Governor said. "Hawaii is adamantly

in favor of secession, and has been ever since the White House pushed through the repeal of gay marriage. But they won't make the first move. They can't."

"Tourism?" Héctor Chavez guessed. "A lot of Americans vacation there."

The Governor shook her head. "No, there'd be enough foreign tourism to make up much of the difference. Governor Kakuda is more concerned with the U.S. Navy. If Hawaii secedes first and no one follows, the federal government will have little difficulty responding in force. Someone else will have to lead the way."

"Alaska, then." Alex offered, though he said it more for the benefit of moving the conversation forward. He already knew the answer.

"Much more likely since the recall of Governor Palin, I'll wager," August said smugly, sitting down again with his fresh drink. "I guess her second go-round was even less successful than her first."

"Perhaps," replied the Governor. "But if the new Governor decides to go it alone, I'm certain he intends to petition Canada for annexation."

"We should do the same," said Gregory. "Canada is the nation that we used to be, or at least imagined ourselves to be."

"Spoken like a true patriot," August said, raising his glass in a mock toast.

"There's more to patriotism than blind allegiance!"

"I believe we are all now very aware of one another's views," the Governor interceded. "Let's continue to focus on practical matters." She gave Gregory a sad look. "I understand your position, Gregory. I love Canada. Tim was a huge hockey fan, and that long ago served as an entrée to Canadian culture for me. In the long run, I think what you propose is a potentially viable option. If," she glanced sideways at Alex, "Canada will have us."

Alex suppressed a smile.

"Of course they'd have us," Gregory argued. "We'd double their GDP, and the value of California-"

"In the end, you may be right," the Governor interrupted gently. "But Canada is never going to entertain a petition from us, at least not when we first secede. Not until –"

"How do you know?" Gregory persisted. "If you look at the cultural and political affinity we have with-"

"Because I've spoken with the Prime Minister."

No one replied as the weight of her words sank in. Finally, August said softly, "That is a very dangerous gambit indeed, Madame Governor."

"I don't see it that way. The discontent of many states, ours included, is out there. Even if the majority of the mainstream media isn't reporting it, alternate streams carry the discussion constantly. The Prime Minister knows this, the President knows this, and we all know it. What purpose does it serve to pretend otherwise?"

"I agree," Gregory said. "But I can't believe that Canada refuses to support us."

"That wasn't what he said. But he was clear that he couldn't risk recognizing us a sovereign nation or to consider any petition for annexation unless our separation from the United States was settled and complete." She looked around the room. "In other words, ladies and gentlemen, with the potential exception of our sister states, we are on our own. No nation is going to risk the wrath of the United States to recognize our independence or otherwise assist us."

"Mexico will," Héctor Chavez insisted.

"That isn't what her President has told me," the Governor said. "In fact, I got the distinct impression that in addition to the concerns that Canada expressed, President Ibanez was also worried about how adding our state would upset the balance of power in Mexico. Not to mention any other states that might follow suit."

"Which New Mexico will consider," Héctor said grandly. "Maybe Arizona, as well. And if we all secede, Texas may even follow suit. The Latino population here in California is fifty-two percent, and in the other states I mentioned, it is now the largest minority. You can't argue with those numbers, ma'am."

"I don't argue your numbers, Héctor. I fully expect our next Governor will be Latino, and I'm happy about that. But what I will say is that Mexico doesn't have the political will to take a risk of this magnitude. At least not right out of the gate."

Héctor shook his head. "I'm certain Mexico would immediately recognize and even ally with us. California represents a majority of her exports. I have many contacts inside the Mexican government, who all assure me –"

"I'm certain you do, Héctor," the Governor said, interrupting once more. "But I've spoken directly to Los Pinos. Both he and the Canadian Prime Minister have veto powers, and neither legislative body is able to overcome that with a super majority."

Héctor pressed his lips together, and glanced away.

"We shall have to agree to disagree, Madame Governor."

"I accept that," the Governor said.

"Other nations, then?" Alex asked her. "Britain, France, the Second Soviet Union?"

"No again. Britain and France for the same reasons as Canada and Mexico. Such an action would be considered too much of a provocation to the United States. And since the fallout between the President and the Russians over the forming of the Second Soviet Union, do you really think it is in our best interest to ally ourselves with them?"

Alex shrugged. "Enemy of my enemy…"

"The United States is *not* our enemy!" snapped August.

No one else spoke for a long moment. Then the Governor said, "I agree. Or maybe I simply hope it is true. But in any event, I won't alienate the White House further by immediately allying with a nation that is an enemy of the United States in all but name. That would destroy any chance of this being a peaceful process. But I think it is clear that any of the nations we might want to support us will not, at least until we've proven we can stand on our own, and those that might support us are likely not nations we want to align ourselves with."

"Most nations will see us as a rogue state, or as rebels. At best." August's tone was dark.

"I wonder about that, too," said the Governor, "so we must proceed carefully. Looking past independence, our most natural geographic ally would be the very nation we're seceding from, and quite frankly, we also represent perhaps her greatest threat for the same reasons. So we must consider every peaceful option available to us. And peaceful also means lawful."

"Secession is not lawful," August murmured.

"So say some," the Governor replied. "But I believe we have some legal precedent. Have any of you ever heard of the Nullification Theory?"

There was no reply. Alex knew the answer, but said nothing. Finally, it was August who once again spoke up. "Are you referring to the theory championed by Senator Calhoun of South Carolina?"

"The very one."

"With all due respect, that's preposterous."

"Is it?"

"Utterly."

James Mallory put his hand in the air. "At the risk of sounding ignorant…what are you talking about?"

The Governor motioned to August to explain. The loquacious senator needed no further prompting.

"The Nullification Theory was popularized in the Southern states before the Civil War. It held that since the federal government existed due to the will of the states, if that government passed any law which a state deemed unconstitutional or detrimental to its sovereign interests, the state could nullify that law within its borders."

"So just ignore it?" James asked.

"More than that," the Governor said. "Label it unconstitutional and null and void within the state."

"The state would be the final authority on the matter," August said. "Not the President, Congress, or the Supreme Court."

James didn't reply, but several of the senators were nodding in agreement with the idea.

"Don't allow yourself to be overcome with excitement," August said. "The very concept flew in the face of the Constitution's Supremacy clause, which states very clearly that federal law cannot be superseded by state law. On the strength of that, President Andrew Jackson ultimately forced South Carolina to back down. And if that weren't enough, most would agree that the outcome of the Civil War settled the matter once and for all."

"Most did agree," the Governor said. "At least until about twenty years ago, when the legalization of marijuana occurred in Colorado, then Washington, and then eleven other states."

August wrinkled his nose. "What does that vile weed have to do with anything?"

She smiled indulgently. "Some would say much the same about what's in your glass, August."

"Heathens, all."

She chuckled. "Maybe. But even after these laws were put into effect in the various states, marijuana remained illegal at the federal level. In fact, it has still never been formally legalized, even though marijuana is legal in fifteen states now."

"And it never should be."

The Governor let a small smile play on her lips for a moment, then continued. "Regardless, the point is that the United States government has chosen not to enforce a federal law in multiple states where state law directly contravenes that law. My legal experts are confident that this action demonstrates that nullification is more than a legal theory. It is fully in practice, and has been for well over a decade."

"Wait," Miriam said. "You're saying that our secession may be legal because of the marijuana laws?"

"Something like that. Look, if the federal government not only fails to affirmatively enforce a law for this long, and fails to take any action whatsoever to counteract a state law that is in direct conflict with federal law, then the federal government has essentially abrogated their right to do so. They couldn't outlaw marijuana now, even if they wanted to. The President tried, remember? What was it, 2021? Right after his first reelection?"

Alex nodded. "Oregon took the case to the Supreme Court and won."

"By the narrowest of margins," August pointed out.

"But the point is, they won," the Governor said. "And U.S. v. Oregon set a precedent."

"Are you suggesting," Gregory asked, "that we cite US v. Oregon as grounds to ignore the immigration laws? To nullify them?"

"Absolutely," said the Governor. "We will use this ruling and the concept behind to refuse to follow unconstitutional laws, and if necessary, to secede. Legally."

The room fell quiet again. Even August waited a long while before finally breaking it. "You sound as if you've made your decision, Madame Governor. Must I remind you that we reside in a democratic state?"

The Governor smiled sweetly, but Alex could see the slightest bit of irritation flash across her eyes. "August, I wouldn't think of acting unilaterally. I am merely expressing my own executive intent. Of course, I want and need the support of the Senate and the Assembly."

"I don't believe there is sufficient support in both houses, Madame Governor," August said.

"Can we at least agree that if this issue were put to a vote, it would pass in the senate?"

"It would," Miriam said. Both Héctor and Gregory nodded in agreement. James, characteristically, remained silent.

"No," August said. "You would not achieve a super majority in either house. Even if James and some of his fence sitters came down on your side, there aren't enough votes."

"A referendum to the people only requires a majority vote," said Miriam. She looked at the Governor. "We could put it to the people as an advisory vote. Not binding, not decisive. But it would give the people of California a voice. When we see the results, we can act accordingly."

"The people of California have already made their wishes known when they elected each of us," August argued. "What you suggest reeks of those old variety shows where the audience texted in their vote for their favorite performer."

Ebby Sounder spoke up for the first time. She was the Governor's Technology Advisor. "There have been numerous polls over the past year. All of them show strong support for resisting federal power, and most support secession, if necessary."

"What polls? I've not seen any such polls."

Ebby gave him a neutral look. "They haven't been run through mainstream media."

"Fringe media, then? I still hear about such things, no matter how diverse the source."

"Some from fringe media," Ebby said. "But many are either deep web or even dark web."

August leaned back in his chair, exasperated. "So we are to believe that a few radicals engaged in illegal communications represent the will of the people? Are you joking?"

"No, sir," Ebby said. "I don't joke."

"No? Not even a little?"

"No, sir. It is a misuse of time."

August stared at her closely, feigning suspicion. "Are you joking with me now?"

"No, sir."

He threw up his hands. "Well, then I will return to an earlier word I used. This is preposterous."

"I think Miriam is right," Alex said. "We should hear from the people directly on this. It's too important."

As he looked around the room, everyone except for James and August were nodding.

The Governor noticed, too. "I would like it if you would move forward on an advisory referendum. Let's make it two pronged – approval to continue to resist federal power, and the question of secession. If it comes back in favor of both, this gives me considerable leverage in negotiating with the White House. The first is an affirmation of the course we've been on, and the second…well, ironically, the real threat of secession might actually be what precludes having to carry through with it."

"Yes, Madame Governor," Miriam said. "We'll get

started in the morning."

"Meanwhile, it is my intent to declare California a sanctuary state for anyone affected by the latest immigration laws that the White House has forced through Congress. We will *not* deport anyone that hasn't committed a violent crime, and then only to their country of origin. While our lawyers are preparing for the legal challenge on this matter, we should prepare for the political fallout."

"Meaning the White House and the New American Party are not going to like this," August said.

"Yes. But we have to follow what we know to be right, even if we perhaps differ on the smaller details." She looked around at the group. "I will be asking all of you for courage in the days and months to come. The prospect of standing up to a tyrant is a frightening one, but if we don't do it, no one else will. California must lead. *We* must lead. Much depends on our leadership."

She let her words sink in for a moment, then said, "I thank you all for coming. I'll leave each to your own thoughts."

Chapter 11

Most people are fortunate to live at a time and in a country where basic questions such as form of government and the roles within it are already answered. Every era, however, sees a scenario in which men and women who were born and lived in the comfort of that stability are subsequently faced with answering these kinds of questions that surround the founding of a new nation.

In the months leading up to crisis and threat of secession with the United States, then-Governor of California Sarandon was asked how she went about selecting the correct structure of government and the roles within it long before either might be necessary. The matriarch of Californian politics famously quipped, "I picked the best people, plain and simple. And if the best wasn't available, then I just picked whoever happened to be there. It is only government, after all."

— From *An Unlikely Phoenix* by Reed Ambrose

After everyone else had filed out, the Governor took Alex by the elbow. "Nightcap, Alex?"

He felt a flash of that nervous shyness. "That would be nice."

She led him back into the study and poured him a glass of wine without asking his preference. When she handed it to him, she said, "This is an award-winning merlot from the Napa Valley. It was a gift from a friend who owns the vineyard."

Alex put the wine glass to his nose and inhaled, then nodded approvingly.

"Wait until you taste it," she said.

He did, and the tastes exploded within his mouth. He soaked it in, swallowed, and opened his mouth to let in the air. "It's delicious," he said. Then he let out a small laugh.

"What's so funny?"

"When I was young, I was more of a beer and brats kind of guy."

"From St. Louis, I should hope so. Along with some barbecue, right?"

"Yeah, well, I never imagined I'd enjoy wine more than all of that."

"Our tastes change as we grow older," the Governor said. She took a sip of her wine, closing her eyes and savoring it. When she opened her eyes, she asked, "Do you think Miriam will get the resolution to the floor?"

"She will."

"August won't block her? Or James?"

"Not James. Blocking her would require taking a stand, and we both know how averse he is to that."

She smiled. "Hopefully, he will come around. But August?"

"I don't think he'll be a problem. At least not overtly. How can any politician oppose asking the will of the people?"

"How indeed?"

Alex looked at her closely. "Pardon me, Madame Governor-"

"Alex, please. Just Susan. For a few minutes, let's just be two people talking and sharing a glass of wine."

"Happily." He raised his glass to her. "To California."

She raised hers as well, and they drank.

"So, now that you are calling me by my first name, I get the sense that there's something else you want to ask me."

"There is."

"Well, then…ask away."

"I've been in a lot of meetings with you, in a lot of different settings. One of the things I've always noticed is that, more often than not, you spend most of your time listening. In fact, it is one of the things I've always admired about you. You genuinely listen to people. Really, that may be what won you the Governor's race more than anything else."

"Thank you," she said quietly. "That's a very nice compliment."

Alex took another sip of his wine, then said, "In the meeting we just had, you did more talking than I can remember. You listened, but not like you usually do. You even cut people off at times. It wasn't typical."

"No, it wasn't. But what's your question?"

"Why? My question is, why?"

The Governor took another long drink of the wine, her

eyes closed while she did. Then she set the glass down on the table next to her. "It's simple, Alex. To prepare them."

He thought about that. "For secession? Or war?"

"For whatever comes. No matter what it is, it will be a challenge. I need to prepare them for that."

"I see."

"I know you do, Alex. That's why I've come to rely on you so much. In fact, that's what I wanted to talk to you about."

"What do you mean?"

"I mean that if we reach a point in which secession becomes a reality, I am going to need to make some changes in my cabinet."

"The Attorney General?"

She waved a hand. "He'll resign. Right after he declares secession illegal, of course. But I'll need to make a few more changes, too. Our mission will have changed substantially, from running a state to running a new nation. So I'll need the best people for that at my side."

"You don't already?"

"For state governance, perhaps. But not for what we'll be facing if it comes to secession, Alex. No, I'll need more." She gave him an intense gaze. "I need you to be my Secretary of State."

Alex blinked, surprised. "Sec…wait, what?"

"You heard me, Alex. And you know you'd be a perfect fit."

"I never thought of it," he said.

"That's part of why I need you in that role."

"I…it's a lot to take in." He struggled to think of what to say, but the Governor rescued him.

"Just think about it, all right? I don't need to know tonight, after all." She smiled, but then gave him a pointed look. "But soon, okay?"

"Yes, ma'am."

She feigned sadness. "And here I thought I was just Susan for a little while."

Alex laughed, bleeding off his own tension a little. "All due respect, Madame Governor, but you just asked me to be your Secretary of State. It's kind of hard to be informal at a moment like that."

She laughed with him, conceding the point. "Well, if you accept, maybe then we can be informal on occasion."

"I'd like that."

"In fact," she said, "why don't you join us tomorrow night? I'm having a few of my advisors here to watch the live feed of the Concert for Freedom."

Alex gave her a confused look. "I didn't think any of the networks were going to carry that."

"No, they're not. I think there might be a fringe outlet that will, but we're actually getting the direct feed from the HSA Arena." She raised her eyebrows dramatically. "Sometimes it pays to be friends with The Boss."

Alex recalled the long-standing friendship she and her former husband had with Bruce Springsteen. "That's a nice perk."

"He's a thoughtful man. We'll be seeing the house feed, with no commentary from anyone that isn't on stage. It'll be almost like we're there."

"How can I refuse?" he said.

"Not a fan?"

Alex shrugged. "I wouldn't say that. But when you

grow up in St. Louis…"

"The blues," she said, matter of factly.

"Nothing better."

"But you'll come."

"Of course."

"Good." She picked up her glass and raised it to him. "To the blues."

He raised his. "And the Boss."

They drank.

"Madame Governor?"

She didn't reply.

"Susan?" he ventured.

She smiled. "Yes?"

"How do you do it?"

"Do what, exactly?"

"This." He waved his hand at the expanse of the Governor's mansion. "All of it. Knowing the right thing to do."

The Governor sipped her wine, her expression thoughtful. Then she shrugged. "You just have to believe, Alex. Believe that your cause is just. Believe that treating people well, that caring for them, is still the right thing to do. That hate is not the answer."

Alex nodded, and sipped his own wine. They sat for a long while, enjoying the silence and the taste of the wine. Alex stole a glance at the Governor, and her eyes seemed distant and cloudy.

"It's a lot, isn't it? The weight."

She nodded slowly. "It is during times like these that I begin to think that I can understand what all of those presidents felt like. So many lives resting on every decision. You described it correctly. It is a weight."

"Why me?" Alex asked. "Why did you pick me?"

"Because you're the best choice," she answered simply.

"That's not an answer."

"Oh, Alex. It's the *only* answer." When he started to speak again, she raised her hand. "Listen, choosing the right person for any position is as much an art as a science. You pick the best person, plain and simple." She smiled wickedly. "And if she isn't available, you ask whoever still happens to be there."

Alex laughed, and raised his glass. "Touché, Madame Governor."

"It *is* only government, Alex, after all," she added, laughing with him.

Alex let himself laugh with her, shedding some of his own weight, and hoping that maybe some of hers slid away, too, for at least as long as the glass of wine lasted.

She deserves that, he thought.

Hell, we all do.

He drove himself home. Since he had a slight buzz, he engaged the auto-drive. He still wasn't sold on this technology, but it was supposedly a learning computer, and he'd driven from the mansion to his own home multiple times, so there was plenty of data there to merge with Google Maps. Plus, traffic was light.

Some of the senior legislators had a driver who also doubled as security. The State Police would provide him a security detail upon request, but since the nationalization of all police, Alex was unsure where the

California Highway Patrol stood. There were white nationalists openly within the organization, and the New American Party exerted its control, but he also knew that a number of commanders and some of the rank and file were not in league with them. In the end, he believed that the CHP would come down on the side of California. Still, he didn't feel the need to have personal security on an ongoing basis, whatever their politics.

Alex considered the question of the police, not for the first time. He believed that the majority of county and municipal agencies would side with California, despite the nationalization. He'd spoken at length with his brother about how the New American Party had taken a firm hold of St. Louis Metropolitan Police. Though Ryan's indictment was scathing, he allowed that even in a department that was almost completely taken over, there were still dissenters. Alex's contacts and intelligence told him that most of the agencies in California gave no more than lip service and some empty gestures to their recent federal membership. Only a few departments went the way of St. Louis. Ironically, Sacramento PD was one of those he was worried about.

Not for the first time, he wondered if, in the event of secession, it made sense to relocate the state capital to someplace more secure. Los Angeles seemed a natural choice. Or San Francisco. He made a mental note to bring it up the next time he spoke with the Governor.

The Governor. The taste of wine was still strong on his tongue, and in the aftermath of their meeting, he felt very much at ease. There was something about being around her that eventually evoked that state, despite that initial case of nerves that he almost always felt in those first few moments.

He thought about her offer. *Secretary of State.* He had to admit that he was flattered by the offer. His first instinct had been to decline, but he resisted it when she asked him to think about it. He wondered why refusal was his initial reaction. As he drove, the answer occurred to him easily.

I don't want to let her down.

He realized that this was exactly why he would have to say yes. If it came to it, and he hoped it did not, he knew he would step for her. For California. He didn't know if he was the best man for the job, but-

His phone rang, cutting into his thoughts. "Answer," he said, and the Bluetooth clicked.

"You have reached Senator Derrick," the auto answer voice intoned.

Alex waited for the caller to speak. If he didn't want to talk to whoever it was, he could tell the auto-answer to guide the caller to the appropriate voicemail account.

"Engage the live line, Senator," a pleasant voice directed him. "My client and I would both prefer not to be directed to voice mail."

Alex hesitated, waiting for more.

"Come now, Senator. I have a Hyperion upgrade to my system. I know for a fact I'm connected to your vehicle Bluetooth, which means in your car. Which means you are listening to this now, or the Bluetooth wouldn't be engaged. So do us both a favor and answer live, please. It's in both our best interests. But especially yours."

"Answer Live," Alex snapped.

"Call is live," the system voice announced.

"This is Alex. Who is this?"

"Ah, thank you for answering, Senator."

"Who are you?" he repeated.

"I'm an associate of some people you know," came the pleasant reply. "But that's not important."

Alex sat up straighter in his seat, bristling slightly. "Listen-"

"No, sir, you are actually the one who should probably listen. You had a visit from Mr. Young recently, yes?"

Alex hesitated. "My affairs are none of your business," finally said.

The man sighed. "I wish you'd had some affairs, sir. It would make things so much easier. But no matter. There are always ways."

"What are you talking about?"

The man ignored his question. "Are you doing as Mr. Young suggested, Senator? Convincing your colleagues? Hmmm? Bringing them into line?"

"We're talking," Alex said cautiously. "It's a delicate subject, and politics move slowly."

"Certainly true. But there are some disturbing reports coming out of Sacramento, sir. Reports that indicate you are perhaps not as diligent as Mr. Young and his clients had hoped you might be."

"Reports from whom?"

The man clucked his tongue. "Oh, don't be naïve, Senator. You know I can't share that information with you. It's not important, anyway. What *is* important, however, is the question I am about to ask you. Are you prepared for my question, sir?"

"Go ahead," Alex said.

"Are you doing everything you can to resolve this impending crisis, Senator?"

"I am," Alex answered with conviction.

There was silence on the other end of the line for a long moment.

"Hello?" Alex said.

"I'm still here, Senator."

"All right. Then you have your answer."

More silence.

Alex waited for a few seconds, then asked, "What else to do you want?"

The man sighed lightly. "I can hear the conviction in your voice, Senator. Very resolute. Very genuine. But…slightly off target. I get the strong sense that you *believe* you are doing everything you can do to resolve this crisis, but in the way *you* think best. And that is not what Mr. Young has asked of you. In fact, he has asked you to do something very specific, did he not?"

"I don't work for Carl Young," Alex said firmly.

"Quite true. But I believe you had an agreement. A very clear one."

"I said I'd do what I could," Alex said, "and I am."

"As you say. Well, if that's the case, then I'm certain what I'm about to tell you will be of little consequence."

"What are you talking about?"

"Your sister-in-law?" the man said. "Nathalie Derrick?"

A cold lance of concern shot through his stomach. "What about her?"

"She's applied for citizenship, as I understand. And has an appeal pending?"

"How do you know that?" Alex asked, then immediately felt foolish. Of course they knew. If it was federal, they knew.

"I get the sense that, as things now stand, her appeal isn't going to receive a favorable ruling, Senator. And time is ticking for her, isn't it? The President's deadline for non-citizens is approaching, just a handful of months away. And if she isn't a citizen when the clock strikes midnight, then we both know she'll be deported to…where? Greece? Or Senegal? I'd think she'd prefer the former, given the way things are going in the latter. Nasty business there, lately. Unrest, military crackdown. It's even spilling into the streets. But of course, if she waits that long, she may not get the choice of her destination."

"I won't be threatened," Alex growled.

"No one is threatening you," came the easy reply. "If anyone is under threat, it is poor Nathalie. And they have a daughter, too, don't they? It'd be a shame if she had to lose her mother."

"I am doing everything I can," Alex insisted. "Leave my family out of it."

"Ah, Senator. If you'd led a more interesting life, perhaps we could. The perils of being a proverbial boy scout, I guess. But rest assured, your erstwhile sister-in-law isn't a mere pawn in all of this. What journalist is? And we have deeper suspicions about her, as well."

"What's that supposed to mean?"

"It means that sometimes people bring down a reckoning upon themselves all on their own. But maybe she can still avoid it. Certainly, your actions will have a lot to do with that." He paused, then asked, "Is my implication perfectly clear, Senator?"

"It is," Alex grunted.

"Very well. Then I'll leave you to enjoy your evening. Oh, and if you're thinking of warning your brother or sister-in-law, I'd advise against it. Communications are so easy to monitor these days, and it would be a tremendous shame if some harm were to befall any of them. The world is such a dangerous place these days."

"Leave my family *alone!*" Alex shouted into the mic.

"I hope to," came the amiable reply. "But that depends on you, sir. Doesn't it?"

The call disconnected.

The rest of the way home, Alex stared out his window, thinking. When he got to the house, he poured himself two fingers of bourbon, but ended up letting it sit on the counter, while he paced through the living room, his mind buzzing.

He wondered who among the senators was feeding information to Young. August Emerson would seem to be the most likely choice, but somehow Alex didn't think so. Despite his reconciliation stance, August had a very refined sense of honor.

James Mallory, then? Did Mr. Undecided decide to be a snitch?

Or some staffer?

He didn't know. But he did know that, moving forward, he would have to be more careful.

They all would.

Chapter 12

History is often an examination of nations, of government, and of the politicians that manage or lead both. Great impact is assumed and frequently assigned to political actors, and with the benefit of hindsight, outcomes are attributed to these same political figures.

What is often overlooked is the influence of the arts upon the political canvas. Even when historians recognize such influence, it is often deemed as secondary or reactionary in nature. Much like historians, artists are thought to be recorders and interpreters of what is happening around them. Only the rarest of instances seems to merit consideration as having a driving impact upon events rather than being merely a reflection of the times. Harriet Beecher Stowe's Uncle Tom's Cabin *is one such exception, as are the works of Alexander Solzhenitsyn.*

In the time preceding the crisis of 2029, dissident views did not have a great many outlets, and were frequently ignored, or dealt with harshly. Filmmakers and television stars (although still non-interactive, these mediums remained the most prevalent of the time), novelists, and musicians trying to attain or maintain popular appeal were largely compliant with the unspoken boundaries that had evolved since the meteoric rise of the New American Party. Dissent was limited to subtle, ambiguous expressions, or outright avoided.

However, some celebrities, the majority of them actors and musicians, seemingly enjoyed a different level of freedom, one that owed its existence to the simple fact that these few were already established icons of America before the President and the New American Party came to power. Each of these artists treated their rare status differently, depending on their individual character, but a handful were exceedingly vocal in their firm rejection of virtually everything in the New American platform.

Given their celebrity status and position in the public eye, there was little direct action the White House could take, aside from the occasional derisive tweet (a message posted online within a widespread social media program called Twitter, a technological ancestor of today's multi-platform Brimsey). But behind the scenes, a hush campaign seems to have been initiated, and while most of the celebrities targeted refused to be intimidated, some did capitulate. Others simply found it more and more difficult to find a stage, both figuratively and literally, and thus became less influential as a result. Certainly, the repeal of net neutrality further stripped these performers of most of their legitimate channels to reach the masses, ultimately causing some to fade into obscurity, while driving others underground.

A select few chose to be more public in their opposition. This approach was the genesis of what was eventually viewed as a watershed moment in the increasing tension between California and the U.S Government: the Concert for Freedom in St. Louis,

Missouri. While no one would make the claim that this affair itself drove subsequent events, per se, few could argue against the symbolism that arose surrounding the incident itself, and in the aftermath, delayed or otherwise.

— From *An Unlikely Phoenix* by Reed Ambrose

Alex spent the next day performing. He performed for his staffers, he performed for his fellow senators, he performed for the journalists, but most of all, he performed for whoever was reporting back to Carl Young and the New American Party. He met with legislators from both the Senate and the Assembly, as well as key business people. In each of the meetings, he took a page from the Governor's playbook, listening more than he spoke. When he did speak, he was cautious, always preaching moderation.

By dinnertime, he was both famished and exhausted, but confident that reports would find their way back to Washington, D.C., or wherever Young was holed up, that he'd been clearly brought to heel and was toeing the party line.

Even if it wasn't his party.

He let his staffers go early, and grabbed a sandwich in the car on his way home to shower and change. Less than hour later, he was outside the Governor's residence again. A tall man with a distinctly British countenance answered the door.

"Sir," he said, by way of greeting. While his tone was formal, the accent was clearly not English, destroying the image Alex had created. "If you'll follow me."

He led Alex into a cozy room. Comfortable looking chairs had been arranged in a u-shape, facing a drop-down screen. A mostly empty stage was projected onto the screen, with the occasional roadie or technician appearing to adjust something before shuffling off stage.

"Alex!" The Governor waved at him. She was standing next to Ebby Lawrence and her husband. Alex tried to remember his name and couldn't do any better than he thought it started with a C. He did remember that he was a software engineer, though.

He shook hands with the Governor, then with Ebby.

"You remember Curtis, my husband?" Ebby asked.

"Of course," Alex said, reaching for his hand. "Software engineer, right?"

"That's right," Curtis said. "I'm impressed that you remembered."

Alex shrugged. "Some things stick and some don't. Good to see you again."

The Governor took his arm and guided him to an hor d'oeuvres table. A small bar next to it was manned by an Asian woman who smiled at him. "Drink, sir?"

"What's the wine tonight?" he asked, and the Governor squeezed his arm and laughed.

"I have a Malbec from Argentina, and a Sauvignon Blanc from the Napa Valley," the sommelier replied.

"I'll go with the Malbec."

"Good choice."

While she poured, Alex glanced at the Governor. "I'm sure it won't be as good as your private reserve, Madame Governor."

The Governor opened her mouth to reply, but the

sommelier interjected.

"Maybe not," she said, "but I think you'll be surprised at the complexity."

The Governor spread her hands. "Well, there you go."

Alex sipped the wine and nodded his approval. "Complex," he said agreeably, and the two of them rejoined the group.

All told, it appeared to him that the Governor had invited about a dozen people. He recognized most, and introductions were made for those he did not. There was the requisite amount of amiable conversation before the house lights on the screen went down.

"Showtime!" the Governor announced, and as if on cue, the lights in the room dimmed as well. The guests found their seats. Alex's seat was between the Governor and Ebby, and he could feel their anticipation as the concert began. In the semi-darkness, with surround speakers filling the room, he immediately felt as if he were in the arena itself.

A spotlight appeared on the stage, and a slightly familiar, middle-aged man in jeans and a casual, collared shirt walked to the microphone. "Hello, St. Louis!" he crooned.

Alex squinted, trying to place who the man was.

"Are you ready to celebrate freedom?" the man asked.

The crowd cheered back.

"Are you ready to show the world who we really are?"

More cheers.

He raised his voice to a near shriek. "Are you ready to *rock*?"

The crowd noise rose significantly at that. The cheering

lasted several long moments. The man stood at the spotlight, nodding with approval.

"Who is that?" Alex asked.

"Jon Hamm," Ebby answered. "The guy from *Mad Men.*"

"That's right." Alex recognized him now. "He's mostly been in movies since then, though."

"There were plans to revisit the TV show," Ebby said. "Don Draper through the Seventies and Eighties. They even shot part of the new season."

"I'd watch that. What happened?"

Ebby gave him a knowing look. "Hamm and some of the other cast members made some comments that were deemed unpatriotic. And the writing was critical of the country back then."

"So the Party squashed the show?"

"Officially, not enough advertisers wanted to support it. And the network claimed the show creators were taking the series in a different direction than what they'd agreed to when they initially approved the project."

"In other words, the Party got to them."

"Exactly. They went where the money is, the same blueprint they used to bust the NFL kneeling protest in the mid-teens."

On the screen, Hamm was grinning at the crowd. "Tonight, I am very proud to be from St. Louis. And I'm proud of the lineup here tonight. We've got a great show in store for you. We've got St. Louis's own, Taylor Vera!"

Cheers.

"And another, hometown boy, Blues man, Nathan Crider!"

More cheers.

"And, of course, we've got a visitor from New Jersey… the Boss, Bruce Springsteen."

The cheers got louder, punctuated by booming boos.

"Why are they booing?" Alex asked.

The Governor chuckled. "They're not booing. They're Bruceing."

"Huh?"

"*Broooooooooooooce!*" she demonstrated.

"Ah. Got it."

"Yes, yes," Hamm said, "Bruce is in the house!" He smiled, and waited for the cheers to subside. Then he said, "Tonight is about music, it's about our desire as a people to say that freedom matters, that every individual matters, and that borders do more to push people apart than to bring them together."

A deafening cheer rose from the crowd. To his right, Alex heard the Governor clapping lightly, and letting out a gleeful, "Yes!"

"So I know you're not here to listen to me," Hamm said. "Let me bring out the first guest, one of the biggest stars to ever come out of St. Louis in the past decade, Taylor Vera!"

The crowd showed its enthusiasm, and a slender woman in a black dress came on stage. Behind her, musicians found their instruments and their marks. Then they burst into an exultant pop song that Alex recognized from its airplay on the radio. The catchy riff and the hook in the chorus had him tapping his foot.

Vera raced through a trio of songs, almost without pause. Alex vaguely recognized them, but pop music really wasn't his thing. He found himself already looking forward to the blues of Nate Crider.

In between songs, Vera punctuated her performance by asking the audience, "How ya doin', Charles?" to significant approval. Alex didn't get the reference. He heard both Ebby and the Governor chuckling each time, but he didn't bother asking why.

As her set came to an end, the singer paced the stage as her band played lightly behind her. "My great-grandfather came to this country from Peru," she said. "He wanted a better life for himself and his family, and he found it here in America."

The crowd cheered in response.

"Thank you," she said. "But you know, I wonder how he would feel about this country today. I wonder if he were a young man in Peru today, would he leave to come to this country? Somehow, I don't think he would, and that makes me sad."

The crowd applauded approvingly.

Vera lowered her eyes. On cue, the band swung into a pop ballad that Alex remembered as her breakout single almost a decade earlier, appropriately titled, "Sad." Piano-driven and guitar punctuated, the ballad seemed as powerful as depression. Vera's crystal clear high vocals served as counterpoint to the music.

And some days it hurts so much I can't even get mad
Only sad
Just sad
And some days it feels like life ain't so bad
Just sad
Only sad

Alex found himself swaying slightly to the music as Vera flowed through verse and chorus, building to a crescendo with a final, long, aching, "Sad…"

The crowd had been on its feet during the song, and now cheered thunderously.

Vera bowed deeply, holding the pose. Then she stood and presented her band, before taking a final bow and leaving the stage.

"Wow," Alex murmured.

"She's pretty good, huh?" Ebby said.

"Better than I thought," Alex admitted. He'd always had her pegged as a bubble gum pop artist, but she turned in a moving performance.

Jon Hamm returned to the stage. "Taylor Vera!" he yelled, and didn't have say any more. The cheering went on for a long stretch. When it was finished, Hamm talked about growing up in St. Louis, and about what it meant to be the gateway to the west. Alex saw where he was going with the comments, but felt like the metaphor was a little forced. He was glad when Hamm finished and introduced Nate Crider as "the blues standard for the better part of a generation."

"Now, this is my sort of music," he told the Governor. She gave him a warm smile in reply.

Crider had a spare backing band, and his music centered heavily around whichever guitar he was playing at the time. He rotated through a half dozen different models, some electric, some acoustic. Alex listened with something akin to joy as Crider performed an acoustic version of his favorite song, "Mama's Sugah." He loved the way Crider used the term in all of the different ways it could be. He first refers to "mama's sugah" being Mama's little baby boy. Then when the singer recognizes his mother has an adult life, too, he sees that the man in her life also has that role. Later, he marries, and refers to his wife as "mama," and he as her "mama's sugah." Things seem to come full circle when he has a son of his own, and realizes his own wife sees their little boy as her "sugah." But Alex's favorite verse came at the end, when his own mother holds his son, and calls him "mama's little sugah."

The entire song played out against a steady blues rhythm that swelled up and fell again in subtle ways, a different instrument driving the ending phrases of each verse. When the song ended, Alex realized he'd been holding his breath.

The Governor leaned over to him. "I see why you like the blues so much."

He couldn't answer, only nod.

Crider went on to play a masterful set, and Alex enjoyed every moment. The singer made no overt statements in between songs, letting such lyrics as "everyone gots to earn respect, but everyone got give some," and "when her beacon fades, so do our hearts" do his talking for him. After the final song of his set, he gave a muted, "Thank you, St. Louis." Then he seemed to hesitate, before adding, "And God bless America, as long she deserves it."

There was a brief intermission. Alex asked for a refill from the sommelier and snacked on a few hors d'oeuvres, chatting with some of the other guests. Everyone seemed to agree that Taylor Vera brought great energy, and that Nate Crider's deeper, understated approach was a perfect counterpoint.

When the lights went down on screen, the sound of the crowd rose noticeably. The room lights dimmed a few moments later, as the guests made their way back to their seats. At the arena, the "Brooooing" began in earnest.

There was no introduction from Hamm this time. Instead a single spotlight opened up on a mike stand at center stage. Bruce Springsteen stepped into the circle of light, carrying an acoustic twelve string guitar and a stool. Without a word, he positioned the stool under the spotlight and settled onto it. The camera switched to a head and shoulder shot, and Alex got his first good look at the Boss in a while. He looked hale, in some ways much younger than his eighty years. But there was a sad wisdom that played in his eyes, one that reminded Alex of how Nate Crider also carried himself.

Springsteen strummed the guitar softly, then more powerfully. After a couple of bars, he began adding in some picking. The resulting music was almost dissonant, just this side of jarring. But each time the dissonance seemed about to overwhelm, he shifted into a brief strum in minor chords, fending off complete musical discord. The effect was transfixing, and commanded attention.

Alex had no idea what the song was, even after Springsteen started growling out the first verse. It was only when he murmured the single line of chorus that he recognized it as one of his biggest hits from the 1980s, "Born in the U.S.A." But the way Springsteen performed it, there was no mistaking it for a celebration, or anything other than what he suspected it was always intended to be: an indictment, one that still stood today, even though the narrator of the song was "ten years…twenty years…thirty years…forty-five years burning down the road."

When the final line of the final chorus fell from his lips, he struck a final dissonant, twanging chord to emphasize the entire song, and the spotlight went black. There was a half-second of near silence before the crowd erupted.

When the lights came back up slowly, Springsteen remained seated on the stool, though he had a different acoustic guitar. He shifted the strap, patiently adjusted the tuning on one of the strings, and then leaned forward to the microphone.

"I wrote that song in the early 1980s," he said, his speaking voice raspier than Alex remembered from the few times he'd heard the man speak. He strummed lightly on the guitar, and his words seemed very deliberate. "Ronald Reagan had just become President, and our country was divided. Back then, it was Republicans and Democrats, haves and have nots, black and white…it seemed like, as a nation, we were really good at finding differences in each other in some fashion. Story of the human race, I guess." He paused, strumming, then began again. "But it slowly got better, through the nineties and into the two thousands. There were a lot of low points along the way, but it seemed to me that things were trending upward. Which was a good thing."

He smiled wearily. "And then…" he trailed off, for a moment, seemingly speechless.

A slow cheer started in the crowd, swelling until it was

loud and raucous.

"So you know," Springsteen said, acknowledging the cheering. "Good."

They cheered louder.

"Anyway, I watched as all of the positive changes in our society seemed to come undone, and be washed away. All of our empathy, our tolerance. And for a long while, I didn't say much about it. I regret that now. I should have said something more, something sooner. We all should have."

More cheers.

"But there's always a second chance to do what's right, I suppose. In some fashion, anyway. And so I wrote this song."

He started playing the guitar in earnest, picking out a melody while strumming a bass note. Alex didn't recognize the song, but that didn't surprise him. His awareness of popular music was limited. Just one of the sacrifices he made to focus on other things.

Springsteen sang about a young woman in an undisclosed foreign country who gets pregnant and leaves home, coming to America. As he listened, Alex imagined she could just as easily have been Taylor Vera's grandfather, as the reasons she cited were very much the same.

I'm looking for a better life
A life without scorn
A better life for my son
He will be American born

The next verse highlighted a young businessman whose dreams of riches came to pass, though not without cost. He only peripherally sees that his fortune is built on the backs of others, many of them immigrants. When a worker dies at one of his factories, he laments the dollars lost, and proclaims that:

For that one poor soul,
don't expect me to mourn
It isn't my fault
She wasn't American born.

During the musical bridge, Alex caught himself wondering if the woman who died in the factory was the same woman in the opening verse. Before he could decide, the next verse began.

This one was from a soldier's perspective, who could very easily be the offspring from the man who narrated "Born in the U.S.A." The soldier spoke of escaping the streets by joining the Army, and finding something important there: duty. That duty led to war, and Springsteen's raspy vocals told a bitter truth about that war, and every war.

We fought for freedom, or so we were told
We were the oasis, we were the storm
And now I can't say if I'm proud or not
To be American born

The final verse was more difficult to follow, but Alex picked up that Springsteen had gone from the individual to the collective. He sang of a nation's identity, of a fall from grace, and finally, of that constant chance at redemption he had alluded to in his introduction.

"Sooner or later," he sang, strumming his guitar fiercely, "we all gotta decide…"

His strumming came to an abrupt stop, and he held the silence for a long moment. Then he whispered, eyes closed, his scratchy voice filling the near-silent arena, "What it means to be American born."

The applause didn't happen all at once, but once it started, the sound of it was overwhelming. To his right, Alex heard the Governor clapping as well, and he joined her. When he glanced at her, he saw her smiling and clapping softly. She caught Alex's eye, and her smile broadened. "If I could say it that well," she told him, "half our problems would be over."

The crowd finally settled, and Springsteen switched guitars again, giving Nate Crider a run for his money in that department. He strummed the black acoustic guitar, then said, "But it can't all be dark, now can it?" Then he broke into a rollicking, upbeat song that Alex didn't know but which had him tapping his foot. The audience got into it as well, clapping along. By the time the song ended, the mood was lightened considerably, and Springsteen didn't stop there. He played another catchy tune, keeping the fun rolling. The guests joined in the clapping and the room truly took on a concert atmosphere. Springsteen even stood up from his stool and swung his hips in time to the song, getting a loud reaction from the crowd.

In the aftermath of the song, Springsteen sat back down, chuckling. "I haven't done that in a while," he admitted.

His guitar technician brought him a different guitar, the same twelve string he'd opened with. Then he handed Springsteen a bottle of water. "Thanks, Kevin," Springsteen said, and chuckled again. "I don't know which is more important at this point, the water or the guitar." Then he quizzed the audience, holding one up for applause, then the other. The guitar won handily.

"The people have spoken," Springsteen said in mock solemnity. He twisted the cap off the bottle and grinned. "But I'm still drinking the fucking water."

After a long draught of water, Springsteen cleared his throat and strummed the guitar. "All right. Back to business." He strummed a few dark chords while gathering his thoughts. "Back during the *River* tour, we played in West Berlin. This was way back, when Germany was still a divided nation, east and west. A couple of us went across the border into East Berlin, and I was struck by how gray it was, and by how different it was from the west. These were the same people, living just miles apart, divided by a wall of concrete and barbed wire, part of an arbitrary line that some politicians drew on a map…and their lives were so very different, east and west. And I remember thinking, it shouldn't be this way."

He strummed some more, working through a few chord changes, then continued. "A few years later on the *Tunnel of Love* tour, we played in East Berlin. The crowd was massive, more than they expected, and throughout the entire concert, the energy was…it was indescribable. You could just feel all of these people out there…*yearning*. Yearning for freedom."

A small, concerted cheer rose and fell in response to that.

"Freedom eventually came to them, too, only a few years later. The Berlin Wall came down peacefully, families were reunited…it was…it was a great time, a great thing to see." He plucked a bass note, strummed a bright chord, then a darker one. "I remember how, at the time, East German state television actually broadcasted our show." He let out a small chuckle. "Well, most of it. They edited out a song or two, and the small speech that I made, but there were three hundred thousand people who heard it live, so I guess it didn't really matter. The men in power had misjudged, you see. They misjudged how much people prize freedom. How much they will always yearn for it, and never give up on it. And they misjudged how long you can keep people from freedom through sheer force. Because, in the end, though sheer, brutal force exacts a terrible price along the way, it will always fail."

A cheered swell up and lasted for several moments.

"About that concert, I said how every once in a while you play a place, you play a show that ends up staying inside of you, living with you for the rest of your life, and that East Berlin in 1988 was like that for me. I think maybe tonight might be, too."

More cheers filled the arena.

"We need to remember our own history as a country, and as a human race," Springsteen continued, speaking deliberately. Alex was too long a politician not to recognize this part as a prepared statement, but was impressed at how effortlessly Springsteen delivered it. "If we forget these things, we will miss those precursors that warn us that those events are in danger of happening again. Forgetting gives us another version of the Nazis, or another round of oppressive communism, perhaps masked as democracy."

There was a swell of cheering, but Springsteen didn't wait for it to go down before saying, "It can happen anywhere. In East Berlin, they edited the broadcast of the concert. But they *did* let me come and play, and they *did* broadcast most of the show."

A couple of quick upstrokes on the guitar, then he added, "Just so you know…here, today, in our country…this concert is not being broadcast by any mainstream media. You should ask yourself why that is. I know I do. But I will say this -- if you'd told me back in 1988 that this could ever happen, I honestly…I wouldn't have believed it."

The cheering was punctuated with some booing and angry shouts.

"Don't get mad," Springsteen chided gently, picking out a few notes. "It doesn't do any good to hate your country for what it's become. Instead, get busy changing what you don't like." He interspersed some strumming with the fingerpicking. "This is a new song. I wrote it in the aftermath of the President's speech about immigration a while back. They say that you can tell a lot about a person by how he treats those less fortunate than himself. I think that's true of countries as well."

The strumming and picking continued slowly, then picked up speed and rhythm, until it was chugging along steadily. "This is called 'Stranded at the Border,'" he murmured, then continued to build the momentum of the music, bringing it up to a near peak and then using micropauses and single notes to back away again. When it finally seemed like it could go on no longer, the driving power subsided into a slow, gentle strum with the occasional accented note or chord.

He sang of a Mexican father who crossed over into the United States every week to work as migrant labor in the fields, only to slip back south again each weekend to see his wife and two daughters. The contrast of his work experience, the wealth around him in the north and the comparative poverty of his own home punctuated the long verse, before the unnamed father finally got caught trying to cross one night, and found himself "stranded at the border."

Alex felt a pang as he listened to the narrative. The plight of migrant workers, especially those who came into the country illegally, was an old one that he was very familiar with. But sometimes the issue seemed so large that it became difficult to keep in perspective. The personal story in the song reminded him keenly.

Springsteen sang verse after verse, each a different kind of story about coming to America, and in every case, the narrator was somehow betrayed or hurt by the process, always stranded at the border in the end.

Alex marveled at how finely drawn the characters were and how easily Springsteen's voice inhabited each of them. He was wondering how the song would end when Ebby leaned across him to speak to the Governor.

"Madame Governor, there's something happening you should know about," she said urgently.

The Governor cast her a curious, distracted look. "Can it wait, Ebby?"

"No, ma'am."

The Governor didn't sigh, but Alex could sense her mild frustration. "Tell me," was all she said.

"Better if I show you," Ebby said, and tapped a few keys on her tablet.

The screen split in half. The concert remained on the left side, but the audio was quickly muted. There was a murmur of surprise and disappointment from the assembled group, but this subsided as soon as the audio from the newscast on the right half of the screen began playing.

The male news reporter straight out of central casting stood in front of the HSA Arena. "-and we are now being told that there is a potential terrorist threat inside the arena."

Terrorist threat? A shot of panic fired through Alex. "Nathalie is at this concert."

The Governor touched him on the forearm. "Oh, Alex."

The reporter continued. "In addition, Lieutenant Potulny of the St. Louis Metro has reported there may have been shots fired inside the arena."

"What shots?" the Governor asked. She looked at the screen and back to Alex. "Did you hear any shots?"

Alex shook his head. "Maybe the music was too loud," he offered, but he didn't believe it himself.

"No," the Governor said resolutely. "Not a chance. The music wasn't that loud, and the crowd was quiet and listening."

"There could have been shots outside of the performance area," someone else said.

She frowned. "Maybe." She turned back to Ebby. "What about the terrorist threat?"

"I only caught the tail end of the original report before I brought it up to you," Ebby said. "But it doesn't seem like there are a lot of details."

"Are they saying the terrorist are in the arena, or the arena is a target, or...?"

"I'm sorry, ma'am. I don't know." She glanced up at the screen where the reporter continued to talk without saying anything new. "Neither does he, I don't think."

"Can we try a different network? Or social media? God knows, people will post there before calling 911. If something is going on inside that arena, it should be all over."

Ebby tapped a few keys and the image switched to another affiliate, this one with a female reporter standing with the arena at a different angle in her background. But after a few minutes, it became clear that she didn't know anything more than the first reporter.

Alex took out his phone and dialed Ryan, but the call went unanswered. He tried Nathalie, but received an error message. Worried, he slipped the phone back into his pocket.

"Nothing?" the Governor asked.

Alex shook his head.

They tried a few other channels, skipping past regular programming that went on, uninterrupted. Only news channels carried anything about the event. A social media search came back empty as well. After ten minutes of searching, they found themselves back at the first channel again, with sparse information.

"We do not know the exact nature of the threat," intoned the reporter urgently, "but authorities have said that it is very credible, and that the suspected terrorists may in fact be inside the arena as we speak." The video feed broke away from the reporter while his voiceover continued. "The event this evening is the so-called Freedom Concert, including performances from known radicals such as Ashely Vera, Nate Crider, and the once-famous Bruce Springsteen. Once known for his patriotism, Springsteen was apparently fomenting dissension and near rebellion in between songs."

"That's ridiculous," the Governor snapped.

The video cut to the house feed of Springsteen performing, with the audio catching him mid-sentence. "…hate your country for what it's become," he said, and then the audio cut away along with the video, returning to the reporter.

"This and other similar statements was met with mixed responses from the assembled crowd," the reporter said, "including significant booing. But reports from inside the arena are that there are some radicals in attendance, which authorities fear will put the remainder of those in attendance in potential danger."

"They took that statement completely out of context," Alex said.

The Governor was seething. "This is what they do, Alex. They lie and twist things to their own agenda." She turned to Ebby. "Are there any alternate news options available?"

Ebby stared back at the Governor, then glanced around the room. "There are," she said. "I can access the deep web. Or even go dark, if you want."

"Are you secure?"

Ebby gave her a look that made the answer obvious.

"Do it, then."

Ebby went to work on her tablet for a minute or so. Alex watched the continued mainstream news coverage while she typed. Springsteen had finished his final song and left the stage while they had been surfing the channels for more information, and the lights had come up on the arena. Rather than emptying, however, the crowd seemed to be milling around.

"Violence has reportedly broken out on the floor of the arena," the reporter stated solemnly. "It is unknown at this time if any of the suspected terrorists are involved, or if it is merely radical concertgoers, incited by the performers. The St. Louis Metro Police Department has secured the entire perimeter of the arena, and are fully engaged in resolving this scenario."

"Violence?" Alex asked quietly. He motioned to the house feed on the screen. "What violence?" He shook his head. "This is some real George Orwell shit."

"It's what things have come to," the Governor said sadly.

"All right, I've got something," Ebby said. "A shadow blogger I follow."

She made a couple more keystrokes, and the screen divided again. The right half had the house feed on top and the newscast on the bottom. Closed captions appeared on the newscast, rendering the reporter's redundant words in clear, white font. The left side of the screen showed a low-res point of view feed from a camera phone as the reporter threaded through the crowd to the side of the stage. The video was full of visual interference and the audio was scratchy. In the background, Alex could hear ambient noise and music playing lightly over the house system. He heard snatches of conversation as the reporter passed by, but nothing to indicate panic by the concertgoers.

"Why is the quality so low?" the Governor asked.

Ebby considered. "My guess is that the authorities have implemented a dampener over the arena. Without the specific access code, all wireless signals are suppressed."

"So how is this transmission getting out?"

"Superior technology," Ebby replied. "Next generation, out of Canada. The dampener still affects it but can't completely interrupt the signal. Or it might be able to burrow in underneath the outlet transmitter, even without the code."

"I don't know what any of that means," the Governor muttered, and Alex agreed sympathetically.

"All that matters is that they can broadcast," he offered.

The reporter reached the edge of the stage and a pair of boots and someone's shins filled the screen. The mute button clicked on for a few moments, and then the reporter was pulled up onto the stage. The camera focused on the back of the person who'd done the pulling as he walked away. The audio resumed, and the reporter began to narrate. The voice was digitally altered to a smooth androgynous tone that betrayed only a hint of emphasis.

"Reports outside of the arena are stating there is a terrorist threat, and that there has been violence within the arena. As you saw moments ago, there is no violence in the crowd. And though I have been from one end of the arena to the other, I have yet to talk to anyone who has heard the gunshots that the mainstream media is also reporting."

"Because they didn't happen," muttered Ebby to Alex's left.

The camera stopped at a door, which was half open. The reporter slid the camera around the edge of the door, and Springsteen's face appeared on screen. The singer had an uncomfortable expression, tinged with confusion. "Oh," he said, then added, "Please, come in. We'll talk."

"It's better if I stay behind the door and you don't see my face, sir," the reporter said, the digitized voice sparking with static. "For your own safety."

Springsteen looked unconvinced, but shrugged. "I'm not sure what you mean, but sure."

"Sir, there are reports of violence within the arena. From your vantage point on the stage, did you see anything like that?"

"No," Springsteen said. "Absolutely not."

"Did you hear any gunshots?"

Springsteen's brow scrunched. "Gunshots? No. Really?"

"Those are the reports, but no one I've spoken to has heard anything," the reporter said. "Sir, the report out there in the mainstream media is that you and the other artists have been inciting the crowd to violence. How would you respond to that?"

Springsteen looked shocked. "Violence?" He shook his head. "No, never violence. Never. All I ever suggest is that people pay attention to what's happening in our country, and make up their own minds about it."

"You aren't telling them how to think?"

"Of course not. There's far too much of that going on, as it is." Springsteen sighed. "People need to think for themselves."

"Are you aware that the arena is surrounded by police at the moment?" the reporter asked.

Springsteen scowled. "What? No." He reached for his own phone and fiddled with it for a moment. Then he looked up. "No reception."

"No, sir. The authorities have probably incorporated a signal dampening device to isolate the people here."

Confusion seeped back into Springsteen's expression. "I don't understand any of this," he said. "This is crazy."

The camera jumped suddenly and pulled out of the dressing room. A security guard's chest filled the screen. "That's going to have to be all," he said gruffly. "We need to secure Mr. Springsteen."

The reporter thanked him, and then the screen went black. The scratchy audio continued, with the digitally altered voice of the reporter explaining, "Stand by for an update as soon as I have anything new. This is Veritas, reporting the truth, live from the HSA Arena."

The audio went silent as well. For a long moment, the assembled group was quiet, and then the room exploded with conversation. The Governor stood, raising her hands for quiet. "Folks, listen for a second. I think the best thing we can do here is call it a night, at least for this gathering. I would encourage each of you to share what you saw on the concert stream tonight, but please…do not mention that last broadcast to anyone. If federal authorities discover that we accessed the dark web and viewed an illegal broadcast, everyone in this room will be subject to charges of treason. I'm not trying to frighten you. I'm just making sure everyone understands what is at risk. Silence is imperative."

The group murmured agreement.

The Governor smiled grimly. "Thank you. All of you." She motioned to the man who had escorted Alex in earlier. "Miles?"

"Of course, Ma'am." He turned to the group. "Ladies and gentlemen, if you'd follow me, please."

Miles led the group out of the room. The Governor reached out and stopped Alex, giving him a short shake of her head. "Stay," she said.

Ebby stayed, too, as well as a young man in a sweater vest, a fashion that Alex noticed had been making a strong comeback recently among the younger set. The man held out his hand. "I'm Paul Keaton," he said. "The Governor's Press Advisor."

"Of course. We met earlier." Alex hadn't initially known him by his face, but had seen his name on some correspondences. As Press Advisor, Keaton did his work behind the scenes rather than being in front of the camera.

"Should we draft a statement?" the Governor asked.

Keaton shook his head. "Not yet, Ma'am. I think we should see what happens next."

"I feel like we should say something. Get the truth out."

"I agree, Ma'am. But you yourself just cautioned your guests against exposing where our information comes from. Even this live feed of the house cameras could be spun by the White House as being part of whatever treasonous activities they are claiming is happening."

"Oh, that's ridiculous," the Governor snapped.

"Of course it is," Keaton said. "But that isn't the point. The point is that the White House would like nothing more than to take an incident like this and use it to discredit his most powerful detractor."

The Governor considered his words. "I can't let the fear of being maligned by the White House keep me from telling the truth, Paul."

"No, ma'am. But we have to proceed carefully. There are large segments of the nation's population who would be very inclined to believe that the Governor of California is surreptitiously engaged in domestic terrorism. It might seem ridiculous, but these types of accusations represent an opportunity for the White House to malign you."

"I don't care what the White House says about me. He can't do any worse than what he called me last Christmas."

The infamous 'C' word tweet, Alex recalled. The President hadn't needed more than 140 characters for that one. He'd somehow managed to avoid being censured by Twitter for that flagrant violation, ironically citing the First Amendment. Twitter executives hadn't put up much of a fight, Alex recalled. Once they'd capitulated to his demand to designate his account as a special

"Presidential" account, allowing him a 1400 character limit, there wasn't much room left for oversight on their part.

Keaton continued his point. "As you've said many times in the past, Madame Governor, this is bigger than you. If the White House discredits you, they discredit our cause. And that is exactly what this concert was about – the cause of freedom."

The Governor pressed her lips together for a moment, then nodded. "You're right, of course. So your advice is not to share that we had access to the house feed?"

"For now, yes." He turned to Ebby. "Did you record that stream?"

Ebby nodded. "Yes. I thought the Governor might want to watch it again sometime."

"Good," Keaton said, then looked meaningfully at the Governor. "That's our ace in the hole, ma'am."

The Governor agreed. "I'm still not sure if I want to wait or not, but you're right about the feed." She turned back to the screen, watching the closed captioning stream across the bottom of the mainstream news channel. "Right now, I am most concerned that this ends peacefully."

Alex sat down, staring up at the blank left half of the screen and the static house feed. He wondered if Nathalie were somewhere safe inside the arena. That moved him to reach for his phone again, but he received the same result as before. No answer from Ryan, and an error message for Nathalie.

The three of them settled into the seats and watched in silence. Ebby turned the volume back on the newscast feed, and they listened as the reporter continued to speculate on the volatile nature of the threat. There were a few stray shots of the police in positions around the arena, and the occasional update that rarely held anything new. This went on for well over an hour, then one of the reporters looked particularly excited as he gestured and spoke.

Ebby brought that feed to the forefront.

"-authorities are now confirming that radical elements of a yet unidentified dissident group are inside of the arena. It is unclear if this is the same group responsible for the terrorist threat or the violence that has occurred during the concert, but what we do know is that this group has been transmitting illegally from inside the venue. Moments ago, the incident commander made this brief statement to the assembled media."

The news cut to a recorded segment. A square-jawed man with blond hair that was gelled even more perfectly than the reporter stood amidst microphones. The caption beneath him read, "LIEUTENANT POTULNY, ST. LOUIS METRO POLICE DEPARTMENT."

Potulny's reedy voice belied his Aryan features. "The transmission from inside the venue was a clear violation of the Internal Security Act, a felony. In addition, it was accomplished utilizing foreign technology that is illegal in this country, another felony. Therefore, as we evacuate the arena one individual at a time, we will be identifying each person, as well as searching him or her for illicit contraband."

"What kind of contraband?" one reporter asked.

"The technology I just mentioned, primarily," said

Potulny. "But anything else that is in violation of state or federal law will also be seized and the person charged accordingly. We are dealing with the safety and well-being of Americans here."

"Sir, are there terrorists inside the arena?"

Potulny shook his head. "I can't comment on that. Anything more than what I've already told you falls under tactics and it would be unsafe for me to share. Please respect the safety of the good Americans who may have come to listen to some music and found themselves in the middle of political rebellion."

With that, Potulny turned away.

"Christ," Alex muttered. "It will take hours for them to empty the arena one person at a time."

"Not to mention that what they're doing is a clear violation of the Constitution," the Governor added.

"Not if they can prove a credible terrorist threat," Keaton replied. "They can suspend personal liberties for the collective good."

"Oh, Paul. I *know* that. They play that card all the time. But when have they ever had to come back after the fact and prove that the threat actually existed? Never. They just stonewall, saying they can't offer the proof at the time because they're focused on resolving the situation. Then later, they can't offer proof because it would compromise the safety of their operatives or of Americans in general, and then everyone shrugs and moves on until the next time they need to violate civil rights. It's a complete sham."

"And yet it works," Keaton said.

"You sound like you admire them."

"The effectiveness of the tactic? I do. But not the intent behind it."

Jon Hamm appeared on the stage on the arena house feed. Ebby switched over to that audio.

"-outside of the arena right now. The promoter received a call instructing all of us to leave through the main doors, single file. Police will be identifying each of us, and conducting a search."

There was a swell of disagreement.

Hamm held up his hands angrily. "I know, I know. This is ridiculous. And I don't know about you, but I'm not planning on showing anyone my identification or submitting to any searches. You all can make up your own mind."

"Oh, no," the Governor said. "That's the wrong move."

"Only if he's alone," Keaton hedged. "If eighteen thousand people agree with him, that could cause serious problems for the police."

"No, it won't," Alex said. "That lieutenant, Potulny? My brother knows him. He is a party hack and a climber. If those people resist, whether violently or passively, he *will* resort to force. From what Ryan has said, he might even enjoy it. But he'd definitely use the opportunity to make a point."

"What point?" Ebby asked.

"That you do what you're told," the Governor answered. "But I think they need to go along with the police in this case. The situation is too volatile for them to risk any kind of greater protest. Especially if the police are being led by someone like Alex described."

The mainstream news feed flashed "Breaking News."

Ebby switched to it.

"-a discredited actor, is reportedly exhorting the crowd to violently resist the peaceful police action to defuse this terrorist situation."

The video and audio cut away to Hamm, whose expression and tone were angry. "I'm not planning on showing anyone my identification or submitting to any searches."

The video cut back to the reporter, live. He managed to look disapproving and grave at the same time. "Now let's shift over to Angela Whitestone, who is standing by with Lieutenant Potulny for a response."

A statuesque blonde woman appeared on screen, her microphone poised. "I'm here with Lieutenant Potulny once again. Sir, how do you respond to the reckless statements made by Mr. Hamm moments ago?"

Potulny scowled. "Look, I don't know who this guy is or who he *thinks* he is, but his actions are irresponsible. We have mobilized in order to secure the facility, maintain the safety of the Americans here, and deal with a terrorist threat in the middle of what amounts to a political protest. There are a lot of moving parts here, and all of them are potentially volatile. Encouraging anything other than absolute cooperation is not only dangerous, but frankly, it may even be treasonous under federal law."

The reporter seemed to suppress a salacious smile at Potulny's words. "What should good Americans inside the HSA Arena do, sir?"

Potulny looked directly into the camera and spoke slowly and clearly. "Move toward the main exit in an orderly fashion. Have your identification ready and be prepared to be catalogued and searched before you are allowed to leave. Cooperate fully with police. Anything less than that merely plays into the hands of terrorists and makes it unsafe for Americans."

The reporter turned back to the camera. "There you have it. Concert-goers are directed to-"

"Turn that sound off," the Governor said wearily. "God, I hate national media."

A tense fifteen minutes went by. Hamm remained on stage, talking to the crowd. Then, unexpectedly, Springsteen appeared on stage, beckoning to Hamm. Amidst some cheers, they stepped offstage. From the camera angle, Alex could see the two of them standing with Taylor Vera, Nate Crider, and several other people. The group was in an animated discussion that seemed to start as a disagreement, but slowly worked into something more agreeable. Springsteen, Hamm, and a woman Alex didn't recognize did most of the talking. Eventually, Hamm returned to the center stage microphone, holding his hands up for quiet.

"Listen, please. Listen. I've given this some thought, and I've talked it over with the promoter and the performers. We believe that the best thing to do tonight might just be to go along with the request of the police."

A round of boos and some shouting met his statement. Hamm raised his hands again. "I know. I realize some of you are against this on principle, and so am I. I also know that some of you are afraid of what violence the police may resort to, whether we go through this process or refuse. We considered this. Listen…"

At that point, Springsteen walked back onstage, carrying a battered guitar. Nate Crider and Taylor Vera trailed behind him. When Hamm noticed them, he smiled, and changed direction mid-sentence.

"Ladies and gentlemen," Hamm said grandly. "Here for an encore…Taylor Vera, Nate Crider, and Bruce Springsteen."

The dissatisfaction gave way to applause and a few bellows of "Brooooooce." Hamm gave way at the microphone and started to walk away but Springsteen said something to him. The actor grinned and joined Vera and Crider.

Springsteen stepped up to the mike, lifting the guitar strap over his head and settling it on his shoulder with practiced ease. Then he strummed a couple of chords before he spoke.

"We live in a country that claims to be free," he said. "And that's something I want to believe in. You're free to believe what you want, and to do whatever you choose. But here's what I plan on doing. I'm going to sing this next song with my friends here…" He motioned toward the three entertainers on stage with him. "…and we're going to encourage you to sing along, too. It's an old song, and an important one. And then after we're finished singing, I'm going to put down my guitar, and I'm going to the main exit. I'm going to leave this arena in a way that is keeping with the purpose of this concert. I'm going to leave freely and in peace."

A mixed response came from the crowd, including a lackluster cheer, and a few shouts of disagreement.

Springsteen ignored the sound, strumming his guitar a

few more times thoughtfully. Then he added, "I figure, if we live in a country where the police will beat up an eighty year old man for playing some music, well then maybe this really isn't a free country anymore."

That brought a concerted cheer of approval. When it died down, Springsteen said, "But I don't think that'll be the case. Not for me, not for any of us."

Next to him, Taylor Vera nodded along, and so did Crider and Hamm.

"So anyway," Springsteen finished. "This is how we win. With peace and freedom. Because that is what this land is all about. And this is a land that was made for all of us."

He strummed quietly, then struck a firm bass note and started the song in earnest. Alex recognized it immediately, and a moment later, so did the crowd. Springsteen's raspy vocals walked through the first verse, and he was joined by Vera, Crider, and Hamm for the chorus.

This land is your land
This land is my land

Alex could hear Vera's higher tones and the low bass vocals from Crider perfectly complimenting Springsteen's folksy lead.

From California to the New York Island

Alex heard a small sound, and looked over to see the Governor covering her mouth while a tear slid down her cheek.

The song continued, and the performers alternated through taking lead on the verses while the crowd overwhelmed their voices and the simple acoustic guitar sound during the chorus. Alex watched on in amazement until the final lines of the final chorus ended, and Springsteen strummed a finally slow chord. Then he and the others left the stage.

He turned to the Governor, who had dried her tears by then. "Will it work?" he asked her.

The Governor nodded confidently. "Oh, yes. Without question."

They sat and watched events unfold over the next several hours, but in the end, the Governor was right. According to the mainstream news, the crowd cooperated, and police were able to secure the facility.

When the Governor asked Ebby to check her dark web source, the computer guru was unable to locate a live feed, but she did find a recorded report that had been archived. In it, the unknown shadow blogger Veritas showed a clip of Springsteen's plea and subsequent performance. Veritas then signed off after reporting that the crowd appeared to be in agreement, and that this was the most advisable course at the time. "This reporter will also comply," came the digitally altered voice. "At least, so the fascists will believe."

The screen went dark.

"I hope he gets out," Alex said.

"They'll never know who it was," Ebby said. "They may not even find the device. There are lots of hiding places in an arena that large."

"We may never know for sure," Alex said.

"Veritas will be back," Ebby assured him. "Even if it is someone else next time."

Alex thought about that for a moment, then nodded his understanding.

They watched for a while longer, all of them seeming reluctant to let this momentous event come to an end. At least that's how he felt, even though they'd never actually been at the arena.

His phone buzzed about four hours after the performance of "This Land is Your Land." It was a text from Ryan.

Saw your call. Nathalie safe. Will call you tomorrow.

"Good news?" the Governor asked.

He glanced up. "How did you know?"

"It wasn't hard. Your face lit up with relief."

"My sister-in-law is out of the arena, and safe," Alex told her.

"Good."

They sat quietly for another long while, watching the propaganda that passed for news strangely line up with some alternate news that Ebby was able to find and stream. Alex wondered at how rare that event must be. Then he found himself wondering about something else.

"What are you thinking?" the Governor asked him.

"About something you said a little while ago, when I

met with you in your office. We were talking about a flashpoint, a catalyst."

"A Sarajevo?"

"Yes."

"I remember," she said.

"This wasn't it, was it?" Alex said, not really asking.

The Governor thought about it for so long that he wasn't sure she was actually going to answer him. But finally she said, "I don't think so, Alex. But it is something. It is most definitely something. As for what that something will become…" She shrugged. "I suppose we'll see, won't we?"

Part III:
SOMETHING

St. Louis, USA

and

California

March 2029

Our democracy must be not only the envy of the world but the engine of our own renewal. There is nothing wrong with America that cannot be cured by what is right with America.

William J. Clinton,
42nd President of the United States

Chapter 13

Almost from its inception, the New American Party (NAP) espoused many of the same principles upon which the United States of America claimed to have been founded; chief among these, freedom and equality. The strict interpretation of the Constitution was another tenet that received a fair amount of attention, with the Second Amendment, in particular, getting a significant amount of consideration. Detractors of the party in its earliest days claimed that it was the outgrowth of an emboldened Alt-Right movement and essentially a thinly veiled white nationalist party. NAP organizers and leaders denied this, and proceeded to walk a delicate line of balance between appealing to its core constituency without alienating the majority and risking political marginalization.

By the late 2020s, this objective had largely been achieved. While the NAP seemed to consistently engage in significant propaganda efforts to highlight its inclusivity and equity toward all Americans, in truth it had suffered the same fate that many such organizations meet. It had fallen prey to its own sense of privilege and become ever more exclusive.

— From An Unlikely Phoenix *by Reed Ambrose*

Ryan hated the desk. After spending his entire career in patrol, where his squad car was his office, being leashed to a desk grinded on him. He wondered for a while if this is what it would have been like if he'd been promoted to detective, but dismissed that thought. Detectives left their desks all the time, following leads, and interviewing people. Good detectives, anyway. But he wasn't allowed to do that. He couldn't leave the police station.

He was allowed to carry his gun, and Lieutenant Potulny had granted that concession as if it were a papal decree, full of sneering magnanimity. The reassuring weight on his hip made Ryan feel only slightly closer to normal, though. He understood that the job involved a significant amount of paperwork, but *only* pushing paper for forty hours a week was slowly whittling away at him.

This was a prospect that Potulny seemed to enjoy. At least, this was what Ryan surmised from the number of times the lieutenant stopped by the Found Property Unit. There was little to nothing for Potulny to do there. He was nominally in command of the unit, along with several other units in the precinct, but Potulny was clearly not limited strictly to his rank and title with the St. Louis Metro Police. His party membership provided him with significant power and influence, and he exploited his federal status at all turns.

Ryan had thought that the promotion to lieutenant would make Potulny even more unbearable, but he couldn't have predicted the meteoric rise to power and influence he'd witnessed over the past few months. The way Potulny handled the concert protest in February, at least in official eyes, made him the darling of both the department and the party. Ryan had even heard rumblings of an assignment to Washington, D.C., though rumors differed as to whether the position would be within the executive branch or the New American Party itself.

As if the two are really any different, Ryan mused, as he thumbed through another mind-numbing police report about a found bicycle.

Sometimes when Potulny visited, he pointedly ignored Ryan. Other times, he gave him some menial task to perform. Frequently, he reminded the officer that he was still under investigation for the shooting incident last year.

Under investigation for what, Ryan wondered. *Getting ambushed?* But he knew that these days, the truth was what those in power made it be, and as long as they could cloak it in something remotely reasonable, most of the people simply shrugged and went about their own business, thankful not to be the subject of investigation themselves.

He thought about leaving the job. Without the shadow of the investigation hanging over him, there was a better than even chance he could petition for medical retirement. His hip ached constantly, and he still walked with a noticeable limp. But he couldn't consider that option until his shooting was resolved.

Likewise, a return to patrol seemed progressively more unlikely, and while he remained under investigation, his position and eligibility on the detectives' list was frozen.

Reviewing found property reports originally looked like a make-work, temporary job, but now it seemed as if it might stretch into a career. At best, he might find himself working as a sworn member of the Crime Analysis Unit, which had been a valuable piece of the puzzle early in his career. The unit even moved to some surprisingly accurate predictive models, based on some software that originated in Vancouver, British Columbia. But as the party members and bureaucrats became more and more empowered, this once-progressive unit was reduced to a glorified statistics collection group, tasked with reporting what crime has already occurred and creating slick graphs and maps to allow those higher in command to more pointedly place the blame for that crime on those lower down the ladder. It had originally been called CompStat, but Ryan simply called it 'scapegoat policing.' Marcus had told him to shut up about it.

"You a lieutenant?" Marcus had asked. "A captain? No? Then put your head down, and do you own job. Let the white shirts do their own thing."

Thinking back, Ryan realized that might have been good advice, even if he was largely unable to follow it.

Aside from the crime analysis unit of years past, there was no place Ryan wanted to land that would accommodate a cop who couldn't leave the station. And whether it was because of his injuries or the open-ended investigation that Gleeson was supposedly conducting, leaving the station was looking more and more like something Officer Ryan Derrick might never be allowed to do.

The idea of leaving police work stung Ryan. On one

level, being a cop was all he'd ever wanted to do. Leaving felt like a betrayal of his childhood dream. In a perfect world, he wouldn't have to. He could resign from SMP and start over somewhere else with another agency. But this world was an imperfect one, and he knew there were several obstacles in the way of that route. His injuries were a significant one all by themselves, but the reach of men like Potulny and the New American Party could easily poison any potential new police employer against him. That left corporate work, which didn't mesh well with Ryan's sense of higher purpose, and private contracts, which lacked any stability.

But there was another reason he resisted the urge to just quit: it was exactly what they wanted. Potulny, Gleeson, the Party…it would be a victory for them to run another so-called shamer off the force. He didn't want to give them that victory.

"*Molon Labe*," he whispered, and the phrase gave him a shot of pride. If they wanted his job, they could come and take it.

In the end, weren't Nathalie and Melina more important than his pride?

They were, of course. Ironically, his family was the reason he hung on, enduring Potulny's antics every time he came by the Found Property Unit. Leaving the police department might eventually be the best move for his family, but right now, keeping his status in law enforcement was the best thing he could do for them. It strengthened her citizenship application, which now rested on the Supreme Court decision regarding the ACLU appeal, as well as Nathalie's own appeal for grandfather status. Both decisions loomed heavily over their household.

As if on cue, the door to the office buzzed and swung open. In strode Lieutenant Potulny.

"Saving the world, Officer Derrick?" he asked, his tone light and sarcastic.

So today wasn't going to be an ignoring day. Ryan kept his eyes on the report in front of him, but didn't focus on the words. "Returning lost property to the citizens of St. Louis, Lieutenant," he answered, his words laced with mock formality. "Just like every day. It doesn't save the world, but I like to think it makes it a better place."

Potulny stopped near Ryan's desk and stood imperiously over him. "It is customary to rise when a superior officer enters the room," he said sternly.

Ryan glanced up. "Is that a custom? Or a rule?"

"A custom that has become a rule."

Ryan considered begging off, using his injury as an excuse. But he knew that would just strengthen the department's case that he wasn't street worthy. So he forced himself to stand, suppressing a wince when his hip flared in protest.

"Lieutenant," he said, once he was standing.

"That's better," Potulny said, then gave him an expectant look. "No salute?"

Ryan clenched his jaw. "That still falls under custom, not rule, doesn't it?"

Potulny shrugged. "For now."

"I thought so." Ryan settled back into his seat, and turned his attention back to the report in front of me.

Potulny didn't move right away. Instead, he said, "You

know that your every action tells us what kind of an officer you are, don't you?"

"I hope so."

"And what kind of an American."

"Again...I hope so."

"You haven't done yourself any favors with your disrespectful attitude toward leadership. Toward the Party and the President, either."

Ryan looked up. "You mean toward people like you, don't you?"

"It's one and the same."

Ryan didn't answer. He knew he could only take conversations like this so far before Potulny would find a way to turn his words into insubordination.

"Nothing to say?" Potulny prodded.

Ryan shook his head mildly. As much as these exchanges burned like acid in his gut, he tried to maintain a flat demeanor on the surface. He didn't want to give Potulny the satisfaction of getting to him.

Potulny waited until it was clear Ryan wasn't going to say anything more. Then he shrugged, "Maybe you're learning, Officer Derrick. Though I somewhat doubt it. But stranger things have happened."

"They have," Ryan agreed, thinking of all that had come to pass in the last decade.

"I have some news for you," Potulny said, changing gears suddenly.

Ryan steeled himself. If Potulny was delivering the news in person, it wasn't likely to be good. Was he being permanently moved from patrol? Or was this about the so-called investigation he was still under? Ryan tried to keep his expression neutral, but he felt himself leaning forward in his seat.

Potulny affected a look of sympathy but it looked foreign on his face. "You'll get formal notification within a few days, but my sources have told me the decision has already been made."

"About what?" Ryan asked.

"About your wife."

Ryan blinked. "Nathalie…what about her? What's she have to do with…?"

An evil smile broke through Potulny's façade of sympathy. "Oh, you thought this was about your case?" He shook his head. "No, Officer. We'll deal with you in good time. But you seem to be forgetting that we are all federal officers."

"I've never forgotten that," Ryan snapped. "What's this about Nathalie?"

"Her appeal has been denied," Potulny said, clearly enjoying being the bearer of this news. "There will be no grandfather clause applied to her citizenship application. She will have to go through the same twelve-year process as any new applicant."

Ryan almost asked Potulny how he knew this, but resisted the urge. He knew the lieutenant was plugged into the various federal agencies through his party membership. He didn't doubt that the information was accurate.

There's still hope, he thought. The ACLU challenged the constitutionality of the law all the way to the Supreme Court. If the court struck down the law, then Nathalie would be eligible to take her citizenship oath in a matter of days.

"Quite a disappointment," Potulny observed. "One of several that people will be experiencing today, I think."

Ryan didn't answer. An image of his wife filled his mind, and he tried to fend off his sense of frustration and defeat.

"You know," Potulny said, his tone conversational now, "as Party members, there are things that we can do within government operations. Especially for other party members."

Ryan locked eyes with Potulny, masking his surprise. This was the first time in a long while that Potulny or any Party member had made such an offer to him, and never had they been so blatant about it.

"This country was built upon the concept of making sure good people were taken care of," Potulny added. "People who see the true way, who are true Americans. Your late partner understood this. That's why he applied to join."

Ryan opened his mouth to protest, to say that this couldn't be more untrue, but he found that he had no words. Instead, he snapped his mouth shut and swallowed, remaining silent.

Potulny smiled. "I can see you're conflicted. But if that's the case, then it also means that you see the benefit and reason in what I'm suggesting. Think it over, Ryan. We'll talk in a couple of days."

Potulny gave him a greasy smile. Then he turned on his heels, and strode out of the room without another word.

Ryan stared after him, his mind racing, a bevy of

emotions battling for first position.

Was Potulny serious? Did he really want Ryan to join the Party? What did they gain from that?

Ryan saw the answer almost immediately. Turning a detractor had significant value as propaganda. He saw it all play out in his mind. A former shamer sees the light. He'd become an example to be repeatedly cited to convince other reluctant officers.

The entire idea was repugnant to him, and he rejected it almost immediately. But a part of him raised some doubt. What if this was the way to save Nathalie? To get her citizenship? He had little doubt that Potulny and the New American Party could find a way to make that happen.

But what then? Could he live with himself? Could Nathalie? And what message was he sending his daughter if he capitulated like this?

Survive, he thought. Maybe that was the message. Do what you have to do to survive, because you can't change the world or anything in it if you're dead or defeated.

Ryan sat at his desk for the rest of the day, trying to decide if there were worse things than death or defeat.

Chapter 14

The philosopher and political activist Cornel West was interviewed in 2036 while under house arrest in the United States on charges of sedition. Though the terms of his imprisonment were gentler than some, the greater punishment seemed to be exclusion from the international discourse on events. When Akimbo, a noted shadow journalist of the time, asked him in a secret interview about the immigration issues that sparked the crisis, he bitterly replied, "Who knew that U.S. v. Fleming would become another Plessy v. Ferguson or Roe v. Wade? We all should have, that's who."

— From *An Unlikely Phoenix* by Reed Ambrose

That night, after dinner, Ryan played a card game with his daughter. It was a simple color and shape matching game with the straightforward goal of getting rid of all your cards. Melina took the game very seriously, and had her mother's competitive streak. Ryan had long ago abandoned any thought of letting her win. He simply couldn't pull it off any more without arousing her suspicion.

After he narrowly won two out of three matches, he sent her to get ready for bed. Nathalie had been working on her tablet once the dinner dishes were finished, and when he leaned down to kiss her on the neck, she closed the file she was working on. He didn't mind. She was a perfectionist, and would only show him her work once it was finished and ready for the rest of the world to see. Even then, she wasn't always satisfied with it, but as a journalist, she'd come to realize that she had to let things go before she deemed them truly "done."

"You want to go first?" he asked, keeping his head next to hers.

"No," she said. She reached up and touched his cheek, caressing the stubble there. "You start, and I'll finish."

It took two of them to tuck Melina in, at least when Ryan was home. That happened more regularly now, having been the only real benefit to his banishment to the Found Property Unit. It made him wonder how Nathalie managed when he was working graveyard patrol.

He kissed her neck again, gave Melina a few more minutes to finish getting ready, then headed to her bedroom. He found her already under the covers, waiting for him. He lifted the covers a little higher on her and kissed her forehead. "You have a good day?" he asked.

She nodded. "Yep."

"What's on deck for tomorrow?"

She shrugged. "I don't know. Something fun."

"I hope so."

"Hope isn't a plan," Melina said seriously.

Ryan smiled. "Where'd you hear that?"

"From you. About a gazillion times."

He laughed. "Yeah, well, it's true. Hope isn't a plan. But that doesn't mean you can't still hope."

"I know. Can we go to another hockey game soon?"

"Sure. I'll check the schedule."

"Okay."

He kissed her again, this time on the top of her head. He breathed in the clean smell of her hair, and smiled. "G'nite, baby girl."

"Night, Daddy."

He left the light on when he left. In the living room, Nathalie saw him coming, put down her tablet and headed into the bedroom. Ryan sat on the couch. "Miri, turn on the TV," he said.

The disembodied, feminine, slightly robotic voice replied immediately. "Turning on television. Do you have a preference, Ryan?"

"Live news," he said. "Set volume to zero."

"Specify - local or national?" Miri asked.

"National."

The TV screen came on and immediately switched to CNN. Miri had learned Ryan's preferences over the years, so even when he made general requests, they leaned toward those preferences. The New American Party had its own channel, NAP News, and Fox News might as well have been an affiliate. While he had no illusions about the compromises CNN had made to remain mainstream, he still found it to be the least sycophantic of the major networks.

Ryan watched, only partially paying attention. Mostly, he was waiting for Nathalie to return from tucking in

Melina. When he heard her footsteps, he turned to greet her. She sat beside him, crossing her leg under the opposite knee. "Time for your daily propaganda dose?" she asked playfully.

"Just trying to be a dutiful servant," he joked back.

"Well, it's less painful when silent and with no closed captioning."

"Do you want closed captioning, Ryan?" Miri asked asked in her disembodied voice.

"No," he said, then shook his head at Nathalie. "I don't know that I'll ever get used to her eavesdropping."

"*She's* not," Nathalie corrected. "*It* is, though. Supposedly only for key words, but some people have theorized that she is actually spying and recording everything we do."

"Everything?" He raised an eyebrow at her.

"Especially that," she said, raising her eyebrow to mirror his expression.

"Miri," Ryan said, keeping his gaze locked on Nathalie. "Are you spying on us?"

"Negative," Miri replied. "My function is limited to the operation of home appliances, entertainment, environmental, and communication devices."

"It's the last part that worries me," he said, only half joking. Then he gave Nathalie a serious look. "Listen, I have to tell you something."

"Oh? You look intense."

"It's important. I got a visit from Pot Belly today."

She smiled. "It is funny that you still call him that."

"It was Marcus' name for him," Ryan said quietly.

"I know. But I've seen this Potulny. He is very fit."

"I guess he was being ironic."

"Our world is full of irony these days. What did *Monsieur* Pot Belly have to say?"

"He said he had information about your grandfather clause appeal."

Nathalie's small smile faded. "If he brought you the news, then it wasn't good."

"No, it wasn't. He said it was being denied."

Nathalie took a deep breath and absorbed the information. "All right. We knew this was a possibility."

"We did."

"And there's still the ACLU appeal to the Supreme Court."

"News alert," Miri said. "Based upon keywords spoken."

Both turned to the screen. "Alert" flashed in red letters in the lower corner of the screen.

"Miri, play alert," Ryan commanded. "Raise volume to normal."

The channel switched to NAP news. A small notice appeared in the center bottom of the screen, reading "Pre-Recorded."

The anchor looked into the camera, his expression carefully grave. "About an hour ago, the Supreme Court issued a decision in the case of Fleming versus the United States, a case brought by the ACLU on behalf of a Belgian immigrant who had applied for U.S. citizenship. As you may recall, the wait period for someone seeking citizenship after being married to a U.S. citizen used to be seven years. Applicants were required to meet other criteria as well, but married status was a positive factor in this process. The President recently proposed legislation, passed by Congress, that extended this waiting period to twelve years. The White House cited security concerns and the ability of the State Department to properly vet all applicants as reasons for this change." The anchor paused dramatically for a half beat. "Today, in a 7-2 decision, the Supreme Court denied the Fleming appeal to this new law, stating in unequivocal terms that, and I quote, 'Fleming offers no convincing evidence that belies the legality of this law, and the right and responsibility of the United States government to regulate immigration for the security and safety of the American people.'"

Nathalie let out a frustrated sigh. "Security," she said. "As long as they tie it back to that, they can get away with anything."

Ryan didn't reply.

The reporter continued. "Moments ago, NAP received this exclusive response from the White House."

The image shifted to the Oval Office, and the President of the United States peered directly into the camera. "My fellow Americans," he said, then held his hands up in an exaggerated shrug. "Was there any doubt that the Supreme Court would agree with me that this is a perfectly legal way to protect true Americans? I'm not surprised. No one who is smart is surprised by this. The Justices understand that we have to control our own borders. Look, I'm not saying that all foreigners are a threat. Some are very, very fine people. But we have to be careful."

"I hate him," Nathalie murmured. "I really do."

"So, I've made another decision that I believe will

continue to protect the American people," the President continued. "I've decided to shorten the grace period for non-citizens to get out of our country. Effectively immediately, this grace period will end the first of July of this year."

Ryan and Nathalie exchanged a surprised look.

"At that point," the President said, "it will be a violation of federal law for anyone who is not a citizen to remain in this country unless you have applied for and received a blue card. And folks, trust me – we are not giving those cards out like candy. You have to be something pretty special to get one, and even then…" He shrugged again. "Remember what I've been saying for years now…America First. Thank you, and good night."

The video switched back to the reporter, who opened his mouth to comment, but Ryan cut him off.

"Miri, turn off the TV."

"Turning off television," Miri replied.

Ryan and Nathalie stared at each other for a long while, neither one saying anything. He knew what was going through her mind. It was the same thing that was going through his. Finally, he gave voice to it.

"Maybe we should just go," he said.

"Go where?"

"Greece," he said. "Or even Canada."

"Shall I search for flight times to either Greece or Canada?" Miri asked.

"No!" Ryan snapped. "Miri, suspend operations."

"Sleep mode or Power Off?"

"Sleep," he said. Powering off affected most of the home appliances.

"Sleep mode initiated," Miri pronounced.

They waited in silence for a few moments, then Ryan leaned forward. Nathalie followed suit. In a hushed tone, he repeated, "Maybe we should go."

She shook her head. "They might let me go as part of this initiative, but they are making international travel hard for U.S. citizens. You might be unable to go. And Melina…"

"I could sneak across the border," Ryan said.

"With our daughter?" Nathalie shook her head. "It's too dangerous."

Ryan felt like some degree of danger was inevitable, but he didn't say so.

"I'd rather Melina was here with you and safe, even if I can't be," Nathalie said. "Her safety is the most important thing."

Ryan agreed, but he added, "All of us being together is the most important thing."

Nathalie shook her head. "No, *amour*. It isn't. She is, and you know it."

Ryan didn't argue. Instead, he went a different direction, and lowering his voice another notch. "What if we got a false identification for you? One that shows you as an American citizen?"

"How would that work?"

Ryan considered. "I'm not sure. I guess we'd set up the identity somehow before you leave. Then you could comply with the law. Leave, and then come back into the country. After that, you just assume the new identity."

"You'd have to divorce me," she said. "To make it look real."

A lump rose in Ryan's throat. "I suppose that's true."

"And move away from St. Louis."

"Yes. But wherever we went, we could be together, and out from under this issue."

Nathalie thought about it for a long while, but finally shook her head. "It's too dangerous. All that must happen is for one thing to go wrong, and both of us would be in prison. Then what happens to Melina? Foster care?"

Ryan scowled at that. "What, then?"

"We could move to California," she suggested. "It's a sanctuary state, and you have a brother there."

Ryan nodded. "That's an option. Maybe a good one."

"We should sleep on it," Nathalie said.

"Yes. For about a week."

She smiled. "We have a little time. Let's use it to think things over. We have to make the right choice."

She squeezed Ryan's hand and then leaned in to put her head on his chest. He draped an arm over her and held her, staring at the dark, blank television and trying to see something of their future.

Chapter 15

In spite of all of the emphasis upon historians, journalists, and celebrities to provide some sort of barometer of the times in which they live, or to examine the past, one sometimes finds particular insight in unexpected places. Comedians and humorists can be particularly perceptive, perhaps because the very core of their work necessarily leads to a study of human nature. This has been true for millennia, as evidenced by the comedies of Aristophanes. Comedy essentially allows one to say things that might otherwise be censured by the government or the prevailing majority. Cloaking these ideas in humor makes them seem less threatening, and permits the thought to pierce the collective mind. Jan Veselý is an more contemporary example than Aristophanes. When faced with the oppressive Communist regime in 1970s Czechoslovakia, one that featured a powerful government official named Čepice, he played on the fact that čepice is also the Czech word for 'hat.' At the beginning of each performance, Jan Veselý ceremoniously and dramatically hung his hat on a hat stand on stage before saying, "There. Now that I've gotten rid of my hat, we can talk."

Along those same lines, but conversely, it is curious that

R yan held out his phone to the door usher at the HSA Arena, who quickly scanned the screen for his tickets.

"To the left, the seventh entrance," he said.

Ryan needed no directions. He'd been coming to this arena since he was Melina's age, back when it was still the ScottTrade Center. He guided his daughter past the swell of the crowd at the entrance, and veered left.

"Hockey dogs!" Melina said excitedly. She loved the arena hot dogs, and had informed Nathalie earlier in the day that she would not be eating dinner that night to save room for one.

They waited in line briefly, and Ryan bought a pair of dogs, one for each of them, and a drink for Melina. Normally, he kept her away from caffeine and sugar, but for hockey games, he made an exception. A Coke ranked only second to hockey dogs as the early highlight of the night for Melina. Ryan went with a cold beer.

Their section was on the first level, slightly off center ice and about half way up from the ice. Ryan settled into his seat just off the aisle, and Melina took the seat next to him. The aisle chair remained empty.

The two of them munched their hockey dogs and watched the build up to the game. Years ago, he and

Alexander used to come early enough to watch the players skate in the pre-game warm-ups, but he hadn't tried that yet with Melina. Maybe when she was older. As it was, he was happy that she usually made it to the end of the game without falling asleep. Right now, seeing the Zamboni finish cleaning the ice and cheering for Louie, the polar bear mascot in a Blues hockey jersey was more than enough to get her revved up. She sat, taking it all in with her half-eaten hot dog perched in her left hand, occasionally leaning down to where her soda rested in the cup holder to sip from the straw.

The player introductions and a bevy of other announcements preceded the national anthem. He and Melina stood for the anthem, and both put their hands over their hearts. Ryan noticed a significant number of fans who held a salute instead, and he heard a concerted rumble of "MAGA" when the anthem singer's long held "brave!" trailed off to applause.

The game began and was a spirited affair from the start. The opposing team, the Houston Renegades, had become a bitter rival in spite of only being in existence for six short years. The two teams had met three times in the playoffs in the last four years, and such meetings often gave birth to a healthy hatred between hockey clubs.

The period ended in scoreless tie. Both he and Melina headed up the stairs to find a family style bathroom. The wait wasn't long, and they made it back to their seats a few minutes before the announcer boomed, "Ladies and gentleman, back for the second period, here are… *your…* St. Louis Bluuuuuuuuuuuuuuuues!"

Houston got an early second period power play, and

managed to blast a shot from the point past the Blues goalie.

Melina groaned, just like he'd taught her.

"I agree," said Wayne, sliding into the seat next to Ryan. "Mooner should've had that one."

Ryan smiled, holding out his hand for a firm shake. "I think he was screened a bit."

"Still." Wayne leaned across Ryan to hold out his hand to Melina. "And how's my favorite hockey fan?"

"Fine, I guess," Melina said, shaking his hand politely, still pouting about the goal.

"Well, don't let that get you down. I'm betting that Lucky will get it back."

Melina brightened at that. Lucinda "Lucky" Conway was her favorite player. Only the third woman to crack the NHL, she was a pure sniper.

Ryan agreed with Wayne. "She just might. Besides, there's a lot of hockey left."

Melina focused on the ice, obviously not wanting to miss the beginning of the promised comeback. Ryan and Wayne settled back in their seats, watching the game.

"How're things?" Wayne asked. He spoke without looking at Ryan, keeping his eyes on the players.

"They've been better," Ryan replied, following Wayne's lead and following events on the ice. At the same time, both men turned their heads slightly toward the other, directing their voices. It was an old habit for them, whether they were at a hockey game, in a desert landscape, or an urban battleground. *You don't need your eyes to hear me,* Wayne had stressed to Ryan not long after the young Marine reported for duty. *Use your eyes for what they were meant for and watch for the fucking enemy.*

"I heard the news on the immigration law," Wayne said. "I'm sorry."

"So are we."

"Her grandfather clause appeal?"

"It's a no go."

Wayne nodded, tracking the play and clapping distractedly when one of the Blues players landed a heavy body check in the defensive zone. "So you're looking at options, I'm guessing."

"Yes."

"There aren't many. You realize that, right?"

"I do."

"Compliance is the most obvious," Wayne said.

"Not an option." Ryan lowered his voice. "We can't be separated. Our family stays together."

"That's a difficult proposition, since she can't stay and you two can't leave."

"That is a problem," Ryan agreed.

"What about your brother?" Wayne asked, and Ryan knew he meant moving to California.

"We're considering that. It might be our best option."

"It might be your only option."

"Our only onside option, yeah."

In his peripheral vision, Ryan saw the corner of Wayne's mouth tick up in a hint of a smile. It was an old code they'd used during their time in the Corps after they'd discovered their mutual love for hockey. Anything onside was by the book. Things deemed offside were not spoken of again after the mission.

"You're thinking of divorcing her?" Wayne asked.

"Marrying another woman?"

"I might have to."

"Thing is, you've always had a type, Derrick. I don't imagine wife number two would look much different than wife number one."

"You're probably right. But she'd have a different name. And she'd be an American."

"Second marriages are tough to come by. Successful ones, anyway."

"I'm confident you could help me."

Wayne sighed. "Maybe But things are getting tougher, brother."

Ryan turned to look at him, violating their conversational norm. "Everything all right with *you?*"

"I'm getting by. But federal service is coming with more and more pressure these days. It's not what I expected when I signed on."

"What do you mean?" Ryan wasn't sure which intelligence agency Wayne had gone to work for once they'd both left the Marines. As a First Recon operator with intelligence training, he had initially been able to write his own ticket, or so Ryan thought. This was the first he'd heard any indication of dissatisfaction from his former lieutenant.

Wayne didn't reply. Instead, he took out his wallet and removed a card. He handed it to Ryan.

Ryan looked down at the dark gray plastic identification. Wayne's face stared up at him with a professional expression. To the right of the photo were the deep red holographic letters N.A.P. and beneath that, the word, "MEMBER SINCE 2028."

His stomach fell. An incredible sense of disappointment and betrayal settled over him, followed immediately by a spike of concern. If Wayne was…

"Relax," Wayne said, taking the card back and replacing it in his wallet. "It was a necessary evil to keep my access."

"Your security access is based on whether or not you're a party member?" Ryan asked, his tone hushed. "Are you kidding me?"

Wayne shook his head. "Technically not my clearance. But you know as well as I do that clearance to know is only half of the puzzle. The other is a need to know. And there's a whole lot of latitude these days where compartmentalization is concerned." He glanced left and right, then at Ryan. "It's a card. It's bullshit. Necessary, evil bullshit, but bullshit all the same. You savvy?"

Ryan stared back, wondering if he could still trust him. After all they'd been through, he wanted to believe so. But he knew how pervasive the party pressure was in the Metro, and could only imagine how much more amplified it was in federal intelligence circles. Pressure like that could change a man, *did* change men, every day.

Was Wayne one of them now?

"I know what you're asking yourself," Wayne said. "And the answer is no. I'm still me. The fuckers haven't gotten me yet, and they won't. But it is getting harder, brother. Harder to find a way to separate what we're doing on behalf of the country, and what is on behalf of the party. But I can still find a way."

Ryan said nothing, but turned his attention back to the ice. A Blues forward knifed between a pair of defenders, cutting toward the Houston net. Ryan would have recognized the player by her stride, even without the number nineteen clearly emblazoned on her back. "Lucky" Conway deked, faking backhand, then snapping a forehand shot over the goaltender's shoulder and just under the crossbar for a goal. The red light went on, the deep goal horn bellowed, and the arena exploded in cheers. Melina leapt to her feet with the rest of the crowd, jumping up and down. Ryan stood and clapped, and Wayne did the same.

As the goal horn gave way to the loud music of the Blues' latest goal song, a re-mix of a Taylor Vera hit, Wayne leaned in close to Ryan's ear.

"You can still trust me, brother. I hope you know that."

Ryan nodded that he'd heard. They stood clapping for a little while longer before settling back into their seats. He and Melina high-fived, and Wayne flashed her a smile.

"Told ya so," he said.

The game resumed, but the energy of the crowd remained electric. Ryan didn't say anything for several minutes, and Wayne gave him the space to think. When he finally glanced over at his old lieutenant, he saw the same man he'd always known. "I'm sorry," he said.

"Don't be sorry for being cautious," Wayne said.

"I've been through a lot," Ryan found himself saying. "*We've* been through a lot."

"I know."

"But I should know better."

"You should. It's a whole new, strange world, though. Your safest bet is to trust no one, so I understand."

Ryan nodded his thanks. "It feels like things are coming to a head."

"That's because they are. We're just about to a point where people who want these changes are going to see the country they want, and those who have been hoping it wouldn't happen are going to realize it already has."

"That's depressing."

"That's real. Things are not what they used to be. These changes have worked their way into every aspect of our world." Wayne waved slightly, indicated the HSA Arena. "Look at the name of this arena, man. It used to be named after the community where it's built. Then a couple of corporations bought the naming rights. And now?"

"Now it's named after a federal government agency," Ryan finished.

"Not just any agency," Wayne said. "*The* agency. Homeland Security. It's the hub of the wheel."

Ryan studied him, wondering if that was where Wayne worked.

"Don't ask," he said, noticing the look. "It doesn't matter anyway. Ultimately, we all work for HSA. Hell, you do, too."

"Not me," Ryan said. "I take the 'community of service' clause of nationalization seriously."

"It doesn't matter," Wayne told him. "Every cop has a federal commission. Every cop answers to the orange fuhrer."

Ryan burst out in a bitter laugh. "Oh, that's good. You better not let anyone you work with hear you say that."

"Why do you think I'm talking out of the side of my mouth just below the sound level of the ambient crowd noise? It's called tradecraft, brother. And I am good at it."

In Wayne's voice, Ryan could hear that age-old genuine mix of self-deprecating humor and mild arrogance that was pure Wayne. That reassured him.

"What would you do if you were me?" he asked.

"I'd get a better haircut, for starters."

"After that."

Wayne was quiet for a long while. Then he said, "Let me think on it for a bit, all right? I'll see what I can come up with."

"We don't have much time left," Ryan said.

"I know." Wayne put his hands into his jack pocket. "In the meantime, you should do what we always did on an op. You remember?"

"Plan for the worst, hope for the best," Ryan recited. "Except-"

"-hope is not a plan," Wayne finished. He gave Ryan a grim smile. "But we can still hope, right, brother?"

"We can always hope, yes."

"Good."

They sat quietly for the rest of the period, reacting with ooohs and ahhhs to Conway nearly scoring another goal and then leaping to their feet after a questionable hit on her just a few moments later. Veteran player and long-time Blues captain Brayden Schenn immediately dropped his gloves and waded into the Houston player. After a brief tie-up and some jockeying, Schenn began landing jackhammer blows on his opponent's face.

Conway was back on her feet. Instead of making her way to the bench, she waved the trainer away and grabbed onto a Houston player who was drifting too close to the Schenn fight. They jerked and pulled on each other for a few moments, but neither one dropped their gloves.

Schenn's pummeling ended abruptly when one of the punches landed on the button and the Houston player's legs gave out. He sank to his knees. Schenn held him from falling to the ice, but stopped raining blows upon him. The linemen got between the two players and guided the Houston player to the bench. Schenn made his way toward the penalty box to the uproarious approval of the crowd, but one of the referees intercepted him and guided him to the Blues bench instead. He left the ice and headed straight down the tunnel to the locker room.

Ryan glanced up at the game clock. There was a little under four minutes left in the period. Fighting was a five-minute major penalty, so that explained why they'd sent Schenn off the ice.

"Old time hockey," Wayne mused. "You don't see that very often anymore."

"True," Ryan admitted. Fighting had become rare in the NHL. He wasn't sure that was a bad thing necessarily, but it was a change from the game he'd grown up with.

"Well, good for Schenner for sticking up for a teammate like that. I guess you can take the boy out of Saskatchewan..." Wayne said, then trailed off without finishing the cliché. He held out his hand. "Listen, I gotta go. I want to beat the traffic."

Ryan grasped Wayne's hand in his own. He felt a small plastic chip press into his palm.

Wayne leaned in and hugged him with this other arm. "You put that in your phone and you can call me secure.

Just in case, okay?"

Ryan nodded. "Thanks."

Wayne broke the embrace and let go of the handshake. He gave Melina a small wave. "Enjoy the rest of the game, kiddo. Blues for life, right?"

Melina gave him a thumbs up.

Wayne clapped Ryan lightly on the shoulder, then turned and made his way up the steps and out of the arena.

Ryan sat back down, slipping the small chip into his pocket. When the period ended, he and Melina stayed and watched the intermission activity on the ice, then quietly followed the Zamboni as it glided over the ice, smoothing over the deep grooves that ran across the ice surface like scars.

"Daddy?"

"Yes, honey?" he glanced down at her expectantly.

"I love you," she said. Her tone was very matter-of-fact.

He smiled, and leaned down to kiss the top of her head. "I love you, too."

"I think we're going to win this one," Melina told him.

"You may be right. I hope so."

"I hope so, too," she said, and went back to watching the Zamboni sweep across the ice.

Chapter 16

History can be a subjective field, and one's own politics frequently mar an otherwise adroit analysis. So when Sage Rasmussen wrote that by 2020, Canada had become the nation that the United States always believed it was, his comments were met with either derision or disappointed agreement, depending upon the political beliefs of the receiver. Certainly, people from any political persuasion would be forced to admit that there was something very similar in Prime Minister Justin Trudeau's early term sentiment that "[w]e have created a society where individual rights and freedoms, compassion and diversity are core to our citizenship. But underlying that idea of Canada is the promise that we all have a chance to build a better life for ourselves and our children."

— From *An Unlikely Phoenix* by Reed Ambrose

Alexander Derrick met with Gregory Bell in the late morning. He agreed to meet at Gregory's office, which was a common ploy by those in power. There were dozens of similar small moves – who set the meeting, who picked the neutral site (making it somewhat less than neutral), who set the agenda, who spoke first, who steered the conversation to his own agenda…all small steps in a dance of dominance and manipulation. He had once reveled in these kinds of political games, but in recent years, he had grown exceptionally weary of all of them. Maybe it was because it didn't seem like a game to him anymore. The stakes had risen from politics to…to what?

Something grander, he decided. Something far more important than the day to day minutiae that had dominated most of his career up until about a decade ago. He just didn't have time to care about these ridiculous power plays.

Power plays. That made him think of the text he'd received from Ryan at breakfast.

BLUES 6, RENEGADES 2 LAST NIGHT. CONWAY A NATURAL HAT TRICK. SCHENN GOT A GORDIE HOWE. ANAHEIM NEXT, THEN YOUR SHARKS.

With everything going on, his brother still took a few moments to jab him about his perceived disloyalty to the hometown team. Somehow that made him feel like there were still things that were right in the world, despite of how the recent Supreme Court decision potentially impacted Ryan's family.

Gregory greeted him courteously, if a little withdrawn. Once they had a very public conversation out in the waiting area, one that enough of his staffers heard or would hear about that minions such as Young would get a favorable report, the two retreated to Gregory's office.

"Something to drink?" Gregory asked.

"Maybe some coffee, if you're having some."

Gregory lifted his phone and made a quick order. Then he leaned back in his chair and waited for Alex to start.

Alex wasted no time. "I'll get straight to it, Gregory. I'm here to secure your vote to back the Governor's initiative."

"She isn't going to wait for the people to vote? The referendum won't be voted on for another week."

"Of course, she's going to wait. But we all know how the vote will turn out."

"Do we?" Gregory asked. "See, I'm not so sure."

"California is still a blue state," Alex said. "And more importantly, we have a culture that prizes personal liberty. That has led to a lot of anti-federal sentiment-"

"Yes, I live here, too, Alex. I don't need a lesson on politics or history from you. I get enough of that from August as it is." He shook his head. "But I'll tell you something. Even if you and the Governor are right about this vote, you're making a mistake."

"What's the mistake?"

"Counting on votes as if they are yours by right. The majority has been doing it for as long as it's been a majority. Democrats always believed they had the black vote locked up without even trying. Republicans counted on the religious right as a *fait accompli*. But when you view a block of people like that, like their vote belongs to you, it shows a lack of respect. It's condescending."

"That's fair. But I'm here in your office, Gregory. I'm not taking your vote for granted – I'm trying to secure it."

"I know. But you've already counted the people's vote, and they won't even go to the polls until next week."

There was a rap on the door, and Gregory called for them to enter. A young man in a sweater vest came in briskly, putting a cup of coffee on Gregory's desk and leaving without a word.

"I hate that," Gregory said.

"What?"

"That stupid sweater vest. It's worse than bell bottoms."

"Those are due for another resurgence soon."

"I know. I dread it." Gregory slid one of the cups across the desk to Alex. "Let's be generous and say that you're not being arrogant or entitled by counting on the public vote. Instead, let's say that you've got a keen feel for the public winds right now."

"That's gracious of you." Alex sparred back gently.

"Where does that leave things? Does the Governor intend to act immediately? To secede?"

"I can't speak for what's happening in the Governor's mind."

"You're here, speaking on her behalf."

"True. All I know is that she wants to have the votes to do it. I don't know more than that."

Gregory gave him a pointed look. "Don't bullshit a bullshitter, Alex."

"I'm not."

"You two have gotten pretty cozy over the last few months. You're going to tell me she doesn't share her plans with you when you go over to the Governor's mansion for dinner? I mean, you do talk politics, right?" A knowing grin spread across his face. "Wait. You're not dating the Governor, are you?"

Alex felt a slight blush of warmth, followed immediately by irritation.

Gregory's eyebrows went up. "Holy hell, you *are*. Alex, she's eight-two!"

Alex cleared his throat. "I'm not. Don't be ridiculous."

"Hey, I'm not judging. Everybody needs somebody."

Alex gave him a dark, weary look. "It's not like that," he said. "Some of it is business, and yeah, some of it is personal. We've become friends. I like her, and I admire her. That doesn't mean I want to sleep with her."

"When a man likes and admires a woman, it usually means he wants to sleep with her."

"Well, call me unusual, then. It's a friendship, and honestly, Gregory, it's one I'd like it if you didn't cheapen it with your silly speculation." His tone had become a touch sharper, not beyond remaining congenial, but Gregory clearly caught the shift.

Gregory held up his hands. "All right, all right. I surrender. You're just friends."

"We're friends," Alex repeated, omitting the *just*.

"My question still stands. Is she going to pursue secession as soon as she has the vote?"

"My answer is still the same. I don't know. I think a lot will depend on what the White House does."

"If we move too fast, we'll lose Canada," Gregory said.

Alex didn't answer. He'd hoped the Governor's revelations about her discussions with the heads of state of both Canada and Mexico would dissuade those who still held to that strategy. He couldn't be sure if this was gamesmanship by Gregory or what he honestly thought was still the best course.

"You don't think Canada is there for us, do you?" Gregory asked.

Alex shook his head. "No. Not yet. Maybe once we're independent. Before that, it's too risky."

Gregory lifted his coffee cup and took a drink, his face thoughtful. "I have come to agree with that position," he said, "or at least consigned myself to Canada being part of the long-term plan, not the short term."

"I'm glad to hear that."

"If my position is no longer viable in the short term, then I obviously have to decide what position to take in the short term." He put the cup down. "Clearly, I can't back Héctor's plan to join Mexico. Just between you and me, I think that might be the only thing worse than the current state of affairs, at least for the people I represent."

Alex didn't reply. He knew Gregory took great pride in being from Oakland. He often drew on the hard, urban roots that he came from, but pointed to the extreme revitalization that had gone on in that city over the past dozen years...ironically, coinciding closely with the President's term in office. He'd pointed that out to Gregory once, who'd given him a death stare before gritting, "Correlation doesn't equal causation. You'd do well to remember that."

"I've never been one to sit the fence, so that leaves me staring down either reconciliation or secession. The two extremes." He leaned back. "When did we become a people of extremes, Alex?"

Alex shook his head. "We always have been," he said. "Once we got this big, it's impossible not to be."

"Maybe you're right." Gregory took another sip of

coffee.

Alex waited, wondering what Gregory wanted. Did he want to be courted? Was he just enjoying his moment of leverage? Or something else?

"Have you been to any of these concerts?" Gregory asked him. "These Freedom Concerts?"

Alex shook his head.

"Me, either," Gregory said. "But they've been cropping up all over the state. From all kinds of musicians. Rap, country, rock, techno, even that new Japanese style. What's it called?"

"I don't know."

Gregory raised a finger. "I remember. They call it *Giru*. You ever listen to any of it?"

"No. I've been busy."

"It doesn't matter. Point is, after that thing in St. Louis, people can't seem to get enough of these concerts, *giru* or otherwise."

Alex nodded. Gregory was right. At least in California, the concerts had been allowed to happen. He'd heard rumblings that in many states, the events had been suppressed. Government agencies refused to authorize permits in some places. In others, a contingent of counter-protestors showed up, threatening violence and giving police the excuse to shut down the show. But the government wasn't able to stop them all. Some promoters had taken to using private property for the shows, even large farm properties, a move that hearkened back to Woodstock.

"People value freedom," Alex said. "You know that."

"I do. And this is why you think the referendum will

pass?"

"Yes."

Gregory thought about it for a moment, eyeing Alex all the while. Then he said, "I will support you, Alex. But I have a condition."

"What is it?"

"The Mexico option has to die."

"I can't promise that. I don't have that measure of control. And Héctor has a lot of support."

Gregory narrowed his eyes. "Let's be real. Mexico is a poor country. A union with Mexico isn't us joining Mexico. It's Mexico joining us."

"That's a little ethnocentric."

"I know it's not PC, but it's true. Joining Mexico is a step backward, and absorbing Mexico into our new nation would be a financial disaster."

"I don't think it's quite that simple."

"Alex, I'm being kind. There are those who argue Mexico is a failed state, and has been for decades. The drug cartels own and run the country."

Alex didn't immediately reply. There was an element of truth to what Gregory said. He wasn't in favor of the Mexico option, either, but he couldn't speak for the Governor. Carefully, he said, "Here's what I can tell you, Gregory. The Governor is not in favor of petitioning any nation for annexation. Not Canada, not Mexico, not anyone."

"Not *now*, sure. But what about two years from now, once we're free and clear of the U.S.? Like you said, Héctor has a lot of votes. And there's a whole lot of brown people living in California. Way more brown than black."

"All of your constituents aren't black."

"Nor yours all white," Gregory replied. "Most are, though. And most of mine are black."

"So what?"

"So it doesn't do any of us any good to join Mexico, that's so what."

Alex considered. "I can promise you that I won't actively support a move to join Mexico. And I'll both advise and vote against it. Beyond that, I can't promise you anything."

Gregory deliberated for a long minute. Then he held out his hand. "Senator, under those terms, I am happy to support the Governor if she should decide that secession is the best course of action for the people and the great state of California."

Alex shook his hand.

That's one more, he thought.

But was it enough?

Chapter 17

In the previous century, Science fiction author Robert A. Heinlein wrote that "secrecy is the beginning of tyranny." The political argument that springs from such a statement is a straightforward one: the more open a government is, the freer its people tend to be. Conversely, the more secretive a government is, the more restrictions placed upon its people.

While there are those who will heartily argue against this maxim, most academics will concede that it is generally accurate. And while the level of governmental secrecy within the United States during the 2020s appears to have spiked considerably, that secrecy was masked with propaganda and other forms of white noise that often served to distract most citizens. While distracted, they did not notice or pay sufficient attention to those actions that they may have otherwise found disturbing.

Another truism throughout human history is that most societies, even relatively free ones, have employed some form of secret police. Certainly the more authoritarian states did. From the Krypteia of ancient Sparta, to the Roman Frumentarii, the German Gestapo, and the Russian KGB, these organizations

---

Ryan and Nathalie spent their anniversary at a small Italian restaurant on the fringe of downtown. They ate pasta, shared a bottle of moderately priced red wine, and tried unsuccessfully to forget their other cares for a few hours.

It didn't work.

To her credit, Ryan could see that she was trying. She laughed at his small jokes, and even tried to make a couple of her own. But she frequently glanced past him, or quickly around the room, and he could see the worry underneath her smiling exterior.

He left it alone. Instead, they talked about Melina, and about how lucky they were in their marriage. Ryan raised his glass, and they toasted in a familiar style.

"Hey, *vous*," he began.

"Who, *moi?*"

"Yes, *toujours toi*." His French was almost nonexistent,

but he'd mastered his phrase.

"Always you," she said back, her tone both appreciative, and a little sad.

When they finished dinner, Ryan left a generous tip, and they left the restaurant. They held hands and walked slowly, partly to savor the moment, and partly in deference to Ryan's injuries. In about a block, he felt his slight limp increase. A muted pain throbbed in his hip.

"Are you all right, *amour?*"

"Hurts a little, is all."

She reached into her purse and took out his painkillers, holding them up.

Ryan shook his head. "No, I think it'll be okay. They make my head fuzzy." He squeezed her hand. "I don't want a fuzzy memory of this."

She squeezed back, hugging his arm. "We'll walk slower, then."

They made their way several more blocks to the park that housed the St. Louis Archway. He noticed her glance over her shoulder twice along the way. Once they found a spot on the railing at the edge of the park where they could stare at the monument, they stood quietly for a while and took it in.

The sound of the city echoed around them, and the lights of the park lit up the grand, white archway. As kids, he and Alex had ridden the small, cramped cars inside the monument to the viewing center at the apex. The whole experience had been disconcerting for him, even as a kid. The ride up to the top seemed like a cross between a submarine and the slow climb of a roller coaster. Then, suddenly, they were exposed to the wide expanse of the view from inside the top of arch. It was jarring, and he never asked to go back after that first time.

Nathalie glanced to the side.

Ryan had finally had enough. "What is it?" he asked.

Her eyes snapped to his. "What's what?"

He shook his head. "Don't do that. Not tonight, of all nights."

She gave him a pained expression. "I'm sorry, *amour*."

"Just tell me."

She bit her lip and looked away. "I should have told you weeks ago, but I wasn't sure. I thought maybe I was crazy."

"Told me what?"

She glanced around again, then back at Ryan. The worry that had been hovering behind her eyes all night came out fully. "I think someone has been following me."

Ryan's surprise was muted by his instincts. Immediately, he followed her gaze. "Who? Do you see someone now?"

"No. I…I don't think so. That is the problem. I don't actually see anyone for certain. It's just a feeling I've been having."

"For weeks now?"

She nodded. "Ever since the concert."

He thought about that. She *was* a journalist. Was it possible they'd put a tail on her after the event?

Then he wondered, who were *they*, exactly? Homeland Security? Immigration? Metro, looking to get to him somehow?

"*Je suis désolé,*" Nathalie repeated.

"I know."

"Am I thinking crazy?" she asked.

"No," he said firmly. "If you feel it in your gut, there's something there. You have to trust it."

"Who is it, do you think?"

"I don't know, babe. But we're going to find out." He took her hand. "Listen, the next time you see someone who looks wrong to you, you tell me right away."

"Wrong how?"

"If the person makes you feel like you're feeling now, that's what I mean by wrong. Okay?"

"*Oui.* Yes. I understand."

"Good." He squeezed her hand. "That's good."

They stayed at the railing, looking out at the archway for another ten minutes. Ryan wrapped his arm around her, and she leaned into him.

"It feels good to tell you," she whispered.

He pulled her closer, and kissed the top of her head. "We're going to get through this," he told her.

She didn't answer.

After a while, they turned away from the monument and walked back into downtown. Nathalie watched carefully for anything suspicious, but didn't see anything. Ryan's senses were on high alert as well, and he studied everything in his peripheral vision. He saw nothing, either. After a few blocks, Ryan was convinced that either they weren't being followed at the moment, or the operatives were too skilled for him to spot.

"I see something," Nathalie said, staring forward as she spoke.

"Where?"

"Behind us, across the street. The man in the blue

jacket. I…I think I saw him before."

"Where'd you see him?"

"At work, on the street outside the office. I think."

"You think or you know?"

"I…I think. I can't be sure."

Ryan's senses were alive. He took Nathalie's hand and they walked down another block, then cut into an alley. Halfway through the alley, he slipped into a deep doorway. They both pressed against the wall of the old brick building, waiting.

For a while, there was nothing. Ryan began to wonder if Nathalie had been wrong, if her paranoia had led her mind to make connections that weren't there. But then he heard soft footfalls in the alley. He knew that logically it could be anyone, but he coiled his body in anticipation.

A man in a blue jacket emerged into view. In a glance, Ryan sized him up. He was medium build and average in almost every way.   There was virtually nothing memorable about his appearance, making the color of his jacket the most outstanding factor.

Perfect for surveillance, he thought.

The man didn't see them right away, and both Ryan and Nathalie remained perfectly still. When the man had taken a couple of steps past the doorway, Ryan shuffled toward him. His intent was to grab onto him with a neck restraint and literally choke some answers out of him. But the night was quiet and his shoes scraped on the pavement.

The man's head snapped toward him.

Ryan didn't stop. He tried to charge toward the man, but he felt awkward and weak. The man sidestepped his attack.

"Hey! What are you doing?" he said, his voice confused.

Ryan reached out and grabbed the man's jacket sleeve. He jerked it away, and stumbled back half a step from the force of it. Ryan charged again, tackling the man to the ground. His hip screamed in protest, and the jarring thud when they both landed forced a painful grunt out of him.

Once on the ground, he wrapped his legs around one of the man's legs, pinning him in place. With both hands, he sought out the man's wrist and elbow, trying for a joint lock to gain control. The man countered his move, though, brushing aside Ryan's reaching hand and then jabbing him toward the throat.

Ryan dropped his chin at the last moment, catching the man's knuckles there. He tried to ignore the sharp explosion for pain, and it dissipated almost immediately. He drove a thumb into the man's right eye in retaliation, but the man was too quick. He dropped his head and Ryan's thumb struck the man in the forehead. Another sharp pain burst from the base of his thumb, and this time he yelled out involuntarily.

The man took advantage of his brief surprise to twist his hips forcefully. The two of them rolled on the hard pavement. Ryan's hip throbbed loudly and he gritted his teeth. Out of nowhere, a punch landed on his cheek, catching part of his nose in the process. He managed to get his hands up defensively while the man rained down several blows. He forearms took the brunt of the heavy punches, but one slipped through and landed square. He saw a white flash momentarily, and felt his body slacken.

Another punch struck him in the temple, and this time he saw an explosion of red light behind his eyes. Blindly, he punched back, and felt his fist land somewhere in the man's midsection. The blow had no real strength behind it, and he'd left himself open on that side. The next punch hooked in from that direction. Ryan tucked down his chin and absorbed it. Fighting through the pain in his hip, he bucked upward to unsettle his attacker, then twisted. The tentative leg lock he had come loose and the man spilled to the pavement beside him.

A foot sailed past his head and struck the man next to him. He grunted as he rose to his knees. Ryan struggled to do the same, but was much slower. By the time he reached his knees, the man was on his feet and running down the alley way.

Nathalie knelt beside him. "Are you all right?"

He nodded, even though he was hurting in several places at once. His hips ached like they'd just been hit with a baseball bat. His thumb throbbed. He could feel the welts and bruises forming on his face and forearms as well.

"Help me up," he said.

Nathalie stood and gave him ballast. Ryan got to his feet, and stared down the alley where the man had gone. He'd disappeared around the corner onto the next street, but Ryan knew he had no chance of catching him.

"Are you sure you're okay?" Nathalie asked.

"It hurts a little," he admitted. "But I'll be all right. Let's just get home."

"Who was he?" Nathalie asked.

"I have no idea," he said, but that wasn't entirely true.

He was starting to form one.

They followed in the footsteps of the man in the blue jacket, even turning right at the end of the alley as he had done, but saw no sign of him. Ryan had expected as much. They continued for another block, then stopped at a bus stop and settled onto the bench. Ryan took out his phone and ordered an AutoUber. Once he entered their location, their destination, and confirmed the purchase, his screen flashed, "ETA 3:19" and immediately began counting down.

He turned to Nathalie, taking her hand. He briefly debated whether or not to share his thoughts with her, but he quickly decided that it was the right thing to do. Not only was she his partner, but she was in this, too.

"Am I just paranoid?" she asked him, before he could speak.

"No."

"I worry that I am. That this man was just some poor soul out for a walk, and my paranoia caused…all of this."

"No," he repeated.

"Did you see how surprised he looked when he saw us in the alley?"

"That doesn't mean he wasn't following us," he said. "Just that he was surprised to see us when he did."

She bit her lip. "What do you think?"

"I think he was an agent of some kind."

Relief flooded her expression. "Why?"

"A couple of reasons. For one, he blended pretty well, and would have been even more anonymous in a crowd. That blue jacket was the most interesting thing about him. He was forgettable."

"He couldn't be that forgettable," she said. "I recognized him from outside of the offices of *The Archway*."

"True," he admitted. "But you said you've felt like you've been being followed for weeks, right?"

"Yes, ever since the concert."

"Then it isn't too outlandish to assume this guy has been part of that effort the entire time. Maybe you recognizing him was a cumulative thing."

"Meaning that I saw him so many times that I finally recognized him?"

"Something like that, yeah."

She thought about it, then shrugged. "It could be. But I'd like to be certain it wasn't simply some coincidence. It would have been nice if he'd dropped a wallet with government identification in it or something like that."

"This wasn't a coincidence," Ryan said.

"How can you be sure?"

"There's something else, too," he told her. "His fighting. He had training."

"Did he? I couldn't tell."

"I could. Believe me."

She took a deep, shaky breath and let it out. "I'll take your word. But to me, it all looked so…brutal. So fast."

He smiled, in spite of everything. "Real fights are like that. Fast, brutal, and ugly." He squeezed her hand. "Thanks for coming to my rescue, by the way."

"Rescue?" she snorted. "All I did was break my foot on his shoulder."

"It was brave of you to join the fight."

"He was hitting you."

Ryan grinned ruefully. "So he was."

She reached out and touched him softly on the face. "I'm sorry."

"Don't be sorry for what other people do."

"No, I brought this on us, *amour*. I-"

A blue Prius glided to the curb in front of them.

"Ride for Derrick, Ryan," a digital voice intoned.

"Confirmed," Ryan said. He held his phone to the small camera on the door frame. The AutoUber camera scanned the screen and dinged brightly. The door locks clicked open and the passenger door disengaged and opened a few inches.

Ryan held the door for Nathalie, then eased himself into the back seat next to her. When he closed the door, the same digital voice advised them both to secure their seat belts. They clicked the belts into place, and a moment later, the automated car began navigating slowly through downtown, and then toward their home.

Nathalie held his hand. "Thank you for believing me."

"You don't have to thank me for that."

"I love you, Ryan."

"I love you, too."

He glanced at surrounding traffic, especially any that followed them, but he couldn't spot a tail. He wondered if the agent had been working alone, but doubted it. Why hadn't his partners joined in once they were fighting? Or did it all happen too fast? Ryan wasn't sure.

Once they were home and had paid the babysitter, he locked the door behind her. Then he systemically walked through the entire house, checking every door and window. All were locked.

He returned to the kitchen, where Nathalie had opened a bottle of wine. She poured and they raised their glasses silently before drinking. Ryan kissed her, and when she kissed him back, he sensed the hunger there, the relief, the fear, the love, all of it.

He returned the kiss with the same urgency, and it seemed to go on for a very long time. When she finally broke away, her cheeks were flushed. She picked up the bottle and walked past him to the living room. He watched her go, admiring her shape and the shine of her deep black hair. He grabbed some ibuprofen from the cupboard, then followed her, and sat next to her on the couch.

Ryan took the ibuprofen with a swallow of wine. His hips still ached, and were the worst of his injuries, despite being punched in the head. His battered forearms felt twice as large as normal, giving him a momentary vision of Popeye the Sailor. When he touched them gingerly, he could feel the lumps there that would become heavy bruises. He inspected the areas on his face that had taken the brunt of the man's punches, but didn't find anything surprising.

Next to him, Nathalie said nothing. They drank in silence for a few minutes, letting the intensity of the evening's events ebb away. After the first glass of wine was gone, he refilled both. Nathalie held hers in her hands, but didn't drink right away.

"I have to tell you something," she said quietly.

"Something else?" he asked, and took another drink. The combination of the wine and the ibuprofen seemed to be starting to gnaw away at his pain.

"Something more," she said. "I know why these men are following me. At least, I think I do."

"Because you're a journalist," Ryan said. "You wrote critical pieces when you were at the *Dispatch* and still do at the *Archway*. They're using the Internal Security Act to -"

"It's more than that," she said.

He gave her a confused look. "Then what?"

"I don't just write for the *Archway*. I...I freelance, as well."

Ryan raised an eyebrow. He hadn't known that. "For who?"

"I'm part of a network of journalists who report uncensored news," she said. "We broadcast about events that the mainstream media either ignores or reports in a whitewashed fashion."

Ryan shook his head in disbelief. "How long have you been doing this?" he asked.

"I started near the end of my time at the *Dispatch*. Once my articles were being heavily edited, I knew I had to do something."

"That long?" He couldn't keep the hurt out of his voice. "And you didn't tell me?"

"It was for your own safety," she said.

"So what you're doing is dangerous, then?"

"Of course it is. Anything anti-federal these days is dangerous. You know this. But we are careful. It's all very secretive. I don't even know everyone who is part of the group. Our identities are cloaked, and everyone broadcasts under the same byline. We are all Veritas."

The Latin word registered in his mind, but he brushed

past it. "The concert," he said. "You were there to report, but not for *The Archway*."

"I did a piece for them, too," she said, then shrugged. "It ran, but the editor toned it down, and let's be honest. Our readership is small, and don't need to be convinced about what is happening in this country. The shadow blogs reach a larger audience, and one that is more moderate, still undecided."

"You reported from the concert on one of these…what did you call it? A shadow blog?" A growing sense of disquiet had settled over him as she confessed.

"I did," she admitted. "I even interviewed Springsteen briefly."

"Who else is part of this group?" he asked, but his mind was catching on the term *shadow blog*.

"I told you, I don't know everyone. Just a few local journalists are in my group. There are other groups, but all of them are kept separate from each other."

"Compartmentalized cells," Ryan said quietly.

"Yes, exactly. Like they do in the intelligence field."

Or like terrorists, he thought darkly, but said nothing.

"Where are these broadcasts, Nat?"

"We use the dark web," she said. "I…I don't know all of the technical details. The handlers set up the technology. As journalists, we just use it."

"The dark web," Ryan repeated, unbelieving.

"Yes. It's the only way to get the message out while protecting our identities."

"I saw another message on the deep web," Ryan said, feeling his jaw clench as he spoke. "Gleeson showed it to me during one of our interview sessions."

Nathalie looked at him, uncomprehending. She gave her head a small shake. "I…?"

"It was posted by a group that called themselves The Bastards of Liberty," he told her, grinding his teeth with every word.

"I've never heard of them."

"Their message took credit for shooting Marcus and me. It was very patriotic." Dark sarcasm filled his voice. "Or so they wanted to seem."

"Oh, *amour*. I'm so sorry."

"These men, Nathalie….these *terrorists*…they used the dark web. They use the same tactics you're describing. And these are the men who murdered Marcus."

Realization swept over Nathalie's face. "You don't think we are-"

"The same?"

"We're not!" she said sharply. "We are not terrorists. We're journalists. We get the truth out there, that's all. We don't harm people."

"You yourself said you don't know all of the people involved. Maybe your cell just doesn't know-"

"You're being ridiculous."

"You didn't tell me!" he shouted. "You lied to me, Nat."

She lowered her eyes. "I know. And it hurt to do it. But it really was for your own safety."

"I don't need you to protect me. I need you to be honest with me. And you weren't. Instead, you were mixed up with…" He waved his hand, looking for an adjective but unable to find one that fit.

"With patriots," Nathalie said quietly. "With people

who believe in truth. People who are opposed to this…regime."

"That," Ryan said, his tone matching hers, "is exactly what I would expect to hear from a Bastards of Liberty broadcast."

Nathalie shook her head. "I know you are angry with me. And I know I didn't tell you the truth about all of this. That was wrong of me. I should have known better. And I also know you are still grieving for Marcus. But *amour*, please…you have to see the difference between what I do and whatever insanity these radical elements have done."

He stared back at her for a long while. Beneath his anger and hurt, he knew she was right. But he couldn't bring himself to say that out loud. The sense of betrayal felt too immediate, too strong. So he said nothing.

"Ryan…"

He got up, and went to bed, and left her there on the couch.

Chapter 18

It has been said that, in history, the ringing cries of dissent are often drowned out by the convenient memories of those who were not there, or who wish they weren't. This cynical remark is usually met with distaste by most historians at first, followed soon after with grudging acceptance. The myths of unanimity are legion when it comes to successful revolutions. The United States, for instance, saw as many as a third of its potential citizenry remain loyal to the British crown, while another third were neutral on the subject, but this was not the 'truth' that most Americans eventually believed about their war for independence. The one third that were revolutionaries slowly swelled in the retelling to include nearly every American, and as it is also said, victory had its thousand fathers.

This highlights three important, relevant facts that also apply to the events of the 2020s. One, that a strong, vocal minority can dictate the course of a nation. Two, that there will always be some dissension, and some apathy. Lastly, three: the ensuing myths are created by the victor.

— From *An Unlikely Phoenix* by Reed Ambrose

A lex sat patiently while Héctor lectured him.

"This is a country of law," Héctor told him stridently. "And, as such, the majority rule of the people is what should drive all of the decisions of the people's representatives."

"You're right, of course," Alex said.

"California is fifty-two percent Latino, Alex. And those numbers are from the 2020 Census! Most estimates put us at nearly sixty percent by now."

"I know."

"Then give me one good reason why, if we truly do secede from the United States, why we shouldn't rejoin Mexico."

"Héctor, this question isn't the one we need to be answering right now. The Governor is focused on our relationship with our own country, and whether or not we should sever that relationship."

He waved away Alex's point. "We'll secede. The immigration issues alone will ensure that."

"It's more complicated than that. There are a lot of issues to consider."

"Is it?" Héctor leaned forward. "Imagine you've come to this country for work, but were forced to leave part of your family behind until you can save enough to bring them to live with you. How big of an issue is immigration to you then? How much does it matter to you? Alex, it is the only issue that matters."

"I'm not denying that it is an important issue. But I'm talking about something else." Alex said. He tried an analogy. "Try to see it from my perspective. I feel like we're trying to make a marriage work here, Héctor, but instead you're already thinking about who should be our next wife."

Héctor laughed. "Well, it's an easy thing to consider when the woman has been your mistress for decades."

Alex had to smile. Héctor had nicely hijacked his own analogy. He tried to take it back. "Fair enough. But can we at least agree that we need to remain single for a little while after the split? Find ourselves, figure out what's best, that kind of thing?"

"Maybe. But who's to say Mexico will wait for us?"

"Sixty percent of California," Alex said. "And growing."

Héctor considered. "I see your point. All right, Alex. In the interests of showing Washington, D.C. a united front, here's what I'll do. I'll tone down the urgency of our message. We won't back away from this course of action, but we'll acknowledge that we have to get our own affairs in order first and foremost. After all," he smiled graciously, "it would be unfair to our future fellow countrymen to do any less."

Alex held out his hand. "*Gracias*, Héctor."

"You're welcome, Alejandro. But make no mistake – California is inexorably bound for reunification with Mexico."

"But not today."

"No," Héctor agreed. "Not today."

For someone who seemed to be perpetually non-committal, James Mallory was remarkably steadfast.

"I think the Governor is being rash," he told Alex.

"You think we should capitulate with the new laws Congress is passing?"

"I didn't say that. I'm just not convinced we should be entertaining the idea of secession as a response."

"What should we do, then?"

"That's exactly what we should be discussing – a wide variety of options. Instead, we have people jumping onto one bandwagon or another, and then the entire discussion is about why it's the right bandwagon. No one is actually listening."

James had a point. Discussions about the future of California had become more polarized in recent weeks, both in political circles and in the public sector. Even on some local mainstream radio and television shows, open discussion about the possibility of secession had grown. The already loose grasp on the California media that federal pressures through the Internal Security Act once had seemed to be slipping one degree at a time.

"I agree," he told James. "But things are coming to a head. You can sense that, right?"

"That's probably true. But that's all the more reason we should be having a reasonable discourse instead of all this squabbling."

"I've already spoken to Héctor Chavez and Gregory Bell. Both of them have agreed that we need to show a united front. They've put their petitions for annexation on hold."

"What about August and the reconciliation crowd?"

Alex shrugged. "I have a feeling the good senator wants to remain the leader of the loyal opposition."

James grunted. "That's my part to play."

Alex realized that James was serious. He really saw himself in that role. For a moment, he didn't know how to reply. Didn't you have to *oppose* something to be part of the opposition?

"The problem with August is that he cares more about being the leader than being concerned about what exactly he is leading," James continued. "If the Governor and the majority of members were preaching conciliation, he'd be on the secession stump, all fire and Southern drawl."

Alex kept his expression neutral, but his mind was racing. This was the first time he had any indication that James didn't care for August. In fact, for most of the last year, he'd assumed the two were natural allies. August wanted to reconcile with the federal government, and James didn't want to commit to anything, which was essentially the same action.

How could I have missed this?

He realized that James Mallory was cagier than he thought.

"You may be on to something," he said carefully. "But let me ask you a different question. If the people's referendum comes back in favor of defying the immigration laws and in favor of secession, how does that impact your position?"

James considered the question for a long while. Finally, he said, "Well, I guess that we'd have some difficult discussions ahead of us, wouldn't we?"

Alex resisted the urge to sigh. He pressed James with further questions, but it was painfully clear to him that the senator steadfastly intended to remain neutral. He wondered if James had already decided on a course of action and if his neutrality was serving as a mask for that decision. He tried to suss out any hints of that during the next half hour of discussion, but ran into dead ends each route he took.

When he finally rose and offered his hand, he had to admit that meeting had been unsuccessful. Despite that, James shook his hand congenially, and said, "Thanks for coming by. I look forward to our next conversation, Alex."

Alex wasn't, but he said that he was, and left the office.

Two out of three ain't bad, he thought, as he got into his car and headed to the Governor's mansion.

His phone rang while he was still en route. The screen told him it was Carl Young, probably one of the last people he wanted to talk to today. Or any day.

He punched the answer button, knowing that Young would track him down if he didn't take the call. Part axe man, part messenger boy, Young was good at his job because he was relentless.

"Senator Derrick," Alex answered, playing the formality card.

"Senator," Young greeted him back. "How are you?"

"Busy."

"Ah. Straight to the point, then. How are your efforts going?"

Alex didn't answer right away. Then he said, "I've convinced a couple of the more vocal senators in favor of annexation petitions to soften the urgency of their positions."

"Soften?" Young clucked his tongue. "Senator, that's

not really progress. Progress would be if all this reckless talk about states' rights and secession were to stop."

"Well, I can't help you there. I can't tell the people what to talk about."

"Don't be naïve, Senator. The people look to you and your fellow politicians, as well as a few ridiculous celebrities, to decide what they should be talking about. Now, trying to convince these so-called artists to be patriotic is a bit like trying to herd a bunch of beatnik cats, isn't it? But you and your colleagues are another matter. You all should be able to show some more discipline, and support for your country."

"I can assure you that every one of us believes what we're doing every day is to support our state and our country," Alex said.

"That is precisely the problem. The Party doesn't care what you *believe* you're doing. The Party cares about what you actually *do*. And frankly, Senator, you're not doing jack shit."

The profanity surprised Alex a little bit. Young had rarely strayed from the role of elegant, refined strong-arm.

"I'm doing everything I can," he said. "But as long as we're speaking frankly, let's talk about the other calls I've been getting."

"What calls?"

"That's funny. You tell me not to be naïve, and then deny knowing about your counterpart's anonymous calls?"

"I'm not sure what you mean?"

"Hell, Carl. Maybe it's *you* making the calls with a

voice filter." The possibility only occurred to Alex as he spoke the words. His gut told him he was probably right.

"I don't know what-"

"Let's pretend that's true. In that case, suffice it to say that some deep, dark voice has called me more than once telling me that if I don't get the job done – the same job you've been pushing me to do, by the way – that something bad might happen to my brother's wife. Now, does that ring any bells?"

"No," Young answered easily, but Alex caught the slightest hesitation that told him he was right. "It must be someone with parallel interests to our own."

"It was clearly someone within the federal government. They offered to help or hurt Nathalie's immigration status."

"Curious," Young said. "I will have to look into it."

"You do that. In the meantime, Nathalie is subject to the new immigration law and her grandfather clause appeal was denied. My sister-in-law is facing deportation."

"That's very sad."

"It's very wrong. And quite honestly, it makes me wonder how motivated I should be pushing for some of the things you want me to push for in the Senate."

"You're playing a very dangerous game," Young warned. "The needs of the entire nation should not hinge on the needs of any one person."

You mean the needs of the Party, *not the nation,* Alex thought.

"I want peace," he said. "I want security. But I also care what happens to the people I love. Now, I've been taking your calls and your meetings for years. I've listened to your concerns, and I've strived to reach fair comprises within the Senate. I've treated you with respect. And what do I get in return? I get the functional equivalent of blackmail."

Young was silent on the other end of the line, an uncommon response for him.

"From now on," Alex said, "if you want my help in conveying moderation to any of my colleagues, I want your help with Nathalie. Otherwise, I might have to just sit back and let things take their course."

"Or go have dinner at the Governor's mansion," Young said, his voice dripping with sarcasm.

"What does *that* have to do with anything?"

"Do you think we haven't noticed the frequency of your meetings with the Governor? We've been suspicious of your relationship with her for a while now, Alexander."

For a moment, Alex heard echoes of Gregory's insinuations. He clenched his jaw.

Before he could reply, Young continued. "I suppose all of those meetings could be about the difficult task of governing the state, but there are those in the Party and the Administration who are wondering if the two of you are contemplating something far less noble. Something downright treasonous, if you want to know the truth."

"I'm certain we're not," Alex said through gritted teeth.

"Well, you're there and I am not, so I guess I shall have to take your word for it." Young's words were spiked with sarcasm. "Just like you've taken me at my word that

I don't know about these frightening calls you have been receiving."

"Are you going to help my sister-in-law or not?"

"I'm not familiar with the situation," Young said. "But if I were to guess, I would say that anyone who is not already a true American, much less an American citizen, is well beyond help."

"Then you no longer have anything to blackmail me with," Alex said. "So stop calling and threatening me."

"I can't stop doing what I've never done."

Alex broke the connection, then immediately dialed Ryan. His brother picked up on the second ring. Alex greeted him and quickly relayed his call with Young and the mystery caller he suspected was Young.

"You should have told me," Ryan said.

"I know. But I didn't want to risk it. Not while there was still a chance that things would work for Nathalie."

"We didn't ask you to do that. You should vote your conscience."

"Family doesn't have to ask," Alex said. "And relax. I never voted against my conscience. The whole thing was just a delaying action on my part. I endured some bullshit meetings and some photo ops, that's all. But now, I don't see the sense in doing even that."

"Probably not."

"What are you going to do?"

"We're still sleeping on it," Ryan said. His voice sounded strange to Alex, but he chalked it up to stress. "But we've considered coming out to see you for a visit. Would that be all right?"

"Sure. I've got the extra space. You can stay as long as

you like. I'll even take you to a Sharks game. Buy you a jersey."

"I have one. It's blue. But thanks, Alex. It's good to know that's an option."

Alex thought it was the only real option his brother had, but resisted the urge to tell him so. Ryan was stubborn, and he knew the man had to reach his own conclusions.

"Just let me know," he said.

"I will."

They chatted amiably about Melina, more hockey, and the Freedom Concerts for a few minutes until Ryan said he had to go.

"My boss just walked in. He went straight to his office, but now he's looking my way. My guess is he's about to call me in for some stupid reason."

"This is that Potulny guy?"

"He's a lieutenant, but yeah."

"Watch that one, Ryan. I've heard his name pop up a couple of times in Party circles."

"You don't have to warn me about him," Ryan assured him. "I've been watching out for him for most of ten years. But I didn't know you traveled in Party circles."

"Party circles are pretty much everywhere, even here."

"Making America fascist again," Ryan muttered.

"Don't let Potulny hear you say that."

"I'm sure he already has. This is probably a recorded line."

Stupid, Alex thought. He sometimes wondered if Ryan realized how pervasive the Party really was. Between them and the passive and apathetic majority, Alex believed that they had greater control than most Americans knew or would like to admit.

They said their goodbyes and Alex hung up, just as his car pulled in front of the Governor's mansion. He thanked his driver, and let him know he was going to be a while. Then he made his way to the front door.

The doorman led him to the Governor's private office. She sat at her desk, engaged in conversation with a tall black man in a simple but impeccable suit. His hair was trimmed short and his facial features chiseled. He had an air of easy confidence about him. Ryan recognized him, but it took a moment for him to place the man. Then he realized it was the clothing. He wasn't used to seeing him in civilian attire.

"Alex!" the Governor greeted him. "You know General Clay Braddock, I think?"

"Of course," Alex said, shaking hands. "I'm just used to seeing him in uniform, that's all."

"I get that a lot," Braddock said in an easy tone. "But given the nature of our discussion, I thought it appropriate."

Alex glanced at the Governor. "Should I excuse myself from this meeting?"

"Don't be silly." She motioned for him to sit, so he did. "Clay and I were in the middle of a productive conversation, I think."

"About?"

The Governor smiled warmly. "Well, perhaps I'll let Clay answer that." She looked to him.

Braddock met Alex's gaze evenly. "Actually, I don't know how productive it has been. Mostly, we've been talking about the hypothetical."

"Have we?" the Governor said. "Well, I suppose that is true. But you can learn a lot of things during a hypothetical discussion."

"I agree," Braddock said.

"What kind of hypothetical discussion are we talking about?" Alex asked.

"One in which California is forced to secede from the United States of America," Braddock said, his tone unchanged.

Alex wondered silently how long ago, for him at least, that idea moved from the hypothetical to the possible and now to the probable. Aloud, he said, "That's on a lot of lips these days."

"Surprisingly so. Not just politicians, but musicians, talk shows. It's gaining momentum. But our discussion centered around the problems surrounding the subsequent government of the new state. Logistics, infrastructure, and the like."

"You mean, like a standing army?"

"An armed force is a necessary component, yes."

"Hypothetically?"

Braddock smiled tightly. "The scenario is hypothetical. The need for a military is not. Every nation needs to be able to defend its borders."

"It does."

"When you came in," the Governor said, "we were talking about what positions were the most key to a new state's success where the military is concerned. I contend that the Secretary of Defense is key, but Clay has a different opinion."

Alex turned to look at Braddock.

"My position is that the commanding officer is crucial. A Secretary of Defense makes policy decisions. A general implements the ones that involve military use. Successful execution is absolutely critical, particularly given that this hypothetical new state would be facing a number of challenges."

"Hopefully war isn't one of them," Alex said.

"Agreed. But a strong defense can help deter others. Better to be prepared for battle and not have to engage, than the reverse."

That made sense to Alex, and he said so.

"This requires coordination and training," Braddock said. "And that would be the responsibility of the commanding officer. It is a crucial role, and would require complete commitment."

"Do you think that will be hard to find?"

Braddock nodded. "In this scenario, you are talking about a lot of competing loyalties. Take the National Guard, for example. Officially, we are part of the United States Army Reserve Group. But most of the time, we fall under the command of the Governor and operate in-state. But we've also been deployed out of country during times of war. I served in both Iraq and Afghanistan as a captain, for example.

"In the event of secession, the President would almost certainly call up the Guard to counter what would essentially be rebellion. That means soldiers who have to decide between their country and their state. If they didn't report for duty, they'd be deemed either AWOL or charged with treason. It's no small consideration. And you face a similar issue with your police services, too. These are the two entities who exist to help maintain order, especially in times of emergency."

Braddock's voice remained calm but the gravitas in his tone was palpable.

"Every member, from senior command down to the newest soldier or cop, would be faced with a very difficult decision to make in a very short period of time. And their collective decisions would go a long way towards deciding the success or failure of the state's action. Hypothetically," he added, without a change of inflection.

"This is something I've dwelled upon long and hard," the Governor said. "And it seems to me that this is the kind of decision that would be good to have already made *before* this short window of time appears. Don't you think so, Alex?"

She was tossing him a softball, and he swung into it. "Of course. It's important to know where things stand before making a final decision."

"I agree," she replied. "But how is it possible to know how all of these individuals will react when the time comes?"

"You can't," Braddock said. "But if enough of the leaders are united in their response, the majority will follow their lead."

Alex nodded. "I suppose that's true. But what about those that don't?"

"I would suspect that a state with a culture like that of California would have a no harm, no foul sort of approach to those individuals, don't you?"

"I can't imagine a different way to handle something like that," Alex admitted. "I mean, they'd be kept away from their rifles and so forth, right?"

"Now you're getting down into the weeds," Braddock said. "But yes, I would think that if the senior leaders of the National Guard called for soldiers to report to duty in support of the state of California, many or even most would respond. Those who didn't agree simply wouldn't come. They might make their way out of state to report to the United States elsewhere if they felt strongly enough about it, or they might just hunker down and do nothing."

"Hypothetically."

"All of this is hypothetical. Otherwise, it amounts to treason, doesn't it? Plotting a coup, essentially?"

"Something along those lines, for certain," the Governor agreed. She sighed, and Alex knew her well enough to know that she didn't enjoy the pretense of this conversation, even if she conceded it was a necessary fiction. "It is a question every person will have to answer for themselves."

"So they will," Braddock agreed. "Though it would hardly be the first time men and women have faced questions like this."

"No," the Governor said. "People had to make hard decisions during the race riots, or during the Civil Rights Movement."

"Similar, but not the same," Braddock replied. "This would be an even bigger question. One that might involve war."

"Well, my generation had the war in Vietnam to

contend with. That divided a number of American households."

"It did. But it didn't change any borders, like secession would."

"You're talking about the Civil War, of course," the Governor.

"I am."

"I've thought about that time in our history a lot, too," she said. "It's the closest parallel, really."

"Do you know who Robert E. Lee was?" Braddock asked.

The Governor gave him an indulgent look. "Clay…do you know who Elizabeth Cady Stanton was?"

He nodded. "She spearheaded women's suffrage."

"That's right. Now, if you are aware enough to know who Ms. Stanton is, can we just assume that I might know who Lee was?"

"No offense intended, ma'am. It's been my unfortunate discovery that most people are not well versed on history."

"Meaning they don't know much, and what they do know is usually wrong. Washington and the cherry tree, et cetera."

"Exactly so. Or that Lee was the general of all Confederate forces during the Civil War. He was, in fact, only the commander of the Army of North Virginia. No more and no less."

"That I did not know," the Governor admitted.

"It's a difference without very much distinction, when you get right down to it," Braddock said. "Lee's forces were very much the core of the Confederate military cause. But that isn't why I asked the question, ma'am. I asked because we were talking about that difficult decision many soldiers would face in the event of secession."

"Lee faced that choice," she said, nodding slowly as she spoke.

"He did. What many people don't know is that privately, even though he felt that the Southern states had many righteous grievances, he was very opposed to the idea of southern secession. He called it anarchy."

The Governor raised her eyebrows slightly, but said nothing.

"When the time came, the Confederacy offered him a command but he ignored it. Then Virginia seceded as well, joining the Confederacy. President Lincoln offered him a top role in the Union Army, defending the capital, but he did not accept. Instead, he resigned his commission and returned home to Virginia. In the end, it came down to one thing for him."

Braddock paused, his gaze going from the Governor to Alex and back again. Then he finished. "Lee asked, quite simply, 'how can I draw my sword upon Virginia, my native state?' And his answer was that he could not."

The three of them were quiet for a long moment. Then Braddock rose and offered his hand to the Governor. "Thank you for inviting me here, Madame Governor. It's been an interesting discussion."

The Governor shook his hand, covering it with her other hand at the same time. "Interesting, if hypothetical."

"Yes. Well, I will share one thing with you that is not

hypothetical." He stopped moving his hand, but still held hers. "I love California, and she is my native state."

The Governor smiled broadly at him. "Thank you, sir."

Braddock didn't reply. He gave her hand another gentle pump, nodded to Alex, and left the office.

The Governor settled back into her seat, then looked at Alex. "And how was your day?" she asked.

Chapter 19

Political advisor and lobbyist Richard Perle famously said earlier this century that, "Dictators must have enemies. They must have internal enemies to justify their secret police and external enemies to justify their military forces." While his somewhat universal observation was made well before the Crisis of 2029, it proved to be prescient. Ironically, the White House was seemingly able to focus on both kinds of perceived enemies – internal and external – at the same time with its immigration policies of 2029.

— From *An Unlikely Phoenix* by Reed Ambrose

Ryan hung up the phone. Normally, it did his heart good to speak with his brother, but that sensation was diminished as he could feel Potulny's eyes on him. He only had to wait a few minutes before the phone rang again and the lieutenant summoned him into his office.

He stood rigidly in front of Potulny's desk, one of several the lieutenant kept throughout the district. There was little in the way of decoration, other than a free-standing flag on one wall and an official photograph of the President behind the desk. The photograph's location gave Ryan the eerie sense of the President watching the conversation from over Potulny's shoulder.

"At ease, Officer," Potulny said, his tone formal but slightly softer than usual.

Ryan relaxed slightly.

"In fact," Potulny said, motioning to the chair next to Ryan, "sit down. I imagine standing too long makes your hip hurt."

'Too long' usually meant three minutes for Ryan, but he didn't intend to admit that in front of Potulny. Still, he took the seat, surprised at how grateful he felt at the gesture. It took him a moment to settle into the chair, and when he had done so and looked up at Potulny, he had to suppress a desire to laugh out loud. The chair sat lower to the ground than most, giving Potulny a sense of dominance and forcing the person sitting to look up at him. Behind him, the President peered down as well. All Potulny needed was *Attila the Hun on Leadership* sitting on the shelf behind him, and the effect would be complete.

"I've given you some time and space, Ryan. A chance to clear your head about things."

Ryan didn't reply. He waited for what was next.

"Are you ready to do what is best for your family?" Potulny asked.

"What would that be, sir?"

Potulny gave him an irritated look. "Are you being sarcastic?"

"I'm being serious."

"Then you're being obtuse as well." Potulny leaned

back in his chair, bringing more of the President into view. "I've been watching you for a while, Ryan. I reviewed your file again, too. You've been good at police work, and from what my friends at the Department of Defense tell me, you were a good Marine, too."

"Thanks."

"That's why I don't understand why you seem bound and determined to ruin your career and devastate your family."

"I'm not."

"Then how do explain the fact that you're not even an associate member of the Party? That you refuse to salute at roll call? I mean, is that really who you are? A shamer?"

"I intend no disrespect."

"The lack of appropriate respect *is* disrespect," Potulny said firmly. He contemplated Ryan for a few moments longer. "The New American Party stands up for America. I know you have to see that. It stands up for true Americans, and we want to stand up for you, too, Ryan. You and your family."

"In exchange for what?"

"Loyalty," Potulny answered immediately. "Loyalty to the Party, to the President, but most of all, to your country. That shouldn't be a difficult thing. I shouldn't have to sell you on it. But here we are."

"Here we are," Ryan echoed.

He'd known this moment would come, and he'd thought long and hard about it. Potulny's implications were clear and made the choice seem simple. Join, and Nathalie stays in the country with him and Melina. Refuse, and she would be deported when the Amnesty period ended. He would lose a wife, and Melina a mother.

How many people faced similar difficult decisions like this? How many Party members were there initially under duress, or was the New American Party as unified as it seemed?

He didn't know. He didn't know any of those people's minds, only his own. And even though he knew that Potulny thought he had boxed Ryan into two choices, he believed there was always a third choice.

"I can't join," he said. "If I did, I'd be lying."

The abrupt change in Potulny's features surprised Ryan. His inviting expression descended into a dark scowl. "That is the wrong decision," he said, biting off each word.

"Probably. I know that's how you see it, certainly."

"You realize the amnesty period is coming to a close in a matter of weeks, don't you?"

"I am."

"Your wife will be deported."

"Maybe."

"Definitely. And neither you nor your daughter will be allowed to go with her. Your family will be torn apart."

"I know what the risks are."

"They're not risks, Officer. They are eventualities. Trust me."

Potulny was the *last* person Ryan would trust. If Judas Iscariot, Benedict Arnold, and P.T. Barnum were all sitting behind that desk, he'd trust any one of them more than Potulny.

The lieutenant continued. "And if you are clinging to the hope that you and your daughter might apply for visas and be allowed to visit your wife in whatever country she lands in, I would like to disabuse you of that notion right now. You won't be." He smiled thinly. "I have friends at the Department of State as well."

Ryan blinked. How in the hell did a police lieutenant in St. Louis get that kind of influence? But Ryan knew the answer immediately. Potulny's true rank lay within the party, not the Metro.

Or he was lying. Ryan supposed that might be true, but he wasn't willing to bet on it.

"I'm disappointed in you," Potulny continued. "I knew you had an independent streak, but you've also got some great talent. You would have been a strong addition to the local Party, and good for public relations. So I offered you this choice, even though you haven't really earned it. And after that, after my generosity, you turn me down." He shook his head. "You know this decision will have a price, don't you?"

"I do. But I once heard someone say there is a price to pay for speaking the truth, but a bigger price for living a lie."

"Who said that?"

"Cornel West."

Potulny's lip curled in distaste. "That's the best you can do? Quote a senile radical?"

Ryan didn't reply. There was nothing more for him to say.

Potulny's face tightened into another scowl. "I think we're done here, Officer. Return to your post."

Ryan stood and left the office. Potulny remained in his office long enough to present the illusion that he had come for some other reason than to talk with Ryan, then strode out of the work area without even glancing his way.

Two hours later, he was summoned to Internal Affairs for another session with Gleeson. The captain walked Ryan through the events of his shooting again with malevolent efficiency. He asked the same questions repeatedly but in different ways, and occasionally dwelled on a seemingly benign point for an extended period.

Ryan answered mechanically, trying to keep his emotions in check. He knew that his own recollection of the incident was irreparably altered by all of this revisiting, and he found that to avoid guessing at whether a memory was accurate or not, he sometimes had to answer with, "I don't recall." Every instance of that met with a slight expression of disapproval from Gleeson.

"Officer, you are aware that full cooperation with this investigation is a condition of your employment, do you not?"

"I am cooperating."

"You've answered multiple questions with the assertion that you don't recall."

"Because I don't."

"Would you be surprised to know that if I were to call up a transcript of you answering this same question months ago, you *did* recall?"

"Then why are you asking me again?"

"You know the answer to that."

He did. As an investigator, Gleeson was interested in

the consistency of his answers. The truth was relatively easy to remember, because it was what happened. It was a real memory. A lie was a story, and a story was harder to keep straight. But after so many times reviewing the shooting, and so many *whys* and *what ifs*, Ryan had lost track of the smaller, objective facts in his own memory. All he knew was that he and Marcus were ambushed, and Marcus was killed. He'd like to think he didn't do anything wrong, but his partner's death belied that opinion.

Gleeson asked some more questions, but after another forty minutes, he ended the interview. As Ryan was leaving, Gleeson stopped him.

"You should know, Officer, that I am rendering my final report tomorrow."

Ryan didn't know whether to feel anxiety or relief. "And?" he asked.

Gleeson just stared at him. "And you'll know the results tomorrow, after the Chief and his Command Staff review it."

Just another twist of the knife, Ryan thought. Tell a hungry man it is supper time, and then make him stand by, salivating, while you set the table and wait on the other guests.

He kept his expression neutral. "I'll look forward to it," he finally managed.

"I rarely hear that," Gleeson said.

"I'm full of surprises."

"Perhaps. But, either way, you are dismissed, Officer."

Chapter 20

Political movements require strong-willed, active people who espouse the philosophy and beliefs of the movement in order to generate the impetus necessary to bring the movement to prominence. Yet, some of these movements eventually reach a point at which the movement itself has gained such momentum and status that this very prominence and control become paramount. This remains the case even if it that means sacrificing truth, or the philosophy and beliefs the movement is ostensibly founded upon. When a movement reaches this point, it will drive mercilessly forward and through any obstacles…including, in some cases, those same strong-willed, active people who initially gave rise to it.

— From *An Unlikely Phoenix* by Reed Ambrose

Captain Gleeson opened the Ryan investigation file on his computer. He reviewed the narrative describing his investigation, as well as his own fact analysis. With only a few revisions and a brief addendum for this most recent interview, he finished the work. As soon as it was done, he sent a mandatory notification to Lieutenant Potulny.

The latter action irked him. Despite holding the rank of captain to Potulny's being a lieutenant, he often felt like Potulny took on a superior tone with him. True, Potulny was in operations and Gleeson was in support, but didn't rank transcend assignment?

Perhaps even more irritating was Potulny's meteoric rise within the NAP. A few years ago, he was the head of one of the three St. Louis chapters. Now he was the regional chief, and seemed to have a direct line to Washington, D.C. And for what? Because he managed to get a bunch of hippie musicians and their fans to surrender? Potulny acted as if it were the equivalent of capturing Osama bin Laden.

Gleeson put aside his thoughts and returned to his work. There was plenty of it. Ryan Derrick wasn't the only person within the Metro that needed investigating. Not even close.

He was surprised when Potulny appeared in his office less than an hour later.

"You didn't send the file," he said to Gleeson by way of a greeting.

Gleeson looked at him, mildly surprised. "I can't do that. Regulations require me to send all Internal Affairs files directly to the Chief's Office via secure server."

"And the Chief then forwards to me via email, which is considerably less secure," Potulny finished, his tone impatient. "How about we cut out the middle man, huh?"

Gleeson shook his head. "Rules are rules, Lieutenant. They are there for a reason."

"Such as?"

"To provide order, for one thing."

"The Party provides order," Potulny retorted.

Gleeson couldn't argue with that. But he made no move to open the Derrick file. The two men engaged in a brief battle of wills, before Potulny shrugged dismissively.

"Fine," he said. "Cling to your petty rules. But I would like a verbal briefing, at the least."

Gleeson considered. To his knowledge, there wasn't a rule specifically prohibiting this, but it seemed a clear violation of the intent of the security in place surrounding his written product. "I don't know if I can do that."

"You can."

"I'd need authorization from-"

"I just authorized you," Potulny said coolly.

"I was going to say from the Chief of Police," Gleeson said.

"Captain," Potulny said, his voice slow and menacing, "you will give me a verbal briefing. Now."

Gleeson stiffened in his chair. "Lieutenant, I don't want to pull rank, but-"

"Then don't. Rank is an illusion, anyway. Do you think your title of captain or your ceremonial bars mean anything in the Metro? They are symbolic at best, a pay grade at most. They don't hold any sway over me." Potulny's gaze bore into Gleeson. "Besides, where do you think real power comes from these days, *Captain?*"

Gleeson knew the answer, but he tried to hold the line. "The Chief-"

"If he had any real power, don't you think it would be

his name people are talking about up in D.C.?" Potulny asked with an arrogant sneer. "And not mine?"

Gleeson hesitated, then relented. Potulny was right, and even though flouting the rules galled him, he knew the lieutenant would get the report eventually, anyway. A preview in the form of a verbal briefing wasn't that flagrant of a violation.

"Very well," he said, trying to regain some measure of control over the meeting. "What do you want to know?"

Potulny let a small, triumphant smile touch his lips. Then he asked, "How solid is your finding of negligence?"

Gleeson gave him a confused look. "Negligence?"

"Your finding, yes. How solid is your evidence?"

"I think there's a misunderstanding," Gleeson said. "My findings regarding Officer Derrick's actions are not that he was negligent. In fact, my recommendation is that he be exonerated."

"Exonerated?" Potulny looked flabbergasted. "*That's* your finding?"

"Yes."

"How is that possible?"

Gleeson felt a slight surge of confidence at Potulny's surprise. "I conducted a thorough investigation of the facts and the evidence available. An analysis of those facts and evidence inevitably lead to that conclusion."

"The man is clearly negligent," Potulny said. "His partner is dead."

"I realize that."

"Yet you have the audacity to somehow conclude this shamer isn't negligent?"

Gleeson pressed his lips together. "I don't approve of his behavior, or his politics. But I don't get to pass judgment on people based on my opinion. I have to follow the facts and reach a logical conclusion on that basis. And in this case, the facts do not support a finding of negligence on Officer Derrick's behalf. To be more precise, the facts do the opposite. They exonerate him."

Potulny gave Gleeson a hard stare. "Hearing that, I worry about *your* politics, Captain."

Gleeson felt a small tendril of anxiety in the pit of stomach, but did his best to conceal it. "I explored every possibility. You'll see that in my report."

"The report you refuse to let me read."

"You'll see it soon enough," Gleeson said tersely. "Besides, you were present for many of the interviews. All are documented on holo digital and audio as well. You know how hard I pushed him. Even at the hospital, I pushed. You *know*."

"Here's what I know," Potulny said. "And here are some competing facts for you. Ryan Derrick is a shamer who refuses to join the Party despite every opportunity. He is married to a journalist, a foreigner, who is under investigation for her own behavior. He was the lead officer on the call for service in which Officer Marcus Washington was murdered."

The news about Derrick's wife was a slight surprise to him, but he supposed he should have suspected it. "All of that is in my report."

"Filed under a finding of exonerated?" Potulny shook his head. "That's no good, Captain. No good at all." He eyed Gleeson dangerously. "Here's something else to consider. Derrick was wounded in that same shooting. There is some sympathy for him out there, both in the ranks of the Metro and in the community. What do you think an exonerated finding will do for those people?"

"I-"

"I'll tell you. It will give them a martyr, that's what it will do. Another local martyr to go along with that pop singer girl and that blues man and that silly actor. That's not what this city needs. It's not what this country needs. What we need is unity. What we need is order."

"I agree," Gleeson said. "But I can't change the facts."

Potulny seemed to ignore his comment. "Do you really want to return to the dark times of a decade ago? To a time when you had to be ashamed to be a white male? Afraid to celebrate the accomplishments of your race or your gender?"

"No, but I don't think this is about-"

"Forget celebration," Potulny interrupted. "How about being blamed for every wrong in the world? Carrying every burden? Are you going to sit there and tell me you *enjoyed* that, Captain?"

Gleeson's eyes narrowed. "No. But that's not what we're talking about here. We're talking about facts. And facts are facts."

Potulny shrugged. "I'm not too worried about facts, Captain. Facts are largely unimportant. How they are interpreted is what matters." He narrowed his eyes at Gleeson. "And your interpretation is troubling."

"I don't know how else to interpret this fact pattern."

"There are always alternative facts somewhere."

"Alternative...?" Gleeson gave him a troubled look.

"Lieutenant, I only see one set of facts."

"Then that becomes a problem all its own," Potulny said. "Frankly, I'm disappointed in you. I wonder, too, how it will look when you send up a report to the Chief with a recommendation in favor of exonerating Derrick and he overturns it in favor of a negligence finding?"

Gleeson's face froze. "Based upon *what?*"

"Based upon his interpretation of the facts," Potulny said, the words dropping easily from his lips. "What else?"

"He's never done that," Gleeson protested. "My findings have always been upheld."

Potulny shrugged. "In the past, perhaps. But every good streak comes to an end. The Chief's decision will be an easy one to justify. Especially when your conclusion is such a shaky one."

"Shaky?" Gleeson sputtered.

"Maybe Ryan Derrick won't be the only one whose career is ruined by this report," Potulny mused.

Gleeson felt his face flush with warmth. He wanted to lash out at Potulny, either with words or a fist or both. But he knew the folly of that action. So he sat still, reflecting on what Potulny had said.

Potulny took that for submission. "You think about it some more, Captain. Revise your report as you see fit. I'm sure you'll do the right thing." He turned to go, then stopped. "Remember this," he added. "What matters most isn't any of one of us, but the good of the people as a whole. Ultimately, everything we do should serve that end."

Gleeson didn't reply, but when Potulny continued to

stare at him, he gave a short nod to signal that he'd heard. Satisfied, Potulny turned away and left the Internal Affairs office.

Gleeson stared after him, his eyes fixed on the plain wood of the door, seeing the faux grain but not processing it. He sat there for a long time before he buried his face in his palms and rubbed his tired eyes.

I've been a good servant, he thought. To the Metro with his investigations. To the Party as well. He was diligent. He was thorough. And he was loyal. He saw the world through the same lens as the NAP. He believed in the precepts upon which the party was founded, precisely because that was the fact pattern that he observed in the world.

But now…now he faced something he hadn't encountered before. Competing facts, Potulny had said. Gleeson found the term distasteful, but here he was, faced with exactly that. And he had a decision to make.

Chapter 21

Politics, it has been said, is the art of compromise. The United States was no exception to this maxim. From the very inception of the nation, when the question of slavery reared its ugly head, the politics of enslavement were rife with compromise. First came the "Three-Fifths" compromise regarding "other persons," a euphemism for slaves, which allowed slaveholders to eat their proverbial cake and have it, too. Slavery was allowed, slaves were not given suffrage, but for purposes of the census (which directly impacted the number of representatives each state would have in the House), each slave counted as three-fifths of a person.

Other significant compromises occurred in the terms surrounding the admittance of both free and slave states to the young country, as legislators strove to achieve balance and instead succeeded only in failing to address one of the core issues (and many would argue, core faults) of the nation's political structure.

Another aspect that all of these compromises have in common is that they were all ultimately unsuccessful, serving only to delay the inevitable conflict and to ensure that the

— From *An Unlikely Phoenix* by Reed Ambrose

Ryan stood at the sink, rinsing the dinner dishes and putting them into the dishwasher. Melina had stacked them next to the sink, one of the small chores that she performed, and then returned to her room to listen to a storybook. He suspected that his daughter could sense the palpable tension between him and Nathalie, and her response was typical of a child – to retreat, and wait.

He knew he didn't have that luxury. So when he'd finished loading the dishes, he sought Nathalie out. She was in the bedroom, curled up on the small chair in the corner of the room, working on her tablet. When he entered, she looked up, and saw the purpose in his eyes. She put the tablet down.

He resisted saying anything about the tablet or her work. Everything about her career had taken on a different light for him since their fight. Where he'd once thought her a perfectionist for not sharing her works in progress with him, now he saw the veil of secrecy. How many of those articles hadn't been for *The Archway*, but were shadow reports?

It doesn't matter, he told himself. *The past doesn't matter. Now matters.*

But he couldn't completely believe that. Not yet.

"Potulny came to see me today," he said, his tone distant.

"And?"

"He offered me Party membership."

"In exchange for what?"

"Your citizenship," he said bluntly. "And using me as a propaganda tool."

Her eyes flared in surprise. "You didn't accept?"

"Of course not."

"Good." She nodded in relief. "That's good."

"It would have been the easiest route," he told her.

She shook her head. "No. It would have been the most expeditious one. There would be nothing easy about it. You know this."

He didn't answer right away. He thought he'd known a lot of things, but over the past year, he'd started to doubt some of them.

"Do you want to talk about the other night?" she asked.

"No," he said.

"All right," she said easily. "When you're ready."

"We have more pressing business," he said. "The amnesty period is ending soon. And you're probably still under surveillance. Hell, I probably am, at this point."

"What should we do?"

"California seems like the best option. Maybe one we should have already taken."

"But you don't want to leave."

He shook his head. "St. Louis is my home. And letting those bastards drive me away from the job...it feels wrong. Wrong for me, and somehow wrong for Marcus."

"You did nothing wrong," she said.

"Tell that to Gleeson. Or Potulny."

"So we stay."

"If we stay, you'll be deported. I'll lose you, Melina will lose you. And Potulny made it clear he'd take a special interest in keeping us from getting a visa to see you."

"He is a rising star in the Party," she said. "I've been researching him lately. There is talk in Washington of bringing him on board as an assistant director of the FBI."

"The FBI?" Ryan said, indignant. "How can they do that? He's not even an agent!"

"All police are national now, remember? Besides, it is an appointed position. The Director can fill it with anyone."

Ryan sighed, then lowered his head and rubbed his eyes. "You know what galls me the most? Even more than a piece of shit like him being rewarded with more power?"

"What?"

"This is a still a good police department. It is full of good people who do a hard job. Yeah, there are a few assholes. But you take any group of three thousand people, I don't care if it's three thousand Buddhist monks, and you're going to have a few assholes. They're an exception. Most of these cops are there, trying to make a difference. And yeah, maybe they made a few political compromises to manage to keep their careers, but life is full of compromise."

"It's full of rationalizations, too," Nathalie said quietly.

"You would know," he snapped back.

Nathalie absorbed the comment without reply.

He didn't apologize. Instead, he continued, "My point is that these are good people. Look how they handled that concert you were at. Very professionally."

"The terrorist threat was manufactured as an excuse," Nathalie said evenly. "And the reported violence inside was an outright fabrication."

"Maybe so, but the cops who were dispatched there didn't have anything to do with that. They responded to a situation, and they handled it. And no one got hurt."

Nathalie hesitated, then shook her head. "I respect what you do, what *they* do, but what you're talking about sounds suspiciously like just following orders."

"It isn't," he shot back. "It's handling a difficult set of circumstances in a safe way. An honorable way. These are the men and women that make up most of my department. I might not agree with the leadership, but I am proud to stand with my brothers and sisters. And it eats at me to think some worm like Potulny or Gleeson can take that away from me."

"So you have a choice, it seems," Nathalie said quietly.

"What choice is that?" he asked, even though he knew.

"Your brethren, or your family."

He shook his head slowly. "You're doing the same thing they're trying to do."

"Who?"

"Potulny. The Party. You're trying to box me into an either/or choice."

"No, *amour*. I am merely telling you how I see things."

Her tablet dinged, then immediately dinged a second time. She hesitated, then lifted it to look at it. Her eyes glided over the alert, then she turned her gaze to Ryan.

"The President is giving an interview to Paula Creighton," she told him. "The White House release said it will contain a major policy announcement."

"Is Creighton another shadow blogger?" he jabbed.

"I have no idea. But I think we should watch this. I have a feeling it will affect us both."

"A feeling? Or do you know something?"

"Just a feeling," she said.

Nathalie rose and went into the living room. Ryan followed.

"Miri, turn on television," she was saying as he entered.

Miri's digital voice responded immediately. "Do you have a preference, Nathalie?"

"CNN," she told Miri. "Volume at fifty-eight percent."

The TV switched on, and CNN appeared on screen. Nathalie sat down at one end of the couch. Ryan sat at the other. They waited in silence for ten minutes while CNN repeatedly announced the impending Creighton interview with the President, along with a few analysts speculating on what the announcement would be. Then intro music played, and the camera zoomed in on Paula Creighton. She greeted the audience as the camera switched to a wider view of her and the President seated next to each other at the high anchor's table.

"Good evening, America. I am here with the President of the United States for an exclusive interview regarding immigration policy." She turned to the President. "Thank you, sir, for appearing here and agreeing to answer my questions."

"You're welcome," the President said. "Happy to do it." Then he wagged a finger at her. "Although, Paula, some people say you're my harshest critic. Some of my advisors told me not to come here tonight. But I told them that you might be a left winger, but you were a smart woman and knew how to behave."

Creighton looked mildly shocked at the word 'behave', but seemingly decided to ignore it. "Well, we're grateful that you took the interview, Mr. President."

"I like your hair, by the way."

"Thank you." Creighton breezed past that comment as well. "Sir, the White House press release mentioned a change in federal immigration policy. Could you-"

"Yes," the President interrupted. "I'm making another change. Not really a big change – that's coming – but more a matter of sewing up some loose ends."

"What loose ends?"

"Well, here it is. One of the things I've become increasingly concerned about is American citizenship. More to the point, about how only true Americans should be granted citizenship. So effective immediately, any child born without both parents being U.S. citizens will not be automatically granted citizenship."

Creighton blinked, clearly surprised.

Ryan felt his stomach twinge in sympathy. If that had been the case when Melina was born, she wouldn't be an American.

Creighton recovered quickly. "What is the reasoning behind this proposed change, Mr. President?"

"Oh, it's not proposed," the President said. "We're doing it. And listen, Paula…this is just to close up some loopholes that a lot of foreign kids were using to take advantage of the wealth of our nation. Some of these kids have grown up to be radicalized, you know, and then we've ended up with terrorists in our own back yard. Not good. Not good at all."

"Have there been documented instances of this?" Creighton asked. "Examples of children born-"

"I'd love to share examples with you, Paula, I really would. Because there are many. Very, very many. But this information is very sensitive, and the CIA and the FBI have asked me to respect the security level attached to this intelligence. And I have agreed, because I don't want to put Americans in harm's way."

Creighton opened her mouth to ask a follow up question, then stopped. A moment later, she seemed to switch directions. "Do you believe this will survive the inevitable legal challenges it will face?"

"Of course. Let the extreme leftists out there take this through the courts. They can go all the way to the Supreme Court for all I care. I trust them to make the right decision, both legally and morally. This is about protecting true Americans, Paula."

"Yes, sir, but we're talking about children here."

"Osama bin Laden was a child once," the President said. "And look, we're not doing anything harmful to any of these kids. We're simply saying, hey – you're not a true American yet."

"Yet?" Creighton echoed.

"Yet," the President confirmed. "They can apply for citizenship, of course. And one American parent is a big plus, a real positive on their side. But this will allow us to vet every citizen before they can become one. It's vital for the safety of this nation, and I'm proud to say I've had the courage to move forward with this."

"So are you saying-"

"Here's what I'm saying, Paula. This is the first step in a massive overhaul with regard to U.S. citizenship. First off, this new rule will be retroactive to the past forty years."

"Forty…excuse me, Mr. President, but are you saying that someone who has citizenship *now* on the basis of one American parent will have their citizenship…*revoked*?"

Ryan's stomach sank. He glanced at Nathalie and saw a mixture of horror and anger in her eyes.

On the screen, the President smirked. "Not revoked. But reviewed, yes. Or call it confirmed. Either way, this gives us the tools we need to ensure the safety of true Americans in what is becoming a much more dangerous world. I mean, let's face it – no leader ever, in the history of civilization, has faced a world this dangerous, like I have. So I've had to take action, necessary action."

"Pardon me for saying so, Mr. President, but this action doesn't seem necessary. It seems extreme."

"Well, I'm not surprised you would say that. But we live in extreme times, so I'm forced to take measures that might seem extreme. But they are necessary, believe me. Very, very necessary."

"Mr. President…"

"One more thing," he interrupted again. "And I will just share this with you so that people can start getting used to the idea. This idea that citizenship is a birthright is outdated. We brought it over from the old country, from some sort of medieval arrangement. Things don't work that way today. I mean, look at me. I'm a self-made man. I earned everything I have, and did it on my own. No one ever gave me anything. And that's the way it should be with citizenship, too. Ideally, what I see us moving toward is no one being born a citizen. Instead, they should have to earn it. And this includes a full review of citizenship for every current citizen, by the way. Let's find out who the true Americans are."

There was a long, shocked silence from Creighton. She recovered, though, and stumbled forward. "In this scenario you describe-"

"Oh, it will happen," he assured her.

"-what would be the criteria? How would someone gain citizenship, or confirm their existing citizenship?"

"I'm glad you asked. It will be based upon a simple question. Can you demonstrate your loyalty and service to this country? If the answer is yes, then bam, you're in. But if not, then forget about it. Not happening."

"What does service look like?" Creighton asked, her tone still slightly dazed.

"We're still working that out," the President said. "But there are some good ideas on the table. Military service, police service. I like the military. I like the police. They're good people. Really good people."

"But you never served in the military, sir."

The President waved his hand dismissively. "No, but I could have. I would've been a good leader, a great general. But I did something different, something very important for this country, Paula. By being wealthy, I didn't put a burden on the government, and with my wealth, I created businesses, and jobs. Tons of jobs. Real jobs that people were thrilled to have."

"Mr. President-"

"And I paid taxes. Lots of taxes."

"So we're talking about…?"

"About driving the economy."

"No, sir. I meant, the criteria for citizenship."

"Oh." He shrugged. "Maybe something like a merit-based citizenship, I don't know. We're still working on it."

"So you haven't completed this policy yet?"

"Not yet. We're close. Still working out the rough edges, but we'll get there."

"What about the people who are not considered citizens under this policy?"

"What about them?"

"Well, will they be deported, for example?"

"No, I don't think so. Not right away, anyway. If they were previously citizens, and they're working towards earning citizenship again, I don't see why we'd deport someone like that."

"But would there be restrictions?"

"Some," the President said. "They wouldn't be able to vote in federal or state elections, for one. Or hold office."

"Own guns?"

The President held up his hands. "Hey, I am not going to mess with anyone's Second Amendment rights. I don't care if you're a citizen or not."

"Sir, that seems inconsistent. If we're going to respect one aspect of the Constitution-"

"Here's what's inconsistent, Paula. Liberals, who for decades droned on and on about the First Amendment while they were trying to grab every gun in sight." He shook his head. "Men had the right to bear arms long before they ever had the right to vote or say what they wanted. It's a sacred thing, and I don't see any reason to mess with it. There's nothing to fear about an armed citizen. Besides, we're the government. We have the biggest guns."

"So a person whose citizenship is revoked-"

"Reviewed, Paula. Don't twist my words."

"All right. What you're saying is that these former citizens won't have voting rights."

"No," he said firmly, "they won't. But it's not like they become invisible. We will count these non-citizens as part of the population for all other purposes."

"As a whole person?" Creighton asked, her tone slightly bitter. "Or three-fifths of a person?"

The President shook his head. "Why would we –"

An advisor leaned into his ear and whispered for a few seconds. The President's eyes narrowed and his jaw set. He shook his head at Creighton in disappointment. "Typical," he muttered. He reached for the microphone at his lapel. "This interview is over."

"When will this new policy go into effect, Mr. President?"

"Not soon enough," he snapped, dropping the small mic on the table and turning away.

Creighton called after him, but he ignored her.

"Miri, turn off the television," Nathalie ordered, her voice hollow.

The two of them stared at each other across the expanse from opposite ends of the couch. Neither spoke, but Ryan knew that neither of them was wondering any longer about what their course of action should be.

Finally, Nathalie slid down the couch until she was

next to Ryan. Tentatively, she put her head on his shoulder, resting against him. He could feel her trembling. For a moment, he didn't move, but then he wrapped a protective arm around her.

"*Mon Dieu*," Nathalie whispered. "How can this be happening?"

Ryan pulled her close, and said nothing. The truth was, he didn't know the answer.

Part IV:
EVERY HUMAN HEART

USA

and

California

June 2029

The desire for freedom resides in every human heart. And that desire cannot be contained forever by prison walls, or martial laws, or secret police. Over time, and across the Earth, freedom will find a way.

George W. Bush,
43rd U.S. President

Chapter 22

Civil unrest has a long and storied history woven throughout the tapestry of the human saga. People have rioted, they have protested peacefully, and they have seen attempts at the latter erupt into the former due to the volatile and unpredictable nature of crowds. There has been civil unrest over bread, over taxes, over drafts, and over basic human rights. This unrest has happened all over the world, through various ages, and under all varieties of government. With this in mind, when the President announced the intent of the Extended Citizenship Act in 2029, it should have been little surprise to the White House that this action initially met with considerable unrest in multiple locations across the nation.

However, in the final analysis, when examining the seeming lack of endurance and fortitude on the part of many of these protests, one must concede that perhaps the administration's initial assessment of American apathy was not altogether inaccurate.

— From *An Unlikely Phoenix* by Reed Ambrose

Ryan woke before dawn, unsure why. He felt Nathalie shift next to him, and could sense by her movement that she was awake, too. He rose from the bed and went to the bedroom window. Outside, he heard sirens from multiple directions. Several cars whizzed by the front of the house, well above the speed limit.

"What is it?"

"I'm not sure." He moved to the living room and directed Miri to turn on the TV. Instantly, he was met with news coverage of rioting across the city. He sat down on the edge of the couch in dull shock. Nathalie exited the bedroom, pulling on her robe. He glanced up at her, then motioned toward the television. "The reporters aren't saying so, but this has to be about the speech last night."

"Of course it is," Nathalie said, gently, settling in beside him. "People can only let things go for so long."

The rioting seemed to be concentrated in the downtown area, and there were multiple clashes with police. The reporters labeled the rioters as 'disaffected radicals' at times, and whenever there appeared to be any form of looting, as "mercenary opportunists."

"I wonder if this is happening in any other cities," Ryan wondered aloud, and so he switched through several different news channels. All of the TV coverage was strangely silent about anything outside of the greater St. Louis area. Even national channels were running local feeds.

Nathalie disappeared into the bedroom for a few minutes while Ryan continued to surf through the channels, searching for information. He was met with local news and standard programming, uninterrupted by events. Some of the channels ran a silent ticker across the bottom of the screen, advising citizens to remain in their homes during this "incidence of minor unrest."

It was good advice, Ryan knew. The safest place in a riot was at home, even in the center of activity.

A thought occurred to him. He looked down to his phone, opening up the app and checking for missed calls. He had one, from Alexander. His brother probably hadn't even gone to bed yet out on the west coast. There was a text from him as well.

Safe?

Ryan texted him back, assuring him that they were all right. He put the phone down as Nathalie returned to the living room. She was about to say something when she noticed his expression.

"What is it?"

He shook his head. "They didn't call me."

"Who?"

"Work. There's a full scale riot going on and…they didn't call." He had a difficult time shaking the emotion attached to those words, though he struggled just as much to properly identify it. Anger? Hurt? Disappointment? Ryan couldn't be sure, but it burned in his gut all the same.

"Oh, *amour*." Nathalie touched him on the cheek. "Of course they didn't. You're still injured. They know this."

"I still could have helped. I could have…" He trailed off.

"This is bigger than just St. Louis," she told him. "It's happening all over the country."

"How do you know?"

She gave him a meaningful look.

He clenched his jaw for a moment, then forced himself to relax his face. "What do you mean?"

"There are reports of crowds out in multiple cities. Some have been peaceful demonstrations, but there are other riots, too."

"Where?"

"Philadelphia," she said. "Savannah, Georgia. Madison, Wisconsin. A few others."

"What about California?"

"There were people in the streets of Los Angeles and San Francisco. San Diego, too. But the Governor came on and urged people to remain peaceful, and that seems to have helped. Only L.A. is still dealing with violence."

Ryan took in the information. That meant Alex was likely safe. But he wondered…

"Will this be enough?" he asked, more to himself than to Nathalie, but she answered.

"No." Her voice was sad. "Not for most. For most people, it will just be another event to get past in the course of their busy lives."

He looked at her. "Such a cynic."

"I'm only telling it true. I wish it weren't, but it is."

"Maybe not in California," he suggested.

She shrugged. "Maybe not."

They were quiet for a while, and then he finally said it. "Maybe it is time to go."

She met his gaze, and nodded slowly. "I think so, too."

He took a deep breath. "All right. We'll wait for things to settle down, and we'll go. I'll call Alex."

"No, don't." Nathalie's tone was sharp, and it

surprised him.

"Why not?"

"I think…I think it would be better if we were quiet about our plans."

"We can trust Alex."

"I know, *mon ami*. But who knows if his phone is under surveillance. Or yours?" She gave him a pleading look. "This is dangerous. As soon as we run, we become felons. Me for violating the Immigration Act, and you for aiding and abetting."

"That's ridiculous. The amnesty deadline is still two weeks away. We can take a vacation to California, if we want. Take Melina to Disneyland."

"We can. Theoretically."

"No, in reality. This is still a free country."

Nathalie sighed. "I don't know what kind of country it is any more. But what I do know is that they've been watching me. You know it, too. And if they're watching me, it is because they've decided I'm some kind of threat. And if I'm a threat, they can justify any action they choose to take. *That* is the world we are living in."

Ryan's objection died on his lips. She was right.

"Let's get packed," he said.

They were careful in what they chose to pack, taking only what they would otherwise take on a vacation to the happiest place on earth. Nathalie put a thumb drive containing all of their family photos into the lining of the suitcase, the only exception to this plan.

Ryan tried to book flights out of St. Louis, but

discovered many had been cancelled and that those few airlines still flying were overbooked. He spread his search, and found a direct flight to Anaheim from Nashville. It was almost a five hour drive away, but he purchased the tickets without hesitation.

While he worked, his phone buzzed. When he'd finished booking the tickets, he checked the message. It was from Gleeson.

Ryan took a deep breath and opened it. The note was brief and came with an attached file.

We don't believe many of the same things, except for this: what is right, is right.

Ryan frowned, wondering what the hell *that* was supposed to mean. He opened the document, and immediately saw that it was the report of his internal affairs investigation. He scrolled through the first few pages quickly until he reached the executive summary. He read in disbelief.

"While Officer Derrick adheres to questionable politics," Gleeson wrote, "the evidence in this case is clear in exonerating him of any wrongdoing, whether purposeful or negligent."

Ryan leaned back, letting out a long sigh. He was cleared. At least that was resolved.

He showed Nathalie, and she smiled and embraced him. "I'm glad this will not follow you."

He nodded. Being vindicated didn't matter anymore for his career. He was leaving that behind. But it felt good all the same.

They watched the progression of the rioting on the news, trying to decipher what was really happening through the haze of mainstream reporting. Things appeared to be tapering off, and most of the activity seemed to be centered around looting more than any protest.

Nathalie consulted her dark web sources only once, around dinner time when web traffic peaked. She said it helped camouflage her activity.

"Most of the protests have ended," she told him. "There's still rioting in Philadelphia and Houston, but it sounds like it is coming under control."

"Just like here."

"Yes," she said, sadly. "It is as I told you, my love. People lack the resolve we attribute to them."

"Not everyone," he said.

She didn't answer.

Two hours later, his phone rang. It was Aaron Fisher, his sergeant. "They want you to come in, Ryan."

"They who?"

"They, they," he said impatiently. "I don't know. The bosses. They're calling in all assets to finish out this goddamn riot. It's mostly under control, so we can activate our civilians and modified duty cops like you."

"Where do I report?"

"Nowhere yet. Stand by for another call. They'll let you know. In the meantime, get ready."

"I will, sergeant."

Fisher disconnected.

Ryan told Nathalie about the call. She didn't like it.

"You can't go. We are leaving soon. You have tickets."

"For tomorrow," he said. "And if I don't go, it'll look suspicious."

"Tell them you're sick."

"It's too late. If I was sick, I should have told Sergeant Fisher."

"They won't know," Nathalie insisted. "They're too busy to notice."

Ryan considered. Then he shrugged. "Let's wait and see who calls me in. If I can book off sick with whoever that is, I will. Okay?"

She agreed, and they settled in to wait.

As one hour stretched into two, Nathalie dozed on the couch, leaning against Ryan. He watched the television on mute, believing less than half of what he saw. He'd half-decided that everyone had forgotten about him when there was a loud knocking on the front door.

Nathalie jolted awake, blinking through her sleep. Her alarmed gaze lighted on Ryan. He held his finger to his lips, standing and shuffling to the door. He tapped the screen to access the porch cam, but it remained black.

Another knock, this one more insistent.

"Who is it?" Ryan called through the door.

"Homeland Security, Officer Derrick. Open the door."

Ryan glanced at Nathalie. Her expression was creased with a frown.

The agents knocked again. "Officer Derrick, open the door!"

Ryan waited a couple moments, then said, "Just a minute. Let me get some clothes on."

There was a pause, and then a reluctant reply. "Make it fast."

Ryan recognized the voice. It was Potulny. His eyes snapped to Nathalie's and he mouthed the lieutenant's name. Nathalie's eyes widened, then narrowed. The two of them stared at each other for a long moment, speaking volumes in silence. Then Ryan nodded briskly. Nathalie slid from the couch and sprinted lightly for Melina's bedroom.

He waited another minute, then opened the front door and stood in the doorway. Lieutenant Potulny stood with two uniformed HSA agents.

"What is it?" Ryan asked.

"Let's talk inside," Potulny suggested.

"Let's talk here," Ryan countered. "Unless you have a search warrant."

Potulny scowled briefly, then shrugged. "Fine. Is your wife home?"

"Why?"

"That wouldn't be any of your business, actually," Potulny said.

"She's my wife."

"So she is. Would you mind getting her?"

He shook his head. "Why do you want her?"

Potulny sighed. "We already covered this, Officer. Get your wife now, or I'll have you arrested for obstruction."

"Obstruction of *what?*"

"Justice." Potulny held out a signed document in the familiar orange color of arrest warrants. He smiled without a trace of humor. "Bring her to the door, so we can resolve this peaceably."

"She's not here," Ryan lied.

"Where is she?"

"She went to my sister's in Nebraska. I sent her as soon as the riots started."

Potulny shook his head, clucking his tongue. "Cops are such poor liars," he said, then turned his gaze to both of the agents with him. "Search the place. Find her."

"You're not coming in," Ryan said, standing in their way.

The agents hesitated, glancing sidelong at Potulny.

"Look," Potulny said. "I have an arrest warrant. That means I can also enter any premise I reasonably believe the wanted person to be. Like her home."

"I told you she isn't here."

"And I think it's entirely reasonable for me to disbelieve you. So if you don't step aside, you're going to jail." Before Ryan could respond, Potulny motioned to the agents.

Both agents stepped forward warily. Ryan considered fighting, but knew he couldn't beat the three of them, especially not since his injuries. All he would accomplish would be to get arrested.

Or give Nat a few moments longer…

"Wait," he said. "At least let me-"

The first agent shouldered him aside, and the second followed quickly. Both drew weapons from their holsters.

"What the hell!" Ryan shouted.

"Relax," Potulny said. "Those are Tasers, not guns."

Ryan gave him an astonished look. *Relax?* He took a step in the direction of the two agents. From behind, Potulny grabbed his elbow and pushed him into the nearby wall. When Ryan turned back to him, Potulny had a Taser in his hand.

"Don't make me use this," he said. "Be a professional."

Ryan shifted gears. "What is the warrant for? What's the charge?"

A light sneer crossed Potulny's lips. "Sedition. Treason."

"What?"

"Your wife is an agent provocateur, Officer Derrick. We have proof. The only question is whether or not you knew about it."

Ryan glared at Potulny for a moment, then pointed past him and through the open door at nothing. "Did you really need him, too?"

Potulny's expression became confused. He glanced over his shoulder.

As soon as he looked away, Ryan stepped toward Potulny and gave him a hard two-handed shove. The lieutenant staggered backward, and fell off the porch, sprawling on the walkway. Ryan didn't hesitate, but turned and hurried deeper into the house. He resisted the urge to call out to Nathalie, then realized it didn't matter at this point.

"Nat!" he screamed.

She didn't answer.

He burst into Melina's room. Her blankets were flipped aside, her bed empty.

"Nat!" he called again, turning and shuffling toward the master bedroom. He ran into one agent coming out of the room. Ryan balled his fist, but before he could throw a punch, the agent raised his weapon. Electricity arced with a sharp clacking sound and fiery pain shot through Ryan's body. His muscles seized and he toppled to the floor. The force of his landing knocked the breath from him and he saw stars. The smell of ozone filled his nostrils.

"Hit him again!" Potulny yelled from what seemed like far away.

More clacking, and the screaming hum of electric pain enveloped him.

Then darkness.

Chapter 23

Not every political movement is entirely transparent about its true core convictions, especially early on its existence. The further away from the cultural norms, the more likely a movement in its infancy will conceal those convictions, or cloak them in euphemisms. Only when the movement has reached a comfortable majority, or at least secured a position of substantial authority, do these convictions become public. Much like the proverbial frog in cold water that is heated slowly, degree by subtle degree, the public, although a numerical majority, sometimes finds itself in boiling water, unable or unwilling to leap out in time to save itself.

— From *An Unlikely Phoenix* by Reed Ambrose

When Ryan woke, he was handcuffed to a chair. The room was bright and stark, and he recognized it immediately. He was in the interrogation room at the precinct.

His first thought was of Nathalie. Did Potulny find her and Melina? Where had she hidden? He tried to imagine someplace in the house where they could have successfully hidden and couldn't think of one. Maybe they'd gotten out of the house in time, he consoled himself. Maybe Potulny's arrogance had resulted in overconfidence, and he hadn't brought along any more than the two agents Ryan had seen.

We can hope.

He tested the cuffs, found them secure, then sat to wait. He knew the cameras in two corners of the room would capture that he was awake. Potulny would be in soon. Or someone would be, at least.

It took another twenty minutes, but he was proven correct. Lieutenant Potulny entered the room, carrying a notepad and a cup of coffee. He sat down opposite Ryan, plopped the coffee cup down on the table and scratched something on the notepad. In spite of everything, Ryan almost laughed at the ridiculous pantomime.

Potulny was serious, however. He finally looked up at Ryan and shook his head sadly. "I don't know whether to feel bad for you or feel like you're bad, Officer."

Ryan wondered how long he'd worked on that opening line. He didn't reply.

Potulny didn't seem to notice. "I mean, either you were completely unaware that you were married to a seditious, treasonous so-called journalist...a *foreign* journalist, at that...or you were in league with her the entire time." He held up his hands, mimicking a scale. "So either you were really dumb," he said, lifting one hand, then the other. "Or you're a traitor, too."

Ryan considered asking for a lawyer, but he knew it would be pointless. He remained silent.

"Now while it *is* tempting to go with the first option..."

He tilted his head at Ryan and gave him a greasy smile. "And entertaining, I have to say. But given your other behaviors, being a shamer and so forth, it seems to me that the second option is more likely. That you're a traitor, I mean."

Ryan said nothing.

"Not talking?" Potulny said. "Tongue fried?"

Ryan glared at him, but didn't reply. More prepared jabs that weren't nearly as witty as Potulny thought.

Potulny shrugged. "It doesn't matter. Your wife is going to see prison if she is lucky, though my recommendation is to simply ship her back to the shithole she was born in. It's at least as much a prison as any of our penitentiaries, and shipping her there is a one-time cost instead of an ongoing one."

Ryan clenched his jaw. He strained against his cuffs momentarily, feeling the cold metal bite into his wrists.

"And if I'm right about you, well then that's already one prison bed we'll be paying for. Plus whatever fostering your orphaned daughter ends up costing us." Potulny watched Ryan for a response.

Ryan forced himself to relax his muscles. Potulny was trying to get to him. If he let that happen, Potulny won.

"Running hasn't made your wife look any less guilty," Potulny said. "You know how a jury will see that, don't you?"

He did. Only guilty people ran. That was the lie that they were always sold.

"And you know we'll find her, right? And charge her for failing to surrender?"

Ryan felt a jolt of adrenaline. That meant she managed

to escape. That gave him hope.

"Funny thing," Potulny said. "I checked your file. You don't have a sister that lives in Nebraska. In fact, you don't have a sister, period."

Ryan shrugged.

Potulny gave him a disappointed look. "That's it? A shrug, a tacit admission of your guilt? I expected some sort of snappy comeback, Officer Derrick. You've always been so full of them." He glanced down at his notepad, then back up at Ryan. "Well, I'll just add it to the list that proves your guilt."

"On what charge?" Ryan asked, finally breaking his silence.

"Aiding and abetting a terrorist, I would think. Or more than one."

"Terrorist? More than one?" Ryan shook his head. "What kind of fantasy world do you live in?"

"Oh, my world is very real," Potulny said. "I don't think it will be difficult to prove that you gave comfort and aid to your wife, or that you assisted in her evading the service of a legal arrest warrant. That goes almost without saying. And when you add to that the results of your internal investigation, the picture becomes quite clear."

"What the hell are you talking about? The internal cleared me."

Potulny gave him a strange look. "What makes you say that? I've read it and I can assure you it says exactly the opposite."

"You're lying," Ryan insisted.

"Why would I do that?"

"It's what you do. It's what all of you do. You cloak your lies in truth and truth in lies, and you present it as reality."

Potulny shook his head sadly. "That's very poetic. And I supposed from the warped perspective you're coming from, that *is* how it looks." A thought occurred to him. "I wonder what we would have discovered if we'd put you through that return-to-duty psychological review? Some paranoia? A skewed world view?"

Ryan ignored his baiting. "Where's Gleeson?" he asked. "I want to talk to him."

"Gleeson? Oh, he's not going to save you, Officer. No, after a long and illustrious career, Captain Gleeson has opted to retire from the Metro."

"Retire?" Ryan couldn't believe it.

"Yes. He's gone."

Questions flew through Ryan's mind like leaves in a windstorm. Did they force Gleeson out? Or did he retire so they couldn't touch him?

It didn't matter. He was gone, and with him, whatever integrity existed in his investigation. Now Potulny could write whatever he wanted to in the report, conclude whatever he chose to conclude. Who was going to say otherwise?

"Not that your career is much of a concern for you, at this point. Or so it would seem." Potulny gave him a knowing look. "Flying out of Nashville? Did you think we wouldn't catch that?"

"It was a vacation," Ryan said, weakly.

"It was a mistake," Potulny said.

Ryan couldn't disagree. "What do you want?" he

demanded.

Potulny shook his head. "Nothing. The time has passed where you have anything I want, Officer Derrick." He frowned. "I guess that's not going to be true much longer, is it? Maybe I should start calling you Mr. Derrick now, so we can both get used to it."

"Get used to this," Ryan said. "I want a lawyer."

Potulny didn't show any irritation or disapproval. In fact, he didn't react at all, except to get up and exit the room, leaving Ryan to wonder what came next.

The first lawyer Ryan tried was Michael Brooks, a longtime associate who he knew had defended people out of favor with the Party. The receptionist told him that Brooks had changed his practice to family law, and was unavailable.

The next attorney he could think of was a prominent criminal defense attorney, Stephen Workman. Workman declined due to what he called "political conflicts of interest," which Ryan took to mean that Workman had joined the NAP.

Finally, two hours later, he settled for the court appointed public defender, Anna Garwin. Garwin proved to be a harried young woman whose nervous disposition did little to inspire his confidence. They spoke briefly on the phone, and forty-five minutes later, she met with him in person.

Ryan told her little, even though he understood attorney-client privilege. His reasoning was that she only needed to know what she had to know to defend him, and what she didn't know, she couldn't betray. If Garwin sensed he was holding back any details, she didn't show it.

After giving him half-hearted assurances that she would return shortly, Garwin left to contact the prosecutor. Ryan settled in for a long wait, expecting to remain in holding for the remainder of the day and be transferred to the county jail in the morning. He was surprised an hour later when Garwin returned as promised.

"You're being released," she told him.

"What?"

"That isn't what you wanted?"

"Of course, but…they aren't charging me?"

"I expect they will, but you were only being held on a charge of obstructing the execution of a lawful arrest warrant. It's a felony, but I convinced the judge that since you're no longer in a position to obstruct or render assistance, there was no reason other than punitive to keep you incarcerated." She smiled uneasily. "The prosecutor didn't like my argument but the judge agreed, and the prosecutor said he wasn't prepared to file complete charges against you yet, so…" She gave a wave of her hand. "You're free to go."

"Are there any restrictions?"

"No further violations. You have to report any contact with your wife. And remain in the county limits, of course."

Ryan nodded. "All right."

"All right, as in you'll comply? Because as an officer of the court, I have to vouch that you'll do so before the release is finalized."

Ryan looked her dead in the eye, and surprised himself at how easily he lied to her.

It had occurred to him that Potulny might have allowed him to be released in order to follow him, in the hopes that Ryan might lead them to Nathalie. So despite the pain in his hip and the overall soreness in his entire body, Ryan didn't take a cab or AutoUber when he left the precinct. Instead, he walked block after block, turning randomly at every corner, but generally going in a serpentine fashion. He checked behind him in the reflection of windows, and with occasional glances over his shoulder, but didn't believe anyone was following him. Then he caught sight of a traffic camera and realized how fruitless his efforts were. Potulny could be following him from his desk, clicking to a new surveillance source every so often.

Frustrated, he got on the subway and took a train to a stop nearest his house. He wanted to run from the station, but the ache in his hip told him that was a bad idea. Instead, he struck a steady pace, and made it home in good time.

The door was unlocked, and when he opened it, he was met with all of the disarray he expected from a police search. There was a time, early in his career, when they were directed to make as little a mess as possible when searching, but Homeland Security clearly didn't adhere to that philosophy. Drawers stood open, closet doors were askew. The floor was littered with a multitude of items, making the place look like the aftermath of a hurricane.

Ryan stepped over the papers and clothing on the floor, calling out for Nathalie.

There was no answer. He went from room to room, anyway, searching and calling. When he'd finished, he started again, going through the entire house a second time. No one answered him, and he saw no evidence of his wife or daughter's presence.

They must have gotten out, he decided. Slipped out the sliding back door and fled. But where?

Then a simple answer occurred to him. Art and Maggie, the next door neighbors. They were good people. They'd hide them, without question.

He reached for his phone, then stopped. He knew his phone had to be tapped at this point. And if he were right, then Art and Maggie had already taken a great risk for them. Calling them now, on a monitored phone, would cast suspicion on them, and bring retribution. He couldn't allow that.

Besides, he realized that Nathalie would not have stayed with them any longer than she absolutely had to. Once the HSA agents finished their search at the house and left, she would move on. But to where?

He stood in the living room, trying to think of an answer to that question. But in the end, he had no idea.

Ryan sank slowly onto his couch, suddenly exhausted. He sat there for a long while, listening to familiar sounds of his home, but taking little solace in them. Finally, he placed his phone on the coffee table, rose and went into his bedroom. His nightstand drawer was removed and upended, the books and other contents spilled onto the floor. He knelt carefully and tilted the stand to the side.

The folded envelope was still there, taped to the underside of the nightstand.

Ryan let out his breath, realizing then that he'd been holding it. He picked up the envelope and spread it open. The small plastic chip was still inside.

Back in the living room, he swapped out his phone's chip with the one Wayne had given him. Then he rebooted the device. When the software came back online, it looked nearly identical to before. He checked his contacts. The list was unchanged, except for the first entry. The contact name was UNIDENTIFIED and the number read RESTRICTED.

Ryan hit SEND.

Chapter 24

Friedrich Zimmer, noted European political historian, has long been considered to hold the American political process in various levels of contempt, depending on the era under discussion. This assessment was only reinforced in 2064, when the abstract for one of his professional research papers stated that, "it is apathy that I find to have been both the most common and the least virtuous tendency among American voters during the 2020s."

When another scholar publicly asked him on an online academic critique forum which tendency he found to be the most surprising, Zimmer's famous reply was as cutting as it was pithy:

"Same."

— From *An Unlikely Phoenix* by Reed Ambrose

Alex sat with Ebby in the conference room, waiting for the Governor. The technology aide gave him a frank stare for a long while, eventually making him uncomfortable enough to ask her, "What?"

"I'm just wondering," Ebby said. "Did she offer you

the position of Vice Governor? Or Secretary of State?"

Alex was mildly surprised, then realized he shouldn't be. If anyone was going to be dialed into the inner workings of the Governor's office, it would be Ebby. He looked back into her intelligent brown eyes, and said, "I'll tell you if you tell me."

"Tell you what?"

"What *your* position will be. I'm thinking Director of Intelligence."

Ebby smiled mysteriously. "If that were true, and I told you, I wouldn't be very good at my potential job, would I?"

"I suppose not."

The Governor appeared at the door, apologizing for her tardiness. "I was on the line with Governor Kakuda."

Alex raised his eyebrow. "And?"

"They are drafting a secession statement right now. The retroactive nature of this latest decision was enough to push them over the edge, and with this nonsense about everyone earning citizenship, the sentiment on the island is that there is no going back."

"You convinced him to wait?" Alex asked.

"I tried." She sighed. "And I believe I was successful, but only for a very short time. He said Alaska was on board as well, but I haven't spoken with the Governor yet. That's next on my to-do list." She looked pointedly at Alex. "You should be with me on that call."

"Of course." Alex glanced at Ebby, who gave him a knowing smile. "Anything I can do to help."

"Good." The Governor turned to Ebby. "Okay, Ebby, give me the referendum results."

"Turnout was relatively high at fifty-two percent of registered voters," Ebby said, as she hit a few keys on her device and a holographic map of the state appeared in front of them. The state was riddled with green and yellow segments, while some remained gray. "This is based upon precincts who have reported, as well as exit polling and predictive models. We won't have the official count until late tomorrow."

"But right now?"

"Right now, it appears that seventy-one percent of the voters are in favor of continued resistance to White House immigration policies, to include remaining a sanctuary state. And forty-five percent are in favor of secession, if necessary."

"Opposed?"

"Thirty-two."

"That leaves twenty-three percent undecided," the Governor frowned.

"True."

"That's a big number."

"So is forty-five," Ebby said.

"Forty-five percent of the fifty-two percent who turned out?" The Governor asked, shaking her head. "Almost half of the eligible voters didn't even bother to vote. If those voters and that twenty-three percent of undecided joined with the dissenters, they'd have a significant majority."

"But they didn't," Alex told her.

The Governor looked down, deep in thought.

Alex waited respectfully for a long while, then finally reached out and touched her shoulder. When she looked up, he said, "Think of it this way, Madame Governor. Those forty-eight percent of the voters who didn't go to the polls weren't saying, 'I don't care.' Neither were the twenty-three percent who abstained."

"No? Because that would seem to be the easiest interpretation."

"Easy isn't necessarily right," Alex said. "What I'd suggest is that maybe what those voters were saying was, 'I trust *you* to decide, Governor Sarandon.'"

She smiled indulgently. "Is that really what you think, Alex? Because I wonder if an abstention is really their way of saying that secession is too unbearable a thought to even vote on."

"Maybe," he admitted. "I didn't say I was right. I just said you could think of it in the way I described."

The Governor laughed lightly, and patted his hand.

"Definitely Sec/State," Ebby murmured.

"Well, Alex," the Governor said, her tone resolute, "if you're right, then I guess I have a decision to make."

Chapter 25

The Crisis of 2029 that prefaced the more tumultuous events of the 2030s forced men and women across the United States to make a slew of personal choices. Albert Dynna, a shadow journalist whose contemporary commentary on the events have proven invaluable to later historians, broadcasted reports on a number of these cases in which men and women were faced with difficult choices and divided loyalties. Dynna offered most of these profiles without commentary, though his single editorial observation cropped up in his patented close to each episode. "Hard choices now," he frequently stated, "because we didn't make enough of them earlier."

— From *An Unlikely Phoenix* by Reed Ambrose

Ryan left his phone at home, as instructed. He drove his own car, but parked it several blocks away from the HSA Arena, and took a circuitous route to the arena. The lights inside the building were dark, and it stood empty. He made his way around to the rear loading dock.

Wayne was waiting for him.

They shook hands firmly, then Wayne pulled him in

close for an embrace. "I'm sorry, brother."

Ryan nodded that he understood. A small part of him held out the fear that doors to the loading dock would snap open and HSA agents would pour out. He could even imagine the expression on Wayne's face, resigned and ashamed at the same time.

Instead, Wayne pushed a padded manila envelope into his hands. "Here."

Ryan tore it open. A fake identification card with his photo and the name 'Robert Hall' was the first thing he noticed.

"Where you'd get this?"

Wayne gave him a look.

"Never mind," Ryan said. "More importantly, will it hold up?"

Wayne nodded. "To a surface check, anyway."

"And this?" He lifted up a plain credit card with no name or identifying marks on it.

"It's a pre-paid card. The currency is BitCoin, so you're going to have to be selective about where you spend it. A lot of places don't accept BitCoin anymore, but enough do. And it's an anonymous transaction, so it's far more difficult to track."

Ryan nodded. That made sense.

"Use the Hall identification and the BitCoin pre-paid to rent a car. Get something middle of the road. You don't want to be noticed. And believe me, brother...the federal government has a lot of ways to notice you these days. Everything from traffic cameras to satellites. Once your name goes public, every law enforcement officer in the country will be helping. And if they're serious about bringing you in, they'll bring in guys like me, too."

"Guys *like* you. Or you?"

Wayne stared at him, not answering. "Just disappear," he said. "And stay off the Interstate."

"Why? It's the fastest."

"It's also thick with cameras wired with facial recognition software. They'll pick you off before you get a state away." He motioned to the envelope. "There's some cash in there, too. And an emergency contact number of a guy I know in Utah. He's good people, but only call him if you have to, you hear?"

"I understand."

"Good. Now, none of this will do you long term, but if your plan is still to head to California…"

"It is. But I have to find Nathalie and Melina first."

Wayne smiled. "I think I can help with that."

The small house was hidden in the center of a solidly middle class housing development. As they made their way through the winding streets, the houses all looked very much alike to Ryan. He felt anticipation building in his chest as they drove. He imagined being reunited with his family, then saw images of Potulny and his lackeys waiting for him in the living room of the house. He cast sidelong glances at Wayne, feeling both suspicious of his former commander and guilty for it at the same time.

By the time Wayne finally turned into a driveway, opened the garage door, and drove inside, tension coursed through him like electricity. He sat waiting while Wayne shut off the engine and lowered the garage door.

"Let's get you to your family," Wayne said.

Ryan opened the door and got out of the SUV. He limped toward the door that he assumed led to the house, but Wayne got there first. He opened it wide and motioned for Ryan to go inside. Ryan didn't hesitate. There was no point. If Wayne had betrayed him, he was lost. But if he remained true…

It was the clean smell of Nathalie's shampoo that told him the truth of it. The fragrance wafted across him, and brought an immediate smile to his face. He shuffled forward and into the living room. Nathalie was there, and Melina. Both of them sprang off the couch and into his arms. Ryan went to his knees and embraced them both. All three of them spoke at once, crying, and laughing.

After a while, he collected himself and rose to his feet. Wayne stood in the doorway, watching them. A sad smile was painted across his face. "You can't stay," he said. "This is an agency safe house. There's no way to know when another agent might bring someone here. We've risked it as long as we can. We have to go."

Ryan nodded, and turned to his wife and daughter. "Get your things."

Nathalie smiled at him, and Melina giggled. "You're looking at everything," she told him. "We don't have anything else."

Ryan smiled back. "Well, we've got each other. That's the most important thing."

Wayne dropped them off near the public library. When he stopped the car in the alley behind the old building,

Nathalie and Melina got out. Wayne stopped Ryan, putting his hand on Ryan's shoulder, and apologizing. "I couldn't get ID for either of them," he said. "There just wasn't time."

"You got them to a safe place. That's more than most people would do in the same circumstances."

Wayne shrugged. "It was a risk, but not as much as you might think." He motioned toward Nathalie. "She's smart. She was careful about how she contacted me. Her email was disguised as spam, and the location they were hiding at was encoded in the message."

Ryan raised an eyebrow. "My wife's a cryptographer?" he joked.

"Don't be too impressed. If anyone suspects, they'll be able to see right through it. But it had to be a little bit obvious to catch my attention. She used your old operator name to manage that. Which, by the way, you weren't supposed to share with anyone for seventy-five years. Classified intelligence and all that."

"She seduced me," Ryan said.

"I always figured you'd crack under pressure, Derrick." He squeezed Ryan's shoulder. "So don't get caught, huh?"

"Aye-aye, sir. And thank you."

The two men didn't speak for another moment, then Wayne clapped his shoulder. Wordlessly, Ryan got out of the car. Wayne immediately pulled away.

"Everything all right?" Nathalie asked.

Ryan nodded. "Yeah." He pointed to the library. "You and Melina wait inside. I'll go up the street and gets us a car."

Nathalie didn't argue. She took Melina by the hand and headed into the library. Ryan walked down the alley and around the street corner to an independent car rental agency. He went through the mundane motions of renting a blue, four door sedan, wondering all the time if his identification would hold up, or if the BitCoin card would work. Every action the sales clerk took had him brimming with suspicion, but in the end, the man handed him the keys and beckoned him outside for an inspection of the vehicle.

Ryan forced himself to walk through the process, then thanked the man and drove away. He found Nathalie and Melina at the library, and they headed west on a secondary road. Ryan felt naked without his phone, and Nathalie had dumped her tablet at Wayne's direction, but at least the car had a navigation program. Unfortunately, it kept trying to route him to the interstate, so he finally exited the guidance feature and just used the system for its map.

In the back seat, Melina fell asleep, and next to him, Nathalie seemed to be fading as well. He drove for another two hours to the outskirts of Kansas City before he started looking for a motel with the BitCoin symbol in the window next to MasterCard, Visa, AmEx, and Paypal. He found one called "The Straight Six" next to a strip mall, and pulled in. Melina didn't wake up, even after he checked them in and carried her into the room. He slid off her shoes while Nathalie drew back the covers, and Ryan put his daughter to bed. Nathalie covered her gently, then sat on the edge of the other bed.

Ryan sat next to her. He didn't say anything, and she

remained silent as well. They stared at each other for a long while, through the fear, the exhaustion, and the relief. Then she leaned into him, putting her head against his chest and throat, and Ryan held her that way until her breath evened out and she fell asleep. Then he slowly lay backward on the bed, cradling her all the way, and finally succumbed to sleep himself.

Chapter 26

Twenty-four hours to Reno, Ryan thought. It sounded like a classic Johnny Cash song, or maybe something Nate Crider would write today. He could almost imagine the blues licks over a montage of the three of them driving across America. It painted a much happier picture than what he faced now.

They filled up with gas at an independent station that accepted the BitCoin card. While Ryan pumped, Nathalie went inside the small convenience store for supplies. Once on the road, they ate breakfast burritos and sipped coffee without a word. Even Melina remained unusually quiet, staring out the window as the landscape scrolled past.

Ryan kept the car radio on, tuned to a news station. They listened carefully to the news reports until the station faded into static, then scanned for another. He wished he'd thought to remember getting satellite radio when he'd rented the car, but it probably wouldn't have mattered. Even with the customary bland and careful reporting of the mainstream media, it was clear to him that there was conflict at the highest level of government.

"That's a good thing," he told Nathalie.

"How is a crisis like this a good thing?"

"It means Potulny and the people he works for have more important things to worry about than finding us."

"You hope," she said, her tone dubious.

"Hope isn't a plan," Melina said absently from the back seat.

Ryan smiled. "But we can always hope."

Occasionally, when they scanned the AM band, which had been virtually abandoned in the last decade, they picked up a renegade station that broadcasted for the better part of an hour before ceasing suddenly. Nathalie found the effect disconcerting, wondering aloud if they were shut down by government forces.

"I don't think so," Ryan said. "I think they limit the time that they broadcast so that their location can't be triangulated."

Nathalie nodded that it made sense, but then turned back to the window, and they remained silent again for a long while.

As night fell, they reached the outskirts of Denver.

They debated whether to push on or find a place to sleep for the night.

"You're exhausted," Nathalie said.

"I'm tired," he admitted. "But not exhausted."

"Well, Melina is. We should find a motel."

Ryan hesitated. "I think we should push on. If Potulny had put out a warrant for our arrest, then we won't be safe until we get to California." *If it is even safe there,* he thought, but didn't add. Instead, he said, "The sooner we get there, the better."

"We won't get there if you fall asleep and drive off the road."

Ryan looked at her, wanting to say that this was the way things were when the operation was ongoing. Sleep was a luxury until the mission was complete. You push through, and you complete the mission. But she was a journalist, not a soldier, and he wasn't sure she'd truly understand.

"All right," he relented. "We'll get a room. But only for a few hours. Six, at most. Then we move on."

She didn't argue.

Ryan found a gas station that accepted BitCoin and started to fill the tank. Nathalie and Melina went into the restroom while he pumped. As he stood, his hand perched on the gasoline nozzle, a state patrol cruiser pulled into the lot and slid up the same island, stopping immediately opposite him.

A shot of adrenaline spiked through Ryan's tired body, but he tried to remain nonchalant. When the driver exited the police car and snapped her round campaign in place, Ryan tensed slightly. Scenarios flitted through his weary mind.

Did she know? Or was she just here to get gas and a cup of coffee?

When she didn't immediately confront him and instead put the gas nozzle into her fuel tank, he knew that she wasn't aware of his identity yet. Still, if Potulny sent out an all-points bulletin, their descriptions would be included. His Robert Hall identification might hold up to a cursory inspection, but if someone was actually looking for them, how many unique indicators were there? A white man traveling with a black woman and their young daughter? Plus his scars and injuries were as good as identifiers as his face.

He avoided looking at the trooper, then started to become self-conscious of this avoidance, so he glanced over at her. She was looking at him, her face a familiar professional visage, a mirror of what Nathalie called his own "cop face." It betrayed nothing.

Ryan gave her a simple nod of acknowledgement, and after a moment, she returned the gesture with a curt nod of her own. He returned to pumping his gas, hoping that Nathalie saw the police car when she left the restroom and waited for the trooper to leave before returning to the car. Neither of them had identification, so if the trooper asked for some, his hand would be forced. He didn't want that. He didn't want to hurt a police officer. And he didn't want to turn the pursuit of them suddenly hot. They were still too far from California for that to end well.

He heard the door to the convenience store ding as it opened, and he glanced up to see Nathalie walking out with Melina. She was leaning down and whispering in their daughter's ear, unaware of what stood next to the island. Ryan tensed, hoping he wasn't putting off vibes that would alert the trooper.

Nathalie reached the car and helped Melina inside the back seat. Then she opened the front door. Only then did she catch sight of the police car and the trooper pumping gas. To her credit, she didn't lurch in surprise. Her eyes flared open slightly, and she glanced quickly at Ryan. He silently begged her to just get into the car. If the trooper tried to stop them, he could get in the car and flee. His rental car was no match for the police cruiser, but at least he'd have a head start.

The gas pump clicked off, signaling the tank was full. Ryan removed it carefully and replaced the nozzle. Because he was facing her and it seemed natural, he gave the stone-faced trooper another nod. She was still watching him, but he couldn't tell if she harbored any suspicion or not.

When he turned away, she spoke. "Sir?"

Ryan craned his neck over his shoulder, giving her an expectant look while he tensed his body for action. "Yes?"

"Is everything all right?"

He nodded. "Yes. Everything's fine. Why?"

She didn't answer immediately. Then she said, "Just checking."

"Well, thanks. But everything's fine."

She watched him carefully for a few moments before giving him a slow nod. "All right, then. Have a good evening, sir."

"You, too, officer," he said, opening the car door. He could feel her eyes on him as he slid into the driver's seat, started the engine, and put the car in gear. Carefully, he pulled out of the lot and onto the road. He didn't look over his shoulder or glance in the rear-view mirror until he was two blocks away. When he didn't see any red and blue lights behind them, he heaved a sigh of relief. Then he glanced over at Nathalie.

"Forget the motel," he said.

She nodded in agreement. "But at least let me drive."

He considered, then nodded. "Let me get us a little ways outside of Denver, and then we'll switch."

They didn't, though. Ryan drove for hours, through the remainder of the night and into the day. Nathalie didn't argue and eventually she stole a few hours of reluctant sleep. Finally, after passing through Colorado and Utah, he pulled into a rest stop just inside of Nevada, where he stretched his hip and back. He handed Nathalie the keys and she handed him a small black phone.

"I bought it at the convenience store," she explained. "It's a pre-paid. I thought you might want to call your brother."

Ryan smiled at her. "Thanks, babe."

She squeezed his hand and got into the car. Ryan thought about calling Alex's private number but wondered about Wayne's warning. They might be monitoring, and he didn't want to put his brother in danger, at least not when he wasn't there in person to protect him.

That thought made him smile ruefully. With his hip, he was going to physically protect Alex? For the first time since they were kids, the reverse was more likely. And considering that Potulny almost certainly filed charges against him, it would take Alex's political influence to protect him on that front, too.

So instead, he dialed Alex's public number. When the staffer answered, "Senator Derrick's Office," he hesitated. Then he asked, "Can I speak with the Senator?"

"I'm sorry, sir. The Senator is unavailable. May I take a message? I can't guarantee that he'll call you back, but I can assure you that he reads all of his messages."

Ryan considered, then said, "This is his college friend, Brayden Schenn," he said. "Will you let him know I'm coming to town and I'd like to see him for dinner?"

"I will, sir," the staffer replied dutifully. "When will you be here?"

"In the next day or two," Ryan said. "Will you make sure he get the message?"

"Certainly, sir." The staffer confirmed his name, then added, "I can't guarantee that he'll have availability while you're here but I'll pass on the message."

"Thank you," Ryan said, and hung up. Despite the staffer's promise, he didn't know if Alex would get the message or not. But he'd tried, and that would have to be enough.

Ryan settled into the passenger seat.

"Did you talk to him?" Nathalie asked.

"I left a message for him. He'll understand." Ryan adjusted the seat until he got it reclined into a position that was vaguely comfortable, and then he tried to sleep.

At first, he thought it would be impossible. Thoughts of the state trooper intruded, and he wondered what Potulny might be doing to catch them. The possibilities haunted him. But the drone of the road finally seeped into him, and he dropped into a dark sleep, plagued by dark dreams.

Chapter 27

In the early morning hours of one of the longest days in the Sarandon governorship, a staffer reportedly asked the Governor if she was certain she was doing the right thing. The Governor's reply may or may not be factual, but it has become a symbolic truth, if not a literal one.

"When has welcoming people home ever not been the right thing?"

— From *An Unlikely Phoenix* by Reed Ambrose

Alex watched Governor Sarandon with growing awe. Each conversation she engaged in seemed more masterful, more powerful. Moreover, she performed this feat in front of a small crowd of advisors. If he'd ever had any doubt regarding her ability to lead, it vanished as the night wore on.

When she ended the vid-call with the Governor of Oregon, she sank back in her seat. Exhaustion suddenly creased her features. Without asking, Alex rose and retrieved a glass of water from the mini-bar and handed it to her.

"Thank you, Alex," she said, taking the glass with a smile.

"Four for four," he said, and gave her the thumbs up.

The Governor took a sip of the water, then nodded. "I wasn't sure about Oregon. That's why I saved that call for last."

"Well…" Alex said. "Not *last*."

She smiled wearily. "I think I'll take a short break before making that particular call."

"It's already almost midnight on the east coast," he said.

"They'll wake him for me," she replied. "Trust me." She turned to Keaton. "Paul, have you lined up the media release?"

Keaton nodded. "Yes, Madame Governor. The stations have all been advised that you'll be making a statement."

"Not just the mainstream outlets?"

"We've included everyone Ebby suggested," Keaton said.

"Good," the Governor said, taking another drink and nodding her approval. "I just need a few minutes, and then I'll call the President. Immediately after that, we'll address the media."

"An address which hopefully isn't interrupted by tactical nukes," General Braddock said wryly.

The Governor gave him a tired look. "If that happens, at least I'll be spared some ridiculous questions from Fox News," she joked, but the delivery fell flat. She sighed. "Let's all take a short break, and reconvene?"

"Yes, ma'am."

Alex poured himself a glass of water and took the

opportunity to page through his text messages from his office. There was the usual fare for the first few, then he stopped hard on one.

YOUR COLLEGE FRIEND, BRAYDEN SCHENN, IS COMING TO TOWN IN THE NEXT DAY OR TWO AND WOULD LIKE TO MEET FOR DINNER. SHOULD WE SCHEDULE IT?

"Holy shit," Alex muttered. There was only one person who would invoke the name of the long-time St. Louis Blues center.

"What is it?" Braddock asked him.

Alex looked up. "It's my brother," he said. "He's coming to California. He's on his way."

Braddock gave him a look of concern. "Well, he better hurry."

"I know," Alex said. "I know."

Chapter 28

Throughout time, the exact words of many leaders during pivotal events have become shrouded in myth. Historical accuracy has given way to paraphrase which has evolved into convenient legends told by the victors. History is replete with examples of this. However, in some instances, what reads as myth or revision for the sake of propriety is actually an accurate depiction of what was said. For example, when American General Anthony McAuliffe of the 101st Airborne responded to the German demand at Bastogne that he surrender, his one word-reply of "Nuts" was truly what the man said, despite later assertions by some that it was a less profane paraphrase of his actual reply.

Similarly, when the last President of the United States was warned that California Governor Sarandon had assembled a coalition of western states and was preparing to secede, his true reply was, "She doesn't have the balls."

— From An Unlikely Phoenix by Reed Ambrose

Ryan woke when the car stopped. He sat up, rubbing his eyes. "What is it?"

"I'm not sure." Nathalie's voice was taut and fraught with exhaustion.

The car in front of them was at a full stop. Ryan noticed a long line of cars spread out on the roadway ahead. "Where are we?" he said. "Are we to Reno yet?"

"Through it," Nathalie said.

"How long ago?"

"About twenty minutes ago."

Ryan tried to remember how far it was from the California border to Reno. He and Alex had taken a road trip once years ago, but he hadn't paid close attention. "Twenty minutes?" he repeated quietly. That seemed about right to him. But there was so much traffic.

Then he noticed that all of the stopped traffic was only westbound lanes. Across the median, a few cars whizzed past eastbound, but westbound traffic was at a standstill.

"Something's wrong," Ryan said. He opened the car door, but Nathalie grabbed his arm.

"Wait."

"I'll be okay, Nat. Just wait here, okay?"

Nathalie gave him a dubious look, but relented.

Ryan got out of the car and looked forward and back. There were a half dozen cars stacked up behind them now. He turned away and looked forward. The cars stretched for at least a half mile. In the distance, he could see the blue and red lights of a police cruiser.

He started walking.

After he passed a dozen or so vehicles, he came to a semi-truck. The driver had turned off his engine, and sat on the huge step leading up to the cab, his arms crossed while he smoked a cigar.

"What's happening?" Ryan asked him. He figured the driver had a CB in his truck and would have news, and he wasn't disappointed.

"The crazy bitch did it," the driver told him.

"Who?"

"The Governor." The driver took a puff on his cigar, blew it out, then spat. "She did it. California seceded. And good goddamn riddance."

Ryan blinked, taking in the information. Woodenly, he asked, "When?"

"A couple of hours ago," the trucker told him. "And not just California, either. Hawaii, Alaska, Oregon, and even Washington. All of 'em."

Ryan swallowed, then motioned toward all the vehicles. "So what's going on here?"

The trucker peered at Ryan, contempt plain on his face. "What do you think? The border's shut down."

"From which side?" Ryan asked.

The trucker snorted. "Both sides. It's a mess, and I'll tell you this. We aren't going anywhere for a while."

Ryan resisted the urge to ask more question. Instead, he mumbled his thanks, and limped back the way he'd come. As he walked, he pulled out the pre-paid phone Nathalie had bought in Denver and texted his brother. There was no need for subterfuge any longer, so he sent the simple text directly to Alex's personal phone.

We're stranded at the border.

When he returned to the car, Nathalie had exited the driver's seat and stood in the open doorway.

"What is it?" she asked. "An accident or something?"

"No," he said, and he told her. As he spoke, her face

became ashen, and she covered her mouth.

"Oh, *mon Dieu*, Ryan. It is really happening, isn't it?"

"It is," he said, and took her in his arms. She trembled as he held her. He looked over her shoulder at their sleeping daughter in the back seat of the car. Melina's face was peaceful, unblemished with concern.

When Nathalie pulled away from his embrace, he was both surprised and heartened to see that her eyes were dry, and her expression was resolute. "What do we do now?" she asked.

Ryan took a deep breath and let it out. "We find a way," he said. "Just like everyone else."

Nathalie took his hands in hers and squeezed. "All right," she said. "All right."

"We find a way," Ryan repeated. Then he added, "There's still time."

Epilogue

When the crisis of 2029 gave way to the tumultuous 2030s, complete with brinksmanship, threats, and ugly politics, singer/songwriter Nathan Crider wrote that:

The last of what was truly America faded
into hatred and mist
like a longtime lover
who forgets how it is to be kissed.

As written here, the lyrics have a somewhat clunky feel to them, but surviving recordings of the bluesman singing them against the backdrop of his signature guitar style have a bittersweet, almost heart-wrenching quality. It is fitting that a uniquely American form of art — the blues — serve as a vehicle to document the passing of an era, and indeed, the passing of a nation.

As Daniel McCollough masterfully chronicles in his classic 2076 work Desolation Averted, *the face of North America was irreparably changed by the secession of California and its sister states in 2029. The events that followed throughout the 2030s were brutal ones, marking this time period as one of the most precarious, not just for America, but for the world.*

But that is another story, and better told by another historian.

— From the conclusion of *An Unlikely Phoenix* by Reed Ambrose, published by Oxford Press. First Edition, 2081

Acknowledgements

Note to the discerning reader: *An Unlikely Phoenix* was originally published as authored by Frank Zafiro, my pen name for crime fiction. It was not a fit, so I transitioned to my more eclectic mainstream name, Frank Scalise. That also was a poor fit, so I finally landed on listing my pen name for science fiction and fantasy for the authorship. It *does* fit.

I'd like to thank a few people for helping me get through this book:

Ashley and Danji for great ideas of events and near future elements to include in this story.

For their careful reads: Jill Maser, Dave Mather, Colin Conway, Brad Hallock, Brian Triplett, John Emery, Silver Chan, and Jackie Reynolds. Your individual and collective feedback was invaluable, and I'm truly grateful. I know this was a tough one for each of you, although perhaps tough for different reasons for different people. Regardless, you all tackled it like champions, and your thoughtful replies made this a better book than it would have otherwise been.

And for her unwavering faith and support, Kristi.

So thank you, one and all.

Frank Scalise
January 2018
Redmond, Oregon

About the Author

In addition to his science fiction and fantasy work, Frank writes gritty crime fiction from both sides of the badge as Frank Zafiro. He was a police officer from 1993 to 2013. He is the author of more than fifty novels, many of them crime fiction.

Frank hosts the podcast, *Wrong Place, Write Crime.*

In addition to writing, Frank is an avid hockey fan and a tortured guitarist. He lives in Redmond, Oregon.

Listen to the Soundtrack

If you'd like to listen to the soundtrack of this novel, which includes performances of the songs mentioned at the St. Louis Concert for Freedom, you can find them on YouTube at the Code 4 Press Channel: https://www.youtube.com/@Code4Press

Understand that these are fictional songs, performed by fictional characters… but the music is real enough.

Other Novels by Frank Saverio

Kemper's House
A Burnt Summer (Book One: Seasons of Wither) (*)

As Frank Scalise

All That Counts
A Village of Strangers
Six Sons (*)
Playing Out the String (*)

SAM THE HOCKEY PLAYER SERIES
(children & middle grade sports fiction)
Sam & the Magic Hockey Gear
The Hardest Hit
Bad Calls
Double Shifting
Line Changes

Non-Fiction

A Street Officer's Guide to Report Writing
Police Body Cameras

As Frank Zafiro

RIVER CITY SERIES
(#1) Under a Raging Moon
(#2) Heroes Often Fail
(#3) Beneath a Weeping Sky
(#4) And Every Man Has to Die
(#5) The Menace of the Years
(#6) Place of Wrath and Tears
(#7) Dirty Little Town
(#8) Dead Even
(#9) Some Degree of Murder
(#10) No Good Deed
(#11) The Worst Kind of Truth
(#12) Chisolm's Debt
(#13) The Cleaner
(#14) All the Forgotten Yesterday
(#16) The Quick of the Night (*)
(#17) Last of the Good Ones (*)
(#18) The Drown (*)
(#19) The Trade Off
(#20) Sugar Got Low

STEFAN KOPRIVA MYSTERIES
(#1) Waist Deep
(#2) Lovely, Dark, and Deep
(#3) Friend of the Departed
(#4) Hope Dies Last
(#5) Think of Laura
(#6) The Sins of Somebody Else Past (*)

(*) *forthcoming*

* 9 7 8 1 9 6 2 8 8 9 0 5 6 *